"Don't you fe healing you?"

What Madison felt was Brandon's body heat radiating through her, tightening her muscles, skimming up her spine. That kind of warmth should come with a warning—exposure might cause side effects. Maybe she could have blamed it on chemistry or like attracting like—called it a lethal injection. She was dying for want of him.

She managed to say, "I see a halo around the sun."

"Feel it vibrate?" he asked, turning to look at her, and his eyes turned molten-blue. Somehow, she didn't think watching the sky had anything to do with it.

The heat had gathered at the sweet place between her legs—another side effect of her being close to him. If this didn't end up in a kiss, she didn't think she'd be able to bear it.

Drawing in a long shaky breath, she said, "I do feel the vibration." Oh, did she!

"Being out in the middle of nature, with the birds and the sea creatures, it does something to a person, don't you think?"

"Amen to Mother Earth," she said dreamily.

"There's harmony in the sounds." His breath seemed to have caught in his throat.

"Yes, a more beautiful melody could not exist."

"Do you feel your eyes blur? It's the sun cleansing you."

Cleansing? Try heating up as if some crazy so-and-so had switched on the gas. She moaned, "My eyes have become pools of marvel." No, that wasn't right. They were pools of longing, no mistaking it.

Praise for Melody DeBlois

THAT APRIL IN SANTA MONICA won first place (under a different title) in the Desert Rose RWA's Diamonds in the Desert Contest.

That April in Santa Monica

by

Melody DeBlois

Love Is a Beach, Book 1

That April in Santa Monica

Cover Art by *Diana Carlile*

The Wild Rose Press, Inc.
PO Box 708
Adams Basin, NY 14410-0708
Visit us at www.thewildrosepress.com

Publishing History
First Champagne Rose Edition, 2019
Print ISBN 978-1-5092-2749-5
Digital ISBN 978-1-5092-2750-1

Love Is a Beach, Book 1
Published in the United States of America

Dedication

To my mother,
who never stopped believing in me

Chapter 1

There are many paths to enlightenment. Be sure you take the one with a heart.

~Lao Tzu

A ringing phone broke through the darkness, and her vision cleared. She raised her pounding head from the carpet. Looking at the office from her position on the floor made her want to cry. The desk was heaped with papers, candy wrappers, and dirty coffee cups. Stacks of files on the right cut off the view out the window. She stepped carefully through the minefield on her way to the chair. What had she read? *A messy desk implies the rest of your life is in a similar state.* Maybe—please God—this office wasn't hers. A girl could hope...

With a turn of her head, she noted a tall man talking on a ridiculously dated flip phone. Did she know him? His posture was as straight as the spines of the books on the shelves along the wall. Was he her lover (nice biceps) or husband (lucky her) or brother? She didn't think so.

Because of this, the obvious hit her. This hunk might be the reason she was flat on her back. If only her heart would stop racing, the fog in her head might clear.

Mercifully—or maybe not—he knelt beside her with his slow, easy moves as he set the phone down and

1

examined her.

"You blacked out and fell." He nodded his head full of raven hair. "Help's on the way."

Her heavy lids closed on their own, and she forced them open. Given the circumstances, no sleep was allowed. Her gaze darted back and forth until it rested on a photo of a woman and man together with two little girls at the ocean. The family was laughing into the camera, the mom and kids' hair blowing in the breeze. Temples thudding, she didn't know who they were. Should she?

"Relax." His tone sounded as if he didn't take her whacking herself in the head and forgetting everything to heart.

She…but wait. What was her name? Sadly, nothing sparked an "aha" moment. To make matters worse, her teeth were chattering like castanets. Her lightweight dress wasn't cutting it in the refrigerated air. "I'm freezing." Did that frightened voice belong to her?

The dear man shrugged out of his jacket and tucked it around a body a little too heavy to be hers. "There you go." He rolled up the sleeves of his shirt, and the tattooed word *samsara* came into view on his muscular arm. "You'll be okay."

"Will I?"

"Yeah." He lowered thick eyelashes over pools of blue—or was it gray? "Breathe. Let all thought melt into your breathing."

"I can't." Not when her stomach was lurching, and she didn't even know her own name.

"Let's try to get your mind off your troubles." He took three sticks of incense from a duffle bag, lit the tips with a match, and they fired up and smoked in trails. "Take a whiff." After a few moments, he added, "What do you think?"

"Hmmm, citrus and pine." She was twelve again and meandering through the peaceful woods. She remembered the way as clearly as if it were still noon on that summer's day, Mom, Dad, her sister, on their way to the sea.

"You've got it. Just kick back and let yourself drift."

Her breathing quieted and slowed, though he was still bent over her, his jeans worn at the knees to near threads. He had that marketable two-days-without-a-shave look. Also, his face, absurdly gorgeous, had movie star potential written all over it.

A landline phone intercepted the moment. *Ching-a-ling-a-ling* and her heartbeat skyrocketed into the outer limits.

The man slid a misplaced high heel back on her foot. "A fashion statement can't appear without shoes, now can she?"

He was on her side, bless him. And he obviously knew her. She didn't recall who he was but could imagine him climbing Mt. Kilimanjaro or ziplining through the Grand Canyon. Had he been a client she'd briefed for an audition? But he didn't appear to have a disability. Now how had those last thoughts popped into her head?

She pointed a finger in his direction. "Do I know you?"

"We met earlier. I'm Brandon Kennedy."

Determined to sit up, she lifted her shoulders. Her head sledgehammered, bitter bile rising in her throat.

He tenderly touched her cheek with his hand, and

tears gushed to her eyes. She blinked them back. This was…embarrassing.

"Hang in there, trouper," he said, and she wanted to hug him. At least thank him for taking such good care of her, but the words got stuck between mind and voice.

Sirens screeched from outside on Wilshire, and he spoke in the reassuring quiet she appreciated. "Give me a few minutes more."

He disappeared into the hall. The distraction he had lent her dissolved, and she took in her surroundings through the aching pulse in her eyes. This was an office, all right. Strange, though, the glossies on the wall were of a man on a stage with hearing aids, a woman with shrunken legs in a wheelchair on a modeling ramp, a child without a left arm. Her heart swelled with emotion, but she didn't understand why.

Time passed with a cell phone beeping, announcing incoming messages, and a jangling landline. The air conditioning wafted chilled air, making her shiver. Brandon's coat had left behind a raw, musky richness, and she cuddled up in its warmth.

Still, it occurred to her she'd forgotten something more paramount than her name. Was it in the familiar people in the many pictures surrounding her?

Thank God, the elevator pinged from the hallway, and in dashed the EMTs.

One of them dropped beside her. "What do you remember?" the man asked.

"It's a blur." She suppressed the tremor in her voice. "I just can't think."

He shined a penlight in each of her eyes. "Do you know your name?"

"Madison Gray." Simple enough now, and from deep within, words from some local newspaper drifted back: *Madison Gray opens InSight, a talent agency that represents actors, presenters, and models with disabilities.*

"How old are you, Ms. Gray?"

"Thirty—no, that can't be right. Thirty-two, I think. Maybe not. I need a second, please." She clenched her hands to stop their telltale shaking. Frustration settled in her throat, closing it up tight. Those missing pieces refused to surface in her head.

He asked her more questions while the other EMTs checked her vitals and her spine for injury. "Time to get you to the hospital."

Her mouth had gone dry as they wheeled her by the paneled walls filled with the press shots of her clients, and she smiled with pride as memories flashed like lightning. She loved them all, loved her work, wouldn't give up any of it for the world.

She motioned to stop before passing by Brandon. She lacked what he had, tranquility in his every move. Being with him was as soothing as sliding into a jacuzzi or listening to rain tap the window. With her job, her life, how long had it been since she felt any sense of calm?

"Brandon, will you come with me?"

"Sure." He said it as if he felt sorry for her. And why not?

Her hand raised to discover a goose egg had developed on the right side of her head. She was being carried from her agency on the top floors of the old Wesley building and out on the palm-studded boulevard while people watched with evident shock.

Her assistant trotted at the end of the gurney with a deer-in-headlights fright. "Ms. Gray?"

Madison sighed. "You better cancel my afternoon appointments." She managed a smile and directed it toward Brandon. "I owe you."

He steepled his hands under his chin. "May you be well."

The EMTs lifted her into the ambulance, and the skull-splitting lights dug into her eyes. To prepare for an IV bag, a paramedic stuck a needle in a vein in her arm and applied tape that tugged at her skin. Throughout the bumpy ride, the team worked on her and explained their procedures. One of them spoke to a doctor about her treatment over a crackling radio as sirens blared and horns blasted. Amid the confusion, Madison clung to Brandon Kennedy's blessing—*may you be well.*

****

More shook up than he cared to admit, Brandon stopped inside a small courtyard. Thirsty, he guzzled bottled water, perked his ears to the bubbling of a fountain, and tried to let go of his tension. With dread seeping down to his bones, he opened his phone and called Madison's sister, Harper McGregor.

"Brandon, how did it go?"

His cheeks burned. He'd done as much as possible, but no matter how hard he told himself otherwise, it hadn't been enough. He thought he'd ascended beyond allowing his emotions to get the better of him. Not true. Not today.

A mist blew from the fountain, cooling his face. He sank his hand into the swirling water, rescued a drowning ladybug, and grinned as it dried its wings and flew away.

"Sometimes, what seems an obstacle is a saving grace in disguise," he said.

"Madison got rid of you before you uttered a word?" Harper's tone cut into him with the trace of doom that dominated a lot of her speech.

He wished he had better news. "I'd just stepped into Madison's office and introduced myself when she fainted."

"Sorry—what?"

"She passed out and hit her head on the corner of her desk. I think she suffered a concussion. The ambulance is taking her to the Good Samaritan."

"For Pete's sake, Madison. You've gone and done it now."

A silence followed, and he thought he heard a muffled sob. Harper appeared tough on the outside, but she loved her sister, he knew.

He shifted from one foot to the other. He was used to people's disasters and had kept his head with Madison, but now his thoughts scattered like startled minnows.

He hated it when a woman wept. "Sorry, I tried to catch your sister. She was too far away."

"No, no, not your fault."

Muted beeps sounded. Most likely a burglar alarm code.

"Madison's working herself to death," Harper continued. "She's gone without sleep for too long. She's bad?"

He didn't want to alarm her. "Your sister could use a rest." The truth? Madison existed in a self-destructive cycle of work with no downtime.

In India, the late Mohan Das taught him the symptoms to look for in a patient. He hadn't expected to find Madison as bad off, but he was mostly judging her after she collapsed. Her face had puckered with fear. Her eyelashes had dampened when she started to cry and fought it with all her might. Something in her grit had touched him.

"I'm texting my brother Andrew," Harper said. "Talk to me, Brandon. Keep it up. Tell me any old thing. Listening to your voice is equal to having a deep-tissue massage. I wanted Madison to be as impressed by you as I am."

A lot of good he'd done. "Your sister's a fighter."

The sound of Harper's car engine rumbled in his ear.

"Got you on speaker phone," she said. "Can you help her?"

"I don't know." He picked up food wrappers from a stone bench and dumped them in the trash. "Not everybody wants help."

"I caught the intro to your show. Brandon Kennedy a.k.a. Guru Brandon. Age thirty-nine. Gave up a medical residency to traipse off to his roots in India—I want to know why."

A flurry of sunbeams flashed off shop windows as he strode down the block. "Conventional medicine isn't always the answer."

"The best way to get Madison to go along with you is to convince her it will be first-page news." She paused, then said, "I make her sound shallow. She's not. The stories I could tell you. When Webster stuck the word *sacrifice* in the dictionary, he was referring to Madison. She's just struggling so hard to make her clients realize their dreams."

"Right."

He knew the facts. Madison worked twenty-four seven, plus volunteering her services at every opportunity. Full disclosure, the woman never stopped to rest.

"She's under tremendous tension," Brandon said, a dilemma he knew too well. "With excess anxiety, the body breaks down and results in disease—a body not at ease. I didn't realize how ill I was until I improved. If I'd learned earlier, I might have avoided making mistakes."

"You? Really?"

"It was another lifetime." One he'd just as soon leave in the past.

"You would have convinced her of your merit if you'd only gotten the chance." She sighed, then went silent. "Crap," she added as if something tragic had dawned on her. "You were my last resort."

He ducked into his electric car. "No worries." He didn't mean it, though. But then, hopefully, he'd still get to help out. "Your sister asked me to come to the Good Samaritan."

"Meet you there."

A half hour later, Brandon sat among the other people in a waiting room. The odor of disinfectant vied with the cafeteria food at the end of the corridor. The television droned the midday news. He focused on his breathing but found himself lost in thoughts of Madison Gray.

Aside from her problems, she was a head-turner. Her hair shone reddish gold, and she wore it up in a trendy twist he had been tempted to dismantle. He wanted to see those waves fall down her back, all natural and soft. Her eyes were the color of Burmese jade. Studying the structure of her face, he'd gotten lost in discovery. He'd never quite finished.

At twelve thirty, Harper steamrolled toward him, wearing her yoga pants and a workout shirt. With her pumped-up body, she might pass for a personal trainer, hands fisted, shoulders pushed back, but her knees clearly buckled with emotion when she saw him.

She sank into the chair next to his. "When will they let us in?"

He saw himself in Harper when he'd been a kid and scared. "Soon." He patted the back of her hand with reassurance. "Let's try reciting the mantra I taught you."

Fifteen minutes later, Harper was flagging down a guy who must be Madison's younger brother. Andrew had her same shade of coppery hair, same eyes. He'd come from the baseball diamond still in uniform and chewing a wad of gum. But when Brandon shook his hand, the mint didn't hide the stench of whiskey. Brandon was all too familiar with the cons of alcohol addiction.

Andrew stuck his trembling hands on his hips. "Thanks for being here, man."

Brandon rocked forward in his chair. "No sweat. Between us, maybe we can work something out to present to your sister when—and if—she's up to it."

****

By two o'clock, Madison lay in a private room on the third floor with a view out the window of the rooftops and sky. She focused on the *blip, blip, blip* of the heart monitor and the saline bag attached to tubes—

tubes everywhere. A breath escaped in a hiss between her teeth.

A hospital stay wasn't an option. What would happen to InSight? Her clients needed her. With a click of her cell phone, she decided to call her assistant. She'd no more summoned her contacts than Brandon Kennedy appeared in the doorway.

His eyes met hers, giving her that same jolt they had in her office. Though she'd been expecting him, something stirred deep within her. One thing she'd learned—he was a man a woman could depend on. Honestly, though, she wasn't foolish enough to believe him attracted to her. Given the situation, who would be?

She hadn't been expecting the long-stemmed yellow rose he gave her.

"How are you?"

"Not bad." Stretching her hand around the tubes, she slid her phone on the nightstand and inhaled the bud's sweet fragrance. "The color of sunshine. It brightens up my hospital gown, don't you think?" His kindness moved her. "Thank you."

He'd opened his mouth to respond when Harper entered. Soon after, Madison's heart expanded at the sight of her brother. Worried about her siblings' reaction to her, she struggled to pull herself together.

A whir sounded as she raised her bed. "Okay, people, don't freak."

The devastating mixture of shock and sympathy in Harper and Andrew's faces made her realize how sick she must appear. She bit her bottom lip to keep it from quivering. Circumstances had to be dire for her baby brother to show up at her bedside.

"I swear on all that's holy it's not as bad as it looks," Madison said.

Harper cocked her head to the side, brown hair cupping her chin. "Seriously?"

Madison forced a lilt to her voice. "Don't worry. I've got this." The prescribed meds were working their magic, and even if she didn't look it, she felt more like her old self.

Harper leaned over the bed rail. "You've been pushing yourself to the limit since we were kids. You always had to be the parent."

"Me?" Madison inclined her head toward her sister. "Look who's talking."

Harper slugged down her mineral drink. "Just let me have my say. We didn't have much after Mom and Dad's disappearance, but we had each other."

Desperation rose in Madison's throat and burned. "I can't do this right now. I—"

"Please." Harper lifted a hand. "Your work habits are out of control." She relaxed her shoulders. "Listen, I found a man who teaches people how to live healthier lives."

"How nice for him." Madison shrugged at Harper. "I don't get the connection."

Harper gestured at Brandon, and he nodded like they were in on a conspiracy. "Maddie, meet Guru Brandon."

"Hold up—" Madison choked. "Did you say, *guru*?"

Brandon nodded. "Harper was frantic when she contacted me. I came to find out if you would be interested in my teachings." He lowered his chin and eyed her with sympathy. "You don't remember?"

A disheveled-looking nurse pressed inside the doorway. "Time's almost up."

Madison straightened as much as possible under the thumb of tubes and monitoring wires leading to machines. "We won't be long." Things were just getting interesting. She waved a hand. "Go ahead."

"Harper, Andrew, and I have come up with a possibility. If you're up to it, I'll explain the idea we want you to consider."

She gave a careful nod.

"You take two months off to work on your health. What this entails is, after your release from the hospital and your recuperation afterward, I move in with you—"

"Hey, did you say move in?" *Holy smokes*! "But there's nothing wrong with me."

Harper chimed in, "No, people always go around dropping in their tracks."

"You're lucky Brandon was in your office when you took a nosedive," Andrew said.

Madison scoured her forehead with the heel of her hand. "Okay, okay, I admit to overworking a little."

Andrew leaned over her. "You never miss a day, Mads."

She blinked. "My job is the love of my life."

"Well," Harper said, "we can write that epitaph on your headstone. 'Here lies Madison Gray, the Hollywood wonder. She married her job, and it has taken her six feet under.' "

The burning in Madison's esophagus worsened. "Oh, give me a break."

Andrew straightened into his six-foot-two frame, his hair awry beneath the ball cap, and she remembered him as a boy, his chin tilted up, crying because his little league team had lost their game. Hadn't that been only yesterday?

"Harper's only trying to help," he said.

Memories fired back to her. Had it actually been sixteen years ago? Mom and Dad had never come back from their diving trip. She had petitioned the courts for custody of her siblings. Raising Andrew brought her both joy and heartache, but she'd done it. Still, their last argument had driven him to stay away for over a year. Unable to sleep, she'd worked more than ever. Didn't matter now. Drew was here! And she had to fight those tears of happiness from exposing how terribly she had missed him.

Madison swallowed over the Mt. Everest in her throat. "Everyone means well, but I'm all right. Please believe me."

Doubt shaded Brandon Kennedy's face, causing Madison to roll her eyes. Who was he to judge? The guru probably sat in a cave and burned incense all the live long day. She should have known he was too good to be true.

She recalled him then. His compelling image had popped up on the plasma screen while she'd been channel surfing. His student had never left her apartment. He'd claimed the woman needed to eat some freaky herbs and manage a yoga pose or two. Madison had laughed out loud. Harper and Andrew asked her to put her trust in a—

"You're a reality TV star." With a sense of triumph, Madison slapped her mattress with her one free hand. "You want me to be on your show. What's it called?"

His neck flushed crimson. "It's *Guru Brandon*—I

tried to tell you. My job is to heal your spirit along with your body. What do you say, Madison? Are you game?"

She narrowed her eyes at Harper. "I can't believe you would stoop to trying to set me up on reality TV. Doing this sort of thing is why I set boundaries. You try too hard. I don't need your interference. I won't stand for it, you hear?"

She shifted her focus to Brandon. "Thank you for the offer, but I'll pass." To keep her hands steady, she fisted them. "I'll be fine, thank you very much, so you can go find yourself a real hopeless case." It was hard to believe he'd gotten caught up in Harper's drama. "I may have suffered a head injury, but I'm not desperate."

"Aren't you?" Harper's voice broke.

"Don't you start sniveling, Harper Lee McGregor. Don't you dare!"

"I'm not crying. Come on, everyone. My sister won't budge." Harper slipped her arm around Andrew's waist. "If you change your mind, Maddie, give us a call."

"I won't, but thanks." Madison's fingers fumbled with the edge of her blanket. Why were they ganging up on her? "I wish I was the sister you want me to be."

Harper dodged around the tubes and kissed Madison's forehead. "Love you, nerd."

Nerd was Harper's pet name for her. Defeated, Madison slumped. When it came down to it, Madison Gray was nothing but the studious girl behind thick glasses.

Andrew hugged her, and she almost blurted, "Don't let me lose you again!" Instead, she watched, her heart aching, as he and her sister skirted around chairs on their way out the door.

Brandon pushed to his feet. "Guess I should let you get some rest."

"I'm sorry they…including me…I'm sorry we wasted your time." To ease the scratchiness in her throat, she crunched shaved ice from a plastic cup. "And please forgive our bickering. Sometimes we're a very dysfunctional bunch."

"Let me help you. I'll give you a diet to rid you of your poor digestion and those itchy patches on your skin."

Her breath hitched. "I told you, I'm not ill."

He flashed her a "you poor, clueless thing" look, but when he ventured closer, his face was an alluring arrangement of planes and angles, a copper Apollo. His blue eyes—yes, the jury was in, undeniably blue—brightened as he studied her like he was coming up with a solution. And the tight anxiety in her neck, that ball of nerves, released.

"So I bet your idea of a health fix is crystals and gemstones," she said before she could stop herself.

To her amazement, he uttered a sexy, just-got-out-of-bed sort of laugh. "I take it you see me as some New Age hippie?"

The man looked anything but.

"God forbid," she said, a grin tugging at her mouth.

He laughed again, all good-humored and charming. "I should take out my tarot cards and see what's in store for my show." He winked at her. "You think?"

Her smile escaped against her will. "It's a gamble. The public is a fickle lot. One can never predict."

"I hear you're a wiz at distinguishing the sellable.

What is it people call you? The lady with the Midas *Hunch*?"

Pleased, she said, "I do have pretty good instincts." Helping clients who, without her, wouldn't get their moment in the sun brought her tremendous joy.

He squeezed the back of her hand. "That you do."

She traced a finger over his tattoo. *Samsara.* "A man or a woman?"

The smile lines at the corners of his eyes deepened. "Neither. It means as soon as you have something, you want something else, or you want more of it. A vicious cycle."

"That's me all right." No amount of food ever filled that deep, aching void inside her. "Just one more piece of cake."

His forehead furrowed. "Let me teach—"

"Visiting hours are over," the frazzled nurse interrupted.

This was Madison's cue. "Thanks, Brandon, for going above and beyond."

His grin could sell toothpaste. "Take care, trouper."

"I'll catch you again on the health network," she said with a slight wave of dismissal. "Bye now. If you ever need good representation, call me."

"Gotcha." He steepled his hands in prayer position, nodded, and then gave her his business card. "Just in case."

Minutes afterward, she lowered her bed and stared at the tiled acoustic ceiling. She might have known Harper would resort to theatrics. Some nerve, using Brandon Kennedy to sway her. At least her brother had come around. Her fainting was a fluke though. A result of getting up too fast and having nothing but coffee for breakfast. She would have to show everyone. Persuading a producer to sock his money into one of her newbies was never easy. Convincing a doctor that she was as fit as a gymnast should be a snap.

Still, tears slid from the corners of her eyes and plopped with hollow thumps on the pillow. Being hooked to a beeping monitor while the odor of antiseptic prickled her nostrils and pain shot between her temples made her doubt herself.

Chapter 2

Two days later, Madison had undergone many medical tests. She received flowers and pep talks from Harper and supervised clients by cell phone. Doctors consulted with her. By noon on the second day, she was dying for french fries. She'd just gotten done speaking to a nurse when the hand sanitizer hummed, and Madison turned to look.

A thin, fit woman with a silver pixie cut and flinty, dark eyes was heading her way. "I'm Dr. Buckley, your cardiologist," she said with a firm, professional handshake.

The doctors had informed Madison she'd suffered a mild concussion, but they kept her over what they called "a more severe condition," thus the prolonged hospital stay.

"So what is the verdict?" Madison lifted the top of the hospital gown that had fallen off her shoulder. "Am I going to live?"

Dr. Buckley pulled up a chair, sat down, and flipped through Madison's chart. "Your test results show you are suffering from malnourishment, anemia, and severe stress."

Madison wet her dry lips with her tongue. "Sounds ominous."

"I'm sorry to say your high cholesterol and blood pressure make you the perfect candidate for a heart attack or a stroke."

"Is it because I've gained a little weight?"

"You eat fast foods, avoid exercise, and sit at a desk for hours on end. Over time, these bad habits have led to some very unhealthy pounds." Buckley's eyes were direct, level. "You're carrying fat in places that put you at risk for coronary disease."

"You make me sound as if I have one foot in the grave." Madison pressed a hand to her throat, trying to ease the strangling sensation. "I'm only thirty-five."

Buckley closed the chart. "That's what worries me. If you don't change your poor eating habits, lose weight, and quit smoking, you won't live to see middle age."

Madison's stomach dropped. "How can it be?" Overwhelmed, she gripped the bedsheet, and her knuckles bleached of color. She'd had weight issues most of her life. "I planned to start eating right when I got some time."

"I suggest you make the time. The truth is excess fat and sodium cuts years off your lifespan."

The sharp metallic sound of Buckley shoving the window curtain along its rod made Madison wince. She flinched at the chill of the doctor's hands.

"You should take precautions, or you'll lose consciousness again," the doctor said and checked her chart once more. "I gather you were working late the night before?"

"Yes." Madison's left eye twitched. Why did everyone insist on making her feel she was binge drinking instead of earning a living?

Dr. Buckley continued to lecture her for a full twenty-five minutes. Madison's head was throbbing.

She should argue, negotiate a deal. Instead, she pressed her fingers to her closed eyelids, allowing the doctor's words to sink in.

Dr. Buckley patted her shoulder. "I'll release you tomorrow. Don't let me catch you in here again. Is that clear?" She wrote something on her pad. "I've recommended some specialists for a follow-up." She ripped off the pages, gave them to Madison. "Do yourself a favor and learn a healthier way of living."

They said their goodbyes. Afterward, Madison tucked in her trembling knees, folded her arms over them, and rested her head. Beneath her ear, the wristwatch her mother gave her ticked with welcomed certainty.

In the next instant, Madison wasn't in her hospital bed on a bright, early spring afternoon. She was in the house that night the police claimed her parents were missing. Somewhere, her baby brother screamed. Madison ran into the yard where, lost and forlorn, Andrew stood in the rain. She fell to her knees and held him, breathing in his sweet toddler scent. On the spot, she vowed to never lose sight of him again.

Madison shuddered at the recollection, slamming back to the sounds of a doctor's name paged over the intercom. She blinked to clear the graininess in her eyes and pushed her lower back against the give of her pillow.

The coast guard had searched for her parents with no results. Never a trace, even after all the rescue divers' attempts.

You won't live... Dr. Buckley's words exploded back into the room.

Madison hadn't given much thought to dying. The

days ticked by, and she just expected they would keep on coming. She'd always pictured herself growing old and being surrounded by lots of kiddos she planned on having when she'd found the love of her life. She wanted that now so badly it hurt.

Oh, God, please! I am not ready to go. Not by a long shot.

She fired up her laptop and Googled Workaholics Anonymous. She could join, but the support group wouldn't teach her the correct way to eat and exercise. Others received epiphanies from how-to books, but did she have the sticking power to stay with their advice? She needed to be held accountable for the choices she made. She mulled over her options. Her sister and brother's plans for her might not be inconceivable.

The biggest draw was Madison couldn't give up on a legal contract.

She swirled a sip of water around her mouth as she brought up Guru Brandon's webpage. The sight of the Adonis in a tight T-shirt made her cheeks flush with heat. *Hmmm.* She researched his credentials, found them impressive, discovered he had treated many celebrities, then checked out all the Internet offered, even his fan sites. Thousands of viewers tuned in to see him each week—*well, yeah.*

Who was more qualified to whip her into shape than Guru Brandon? And a reality show would put her agency in the public eye. Plus, she'd turn misfortune into a means of inspiring others in a new and relevant way. A win-win situation.

An hour later, her lunch sat untouched on her bed tray, but she had reached a decision. She'd do the reality show and have Brandon move in with her. A small part of her rejoiced at the idea of seeing him again, a reaction she tried to ignore.

She made a three-way call to Harper and Andrew and waited for her sister to quit scolding her kids for dressing their house cat in a tutu. Moments later, Madison gave them the news. Andrew whooped, and Harper cheered.

"You'll have to stay at my house," Harper said. "That way I can keep an eye on you."

Her sister's comment made Madison glad the nurse arrived with an arsenal of capsules. She grasped for the excuse to conclude the conversation. "Time for my meds."

Within minutes, she found Brandon's business card and tapped in the number. "Hey there," she said after he answered, and his comforting voice reassured her. "Are you still looking for a guinea pig for your show?"

"Madison." He sounded surprised. "It depends on who's asking."

"I am." Her breath caught. "How long would it take for the TV crew to set up production?"

"It's possible for pre-taping to start in as little as two weeks."

"Perfect." She was making headway even if he thought her fickle as rain. "In the meantime, I can strike a deal with the producers." She was organizing her pills while talking in little rushes. "I have to approve of the storyline. And help arrange the scenes. The same with the episode outline. I need the freedom to plug my agency."

Did it sound like she was taking charge? Well, perhaps she was, but then a silence lingered for so long she worried he'd decided her not worth the trouble. Her helplessness in those moments proved unbearable.

"Brandon, it's my doctor." Her eye had started its frenzied twitching again. "I'll be forever grateful to her for mentioning I can turn this thing around. Before it becomes ugly, I mean. All I want is to have one more birthday, one more Christmas with my family." She shoved her hand through her hair. "Guess you're not interested in such a—such a—"

"A hot mess?" The teasing grin in his voice was clear.

She feigned a long-suffering sigh. "You only want me for my name."

He laughed. "Ah, you found me out."

"I guess there's no other reason you'd bother with me."

A pause. "Let's just say it's payback and leave it at that."

Her instincts told her to believe Brandon Kennedy. It was important to trust—in a world where death struck when you weren't watching.

Chapter 3

Three weeks, five days, and eight hours into preproduction, Brandon was mindfully counting to ten.

Madison Gray posed for the cameras on a rattan throne in the patio of the house she'd inherited from her parents. Brandon had advised her to quit taxing her strength. Not her. One take, another, hour after hour, waving her hands as she spoke, fingernails an ivory that matched her flowing tunic and pants.

So pretty, so in tune to helping others, yet so clueless about her own needs.

It didn't matter how much he griped. The TV crew kept fluttering like crazy-ass moths, giving in to her every whim while she insisted on perfecting her profile interview. Frankly, he wasn't for Madison being on his TV show. He told her he'd move in without the cameras, but she insisted on them, claiming InSight would profit from the press.

In his opinion, the concept of his show had gotten lost in the last few years. He'd started out with an idyllic vision of teaching people as his guru had him. Television provided the potential to touch a worldwide audience. The first episodes met all his expectations, but soon his producer wanted him to create drama when there was none. The "black moment"—a time when it looked like his student would fail—lent a forced quality. His program had become as formulaic as all the other reality shows.

He had quit being as happy with *Guru Brandon*. As it was now, only he seemed to get Madison Gray hadn't landed in the hospital by accident.

And the camera operators were doing it again, zeroing in for the umpteenth time.

"My name is Madison Gray. I was born in a small, coastal town in Oregon, but we moved to Santa Monica. I started as a secretary at Christopher Black Casting. The head honcho told me I didn't have the right personality to be a talent agent. By the time I was twenty-five, I had become the president of his department.

"One day, I was stumped when a businessman asked for disabled models to promote his wheelchairs. It became obvious to me that models with a disability were more representative of the consumer. One thing led to another, and I sent out a call for disabled models and actors interested in representation. I found myself flooded with hundreds of requests. On a hunch, I quit my last job and opened a company that introduced a casting agency to a workforce that's becoming more open to embracing diversity. It hasn't always been easy.

"Three weeks back, I collapsed from exhaustion. I found myself at the hospital and afterward going to follow-up doctors. After my fall, I reevaluated my life. I'd been working eighteen hours a day, seven days a week, trying to build a business, but along the way, I destroyed my health. Rather than succumb to premature death, I called Guru Brandon.

"I asked him to help me find a new way of living. The reason I chose to tape my progress is to inform others. My cardiologist gave me the statistics of the population who make poor choices when it comes to their health. I think it's important to show people that, with effort, you can overcome most anything."

The light faded. Madison dipped her chin, dark-lined eyes on the field producer, Willie Stravinsky. "I wasn't at my best. Let's try again."

"Madison, your last take was perfect," Willie said.

"Sorry to be such a bother." She clasped her hands together in her lap. "How's your wife? Eight months into her pregnancy you said. Isn't that lovely?" She raised a finger in a syncopated pause. "How about one more take, and we call it a day?"

Before Willie responded, Madison beckoned to Lilly, the pink-haired makeup artist, the best of the best. "Let's dab on a touch more camouflage." She lifted her face, allowing Lilly to work miracles on the rash across her forehead.

Brandon asked Lilly to step away, then he knelt to speak to Madison with confidentiality the microphones couldn't detect. "Try to cut back on the makeup. Toxins in it exacerbate your eczema."

"But I need the war paint to cover my blotchy skin."

"Take care of yourself, and your outbreaks will disappear."

She cocked an auburn brow at him. "You know how important profile interviews are to the overall picture. A good first impression is everything."

Although he understood her reasoning, he had to make her see his side. "You're on a mission to sell yourself; I get it. That's how you roll. Market and deliver. But it's my job to make sure you're well enough to tolerate the strain of constant filming."

She saluted him. "I'm fit for duty, sir."

"Oh, Madison." His fingers examined the skin on her forehead. "You're supposed to be recovering at your sister's house. Instead, you show up here each day. It's not like I don't enjoy seeing you." He was so close to her now it tempted him to rub off all the pancake to discover what lay beneath.

She lowered her chin. "Once we start production, I'm putty in your hands, Svengali."

The sprinkling system picked then to click on. Soon a mist clung to Madison's hair. On impulse, Brandon found her shawl on the back of her chair and draped it over her head. She looked up at him, her face so incredible his breath stuck in his chest. He'd like to see her dressed in nothing but that gauzy shawl. He'd strip it off her to see the green of her eyes darken the way they were now. With his hands stroking her cheeks, he forgot she was his student.

She turned on a shy smile. "If you don't mind, I'd like to know where all the cameras have been placed in my house."

"Hidden cameras make for a better story."

"I know, but I wrote up a clause objecting to the little devils."

She was trying to manipulate him, he realized, and dropped his hands to his sides as he inhaled a long breath.

"The network lawyers denied the request," he said.

She rose from her chair and tipped back her head to get the last drop of coffee. Her high-heeled boots wobbled precariously, then went out from underneath her. Brandon caught her. His hand lingered on the softness along the small of her back. The exotic scent of her skin fogged his head with visions of wild orchids as he lowered her to a stool.

She rested against a window. "You're my knight in shining armor, Brandon Kennedy."

He shook his head, blocking out the seductiveness in her tone. At this point, she'd kiss a rabid bat to get her way.

He refused to be drawn in. "Ms. Gray, you might want to lose those shoes."

She stretched her legs out in front of her and tapped her ankle boots together. "But presenting an illusion is my specialty. It's part of what I do." She glanced up, eyes dialing down to emerald slits. "So why not allow me to sell your show to the best of my ability?"

"If you don't pass the medical evaluation, the network will cancel the production date, and you'll be out." He folded his arms in front of him. "What will you do then?"

Her face flashed with something dark. Was it fear? Just a trace. Fear he could use, play on it to get her to see logic. Still, her fear disturbed him, blocked him, stirred him with a racing prickle beneath his skin.

"The yogic life will give you peace if you work at it, Madison."

"I—" she said when a tinny rendition of "Empire State of Mind" rang out, and she yanked off her shoes and paced the floor barefoot, ruby toes glistening on cement, her jeweled-cased cell phone tucked between neck and shoulder.

"Kristen, thank God you got back to me. The new hire is as marketable as sin on a popsicle stick. Securing him might prove one of our most significant finds."

Brandon heaved a sigh. In two more weeks, she wouldn't be any closer to stable health than she was today. She'd fail to thrive if someone didn't intervene. The sinking sensation in his gut waylaid him. He'd be no help to her if she resisted him, although he'd do everything possible to make it easier for her to comply with what he expected from her.

One of the network execs had met with the field producers in the small office. Brandon motioned him into the privacy of the hall.

"Rob, I want you to get the legal department to draw up a new article stating Madison must give up all digital gadgetry for the two months we're in production."

"Are you kidding? No cell phones or laptops or tablets? Madison will feel like you ripped off her arm and poked out her eye. What if she doesn't agree to the terms?"

Brandon shrugged. "There'll be no show."

****

April 1st. Ah, yes, April Fool's Day. Late afternoon. The weather breezy at eighty degrees, the debut of *Guru Brandon* started production.

On a coastal stretch of Pico Boulevard in Santa Monica, Brandon met Harper's CRV as it parked on the drive flanked by flowering cherry trees. Madison exited the passenger side. She sprayed breath freshener in her mouth, and the air filled with the stench of chemicals.

Her face was more bloated than before, her body frailer. Brandon's hand clasped her elbow as he escorted her. He worried if he let go, she might not make it to her house. But as he guided her around the staff vehicles blocking her driveway, he got a whiff of tobacco.

He held her suitcase in his other hand. They made their way through the dark shadows of the trees, the wind carrying the scent of the sea. A rustle shook the bushes, and the paparazzi sprang toward them. Cameras erupted in bursts of light.

Madison shielded her eyes, and he darted in front of her.

"That's enough, you guys," he said, not wanting to sound as territorial.

She gave him a slight shove. "It's all right." She nodded at the cameras now orbiting around her, flashing, dead leaves crunching underfoot.

Within minutes, she was blinking like the reporters had blinded her, or at the least, left her with spots before her eyes. The sound crew snapped a microphone to her collar, and she flinched but maintained her plastered smile.

He removed a leaf that had fallen into her hair. Her skin was pallid, the paleness of her face accentuated by the shadows of the pines. If only he could whisk her off to a hidden island on the other side of the world, he'd teach her how to live without interference.

As if oblivious of his efforts, she twisted away from him. A woman on a high wire, swinging a clipboard like mad at her side. With her gaze directed straight ahead, she missed the sight and sounds of the ocean peeking through the trees. The sun hung thinly in the sky, and the glare came off the water, pleasantly filling his eyes.

"Look around you," he said, trying to slow her down. "See all the beauty?"

Her feet jiggled in her killer spikes. "Uh-huh, that's

fine, but I—"

"Check out the color from the flowers in the shade among the moss and dense ferns." Her indifference spurred his rant. "Look at the climbing vines. The stepping stones in the ivy and the meandering pathways. Do you see the seagulls circling above the chimney on the north corner of your house?"

"Uh-huh," she said, raising her tablet. "I thought you'd begin with a lesson."

Her rebuke struck a nerve. "I did. I gave you a lecture on celebrating the miracles in your everyday world. And another on living in the now."

She turned her head out of microphone range. "I beg you not to go all woo-woo on me."

Was this the same woman he'd treated in her office?

"A prescription for good health," he said as she scribbled notes. "Pay attention, Madison. Pay heed to nature and all it has to teach you."

She stifled a yawn as she dropped her clipboard to her side and pivoted in the doorway of her house to face the cameras. "Here we are, home sweet home."

To reach her, he quoted from a local historian's diary he'd come across. " 'Here in these almost holy hills, an ennobling stillness makes the mind ascend to heaven.' "

She rolled her eyes. "Go for it, Guru."

With cameras shooting, in front and in the back, the caravan traveled into the deep, still blueness that was Madison's home.

Harper's weary voice drifted from the open doorway. "All right, I'm heading out," she said as if glad to leave. "Maddie, you do everything Brandon says. Get enough sleep. Eat right." She ventured toward him, her lips pressing against his ear. "Don't let my sister get an inch."

The warning echoed in his head like a danger sign at the end of a rocky ledge.

"Thanks for everything," Madison said, hugging her sister.

Harper left soon after, and Brandon was alone—well, not entirely alone—with Madison. Staff members murmured as they worked behind the scenes. Footsteps shuffled as camera operators made their way down the hall and into a bright, spacious great room.

Here it smelled of floor wax, fresh cut flowers, and old books. If he had time to himself, he'd have explored the shelves. Be it a volume with a printed scent or leather worn with use, he'd treat each with the reverence it deserved.

"A home without books is like a body without a soul," he said but realized he was alone and talking to himself.

He found Madison with her back to a floor-to-ceiling window that allowed glimpses of the ocean. She was going through her mail. The late afternoon light made the bluish shadows beneath her eyes even more noticeable. He noted the hard line of her shoulders and the weary set of her head as she smoothed an invisible wrinkle from her sleeve.

Madison Gray hadn't changed one iota. Her self-annihilation was imminent. He had to look away. So far, he seemed unable to do anything to stop it.

****

Madison spotted Brandon studying her, and her shoulder blades jetted sharply against the cold glass. He was giving her that "you pathetic thing" look again. She hated it when he did that. It was like the man was looking at her without her clothes—a fate worse than malaria.

He clapped his hands. "So, Madison, are you ready to begin your new journey?" He had that kooky New Age jargon going on again, which irked her to no end.

"I am," she said and allowed him to pull her to her feet. Honestly, she wasn't sure of anything except how damned good he looked.

Not many guys got away with mixing an ecru silk shirt with distressed denim and flip-flops. His hair shone, a mixture of ebony and bronze. She admired the elegance in his face as it fought with his imperfections. Those flaws drew her eye. The small, thin scar through his left eyebrow and the two-day bristle with its hint of amber. A look few men were able to pull off, his blending class with grit.

In her book, a man was close to perfect when he wasn't trying. Too bad for the camera vultures. Hold on a sec, what was she thinking? This was strictly business. And reality check, her new live-in was steering her through her house as if she had lost her way.

"It's after five," he said.

"I can't wait to eat something besides hospital food. I'm game for anything that's not saltless and plain."

"I think I've got just what the doctor ordered without sacrificing taste."

They entered the white and indigo kitchen, colors her mother had used. This was her childhood home, after all. The place where she'd ruled the roost after her parents' disappearance. Her arm rested on the slate countertop, and a whirring came from the far corner with a *click, click, click.*

A muscle in Madison's neck cramped when she turned her head. "I see the house has acquired a thousand eyes," she said, all devil-may-care.

No one would allow her a script. She supposed the producers wanted to catch her off her game. They were in for a disappointment. If Madison Gray excelled at anything, it was keeping her cool under pressure.

Brandon dipped his head in her fridge. "What do we have here?" A screech rang out of objects being slid along the glass. "Ketchup, mustard, and that's it?" He surfaced with one of his million-dollar smiles.

She peered around his shoulder. "You missed the champagne on the inside of the door. A little bubbly keeps a girl in the pink, don't you agree?"

He took the bottle from her and displayed it on the counter as if making it an example. "Let's begin by observing what your attitude is toward food, drink, and your routine."

"I usually eat in." Her hand flitted across the takeout menus attached to the refrigerator door. "What are you in the mood for?"

"Excuse me?"

"Pizza, tacos, Chinese?" Ordering out would take the burden out of his having to cook. "There's a little French bistro that makes a steak that's fabulous. Your taste buds will whimper in delight, then beg for more."

"Takeout is not how we do it."

She tried to hide her disappointment. "It's not?"

"No." He headed to the island in the middle of the kitchen. "Let me show you."

A cigarette would calm her nerves right about now. Despite her good intentions, she'd stashed the only pack she had in a desk drawer when she checked her mail. What she wouldn't give for a flute of champagne. Shoot, she'd just as soon down a double shot of tequila. A stiff drink might help her deal with Brandon Kennedy.

She kept getting sidetracked by his well-defined, well-endowed biceps in his clingy shirt. Did he pump iron? He must get paid big bucks for being Guru Brandon of the faultlessly masculine physique. Performing a few yoga poses didn't build muscles, now did it?

She gawked at him, heat traveling up the back of her spine to her neck. It must be her out-of-whack hormones due to stress and God knew what else. After all, he wasn't doing anything but taking containers from one of those cloth bags people endorse to save the planet.

"Relax." He said it in the same mild way he had three weeks ago in her office. When he'd been her savior, the person she most wanted to emulate.

Madison peeked inside a bag. "Ah, so we *are* eating in."

"Not quite. Tonight, we're cooking."

"I think I'll leave cooking to you."

She noticed him keeping track of her out of the corner of his eye. She wanted to appear at her best, but that icky stomach acid rose to her throat and all but choked her.

He passed her a serving spoon. "Nothing to it, trouper."

Her heart did a little jig. "Trouper" was what he

had called her before—before the fallout of discovery.

He's trying to make everything easy for me, and I adore him for it.

What struck her the most about Guru Brandon was how nice he was. She'd been expecting him to turn into a jerk once the cameras rolled. But no, it hadn't happened.

The least she could do was sling on an apron. "What's in the cartons? I suspect it isn't pork dim sum or beef á la Sichuan."

"It's all-natural ingredients."

"I'm not a big fan of tofu and sprouts." Her voice sounded high pitched and bitchy.

Let's edit, pretty please.

"I'd like you to observe yourself, Madison. See if your resistance is to change or to deeper issues you need to explore."

She winced at that. "So what's the plan?"

He popped open a carton. "For the next few weeks, you'll have a wonderful time letting go of toxicity in your body and mind."

She stuck her tongue in the side of her mouth as she observed a bowl heaped with broccoli spears. "I thought you'd cut my calorie intake." She adjusted the twisted waistband of her black organza jumpsuit. "I know I need to lose a few pounds." That was a good part of what all this fuss was about. "Okay, bring on the lean beef."

"You'll want to stick to a small variety of foods and drinks to regulate your digestion."

"Oh, will I?" Wasn't a big dose of protein what she needed? "I guess this means no charbroiled steak tonight?"

"In your time with me, no meat shall pass your lips. I want to start you on the right track. It's the only way to get rid of the poisons you've stored in your body."

She licked her dry, cracked lips. No meat, poultry, fish, no booze, or cigs. How would she last? Her head spun like she was on the Tilt-a-Whirl, and the world went fuzzy. Dark. Her legs buckled, the floor coming up to greet her.

Brandon wrapped an arm around her waist as she grabbed his shoulders with both hands to keep from taking still another tumble, this disaster displayed on national television.

In the name of all that's holy, stop the film!

Their heads lowered, and their eyes locked as they stood close, bodies brushing before she jolted away like she'd touched a high-voltage wire.

"Sorry!" she cried.

His eyes had darkened to navy. "You'd better take a seat."

As he pulled out a barstool for her at the island, an unbearable warmth flooded her face. Up to now, for publicity's sake, her life had been a reality show—one she'd made sure displayed no true-life complications. That's why it had been imperative she keep tabs on the promo. Her reels of film tape must sizzle with a version of Madison Gray she sanctioned. What she hadn't bargained on was falling on her face.

Brandon had warned her. She'd been a moron to ignore the signs. Standing and walking seemed like such trivial things until her body stopped allowing her to do either of them. If she didn't pay heed, the network's medical team would cancel the show. She'd fail before she began. Madison would be back to square one. Square zero to be exact. Then what would happen to her? Worse, what would happen to her clients?

****

Before Brandon got in another word, the chief executive producer, Spencer Hugo, was marching toward them with a scowl on his face.

He set both hands on the butcher block, his sausage-like fingers splayed. "Ms. Gray, we can't have you passing out like you did in your office. Brandon aided you then, but that won't wash here on the show. If you're sick, we'll call off production. Lawsuits and all that mess. You get my drift?"

Madison hadn't stood to confront Spence, which bothered Brandon more than if she would have jumped to her feet and bared her teeth. It proved she was leery. She dealt with showbiz execs on a daily basis, but she might need a hand this time around.

Brandon snagged a binder and turned to Spence. "Have you gone over the preliminary outline since you got back from vacation?"

Madison raised a hand. "That's not what Spence wishes to address. It's those safety clauses, but then he didn't see the promo where I was wearing those high-heeled boots and would have fallen on my rump." She crossed her legs at the ankles. "If you hadn't caught me, Brandon, I'd have hurt myself."

Spence shook his head. "No, I didn't witness that."

Madison's manicured index finger drew a circle on the butcher block. "People have their vices, and mine has always been fashion." Her head tilted to the side. "Let's face it. A poor choice of shoes can ruin the effect of the most artfully composed outfit." She hung her head and let out a sigh. "To tell the absolute truth so help me God, heels, the higher the better, make my legs appear thinner."

"What does this—?" Spence started.

"I now realize my choice in shoes might be a stumbling block, shall we say? So, Spence, from now on, I vow to wear only Nikes or ballerina flats."

Spence centered his attention on her. "It wasn't your shoes that made you take a spill."

"Well, that depends on your perception." She slanted a hopeful glance Brandon's way. "What do you think? You were the one who rescued me. You be the judge. You want what's good for all concerned, don't you?"

What he didn't want was for her to continue the show if she wasn't strong enough. But if they stopped now, what would become of her? Torn between his ethics and his concern for her, he stalled.

And then he caught sight of her mutely pleading with him, prompting him to take her in his care—to mend her.

How could he turn his back? "Spence, it's those five-inch daggers. They need to go." Conflicted, he turned the bowl full of fresh veggies over with a little too much enthusiasm. "Time to eat. Are you with me on this, Madison?"

She kicked off her heels and shot up. "Ready and willing."

Spence didn't move from his hunched position over the island. "I don't know. I think Ms. Gray is playing us."

"Hmmm, you could have something there." Brandon picked up a spoon. "But if she were perfectly healthy, we wouldn't be here."

Spence exhaled out his nose, nostrils flaring, then backed off. "You better believe I'll be keeping an eye on things."

Madison slid in beside Brandon. "I may not win a Betty Crocker Bake-Off anytime soon, but I'm handy with a knife."

"Have at it." His back stiffened. "We're going to add our sprouts. They possess a cooling energy."

"Energy I understand," she said, her nose wrinkling. "But a *cooling* energy?"

"It's an Ayurvedic term. You'll be learning about it." He poured from the bowl. "Now we stir in some mushrooms. They take away the toxins. Give it a dash of sea salt and two sprigs of rosemary. And blast off."

The blue ring of gas flame kicked up with a woof, and Brandon placed the pan on the burner. *Sizzle, sizzle, spark, spark, boom*! Soon the kitchen steamed, smelling deliciously of spices and seasonings.

She bent over the warm stove and inhaled. "Smells scrumptious." She straightened. Without her heels, she was shorter than him by a few inches.

He found he liked it that way. "You hungry?"

"You have no idea." She turned, the twilight filtering through the window touching her face with flattering pink light. "I don't suppose you changed your mind. Is there maybe roast chicken or broiled lobster in the works for tonight?"

"No, but I think you'll like what we have prepared." But would she?

"Veggies make a perfect appetizer, but on the horizon, I see noodles or potatoes—something of substance."

"Didn't you state in a questionare you needed to lose weight?"

Her shoulders slumped. "I suppose I did."

While he dished up the meal, she dimmed the starburst of a chandelier and lit candles on a smoky glass table top. Soon, soft jazz floated from someplace hidden, and she had grabbed a pair of cloth napkins and a vase filled with ivory roses without his being aware.

Her breath caught as he pulled out the Renaissance-style chair for her, and again he caught the drift of her scent—that touch of the Orient and the exotic.

"There you are, Madison." He took the seat across from her. "Bon appétit."

Chapter 4

"I'm not a bird," Madison said, though the aroma made her mouth water.

Brandon shrugged. "It may surprise you to know how little you need to eat to be full."

"I can't see myself as a vegan." She stabbed a broccoli spear he had arranged on her cream-colored Lenox plate. "Not ever."

"What if your life depended on it?"

Her fork paused midair. "You got me there, buster. But I've always heard the body needs protein." She all but tasted the baked potatoes, chives, and sour cream she was giving up. "If left to my own devices, I'd have gone for a lean-beef burger."

"Hmmm, not the best choice, and you already know it, so you can quit making a fuss." Brandon got up, and with the finesse of a leading man, closed the french doors she had opened to the flagstone terrace. "No need to waste energy."

"I'm sorry?" She frowned in confusion. "What did you say?"

"The air conditioning is on."

"I'm a little too warm."

"When you steal from the environment, Madison, you take from every living creature on Earth, including yourself."

"I see." No, she saw nothing of the sort but nibbled

a bite of broccoli. "Hey, this is yummy." Unable to believe it, she waved her fork. "Who'd have thought?"

"I'll take that as a compliment, coming from the woman who doesn't eat her vegetables."

The candlelight was doing remarkable things to Brandon's face. His eyelashes were to die for. How come men always got the crazy-thick lashes? Too bad he was such a go-green sort of guy. Talk about different lifestyles. Her head hurt just thinking about it. Two months stretched before her, and she wondered how she'd get through them, but this wasn't the first time she'd dealt with difficult people. No. The idea was to find common ground.

She sipped from Waterford crystal. "Since we'll be roomies, I'd like to know more about you. Why not give me your bio?"

"My bio?" Grinning, he tapped the rim of his glass with his knife. "Are you hiring, Ms. Gray?" He sat back, discipline in his bearing. "There's nothing too remarkable. My mother was from India, which is how I got my olive complexion. The Irish from my father gave me the blue eyes, not to mention a temper that used to flare up now and then."

"I take it you've got your emotions under control?"

"Most of the time. I try to apply right thinking."

"Right thinking, I suppose that means being a Pollyanna?"

He laughed then, warming up the room. "There's more to it than positivity."

She propped a wrist on the table. "What was your childhood like?"

"Ordinary. That is until a talent scout spotted me in a Pasadena theater gig and signed me in what would be a three-year hitch in the soap opera, *Life and Destiny*."

She almost fell out of her chair. "I thought I recognized you right from the beginning. Matthew Post. You were every teenage girl's idol."

He shrugged as if he hadn't known of it. "No big deal."

Oh, the things she longed tell him. *I had a gazillion pictures of you plastered on my walls.*

She cleared her throat. "That role earned you an Emmy. I don't understand it. Why are you slumming in reality TV?" That sounded mean, and she hadn't meant for it to. She was just maddeningly curious.

"I was tired of acting with all its snares."

"Go on." She leaned closer. "I'm dying to know more."

"There's not much to say." And he repeated the taped monolog from his show. He talked about his medical residency and the disillusionment that drove him back to his birthplace in Bombay.

She waited for him to finish. "You gave me your bio all right, rehearsed and film-worthy, but not at all personal. I asked about your childhood."

"Perfect." He gave his shoulders a noticeable squeeze. "I can't complain." He uttered too quick a laugh. "My parents didn't beat me or hide me in the basement."

She always asked her impending clients the next question. "Answer me this. What one person was more influential than all the others?"

"That's easy." His face lit. "My mother."

His response surprised her. She'd have expected him to give the name of some high muck-a-muck guru something or other. "Why your mom?"

"When I was a kid, she told me stories about India. She had a way of bringing her prose to life with such lucid imagery I imagined I was there. You might have liked her fables. Her heroines were fighters, pretty much like you."

She felt flattered. "Thank you."

"What about you, Madison?" He paused, eyeing her. "Do you have a tale to tell?"

She set her elbows on the table and peered at him through the blue veil of smoke rising from the candle flame. No one ever asked her about herself. Just how much should she tell him without exposing her past?

Pay attention to the cameras. Remember where you are.

She toyed with her napkin. "I grew up in this very house. It was as idyllic as a Thomas Kincaid painting." Glittering generalities wouldn't help anyone. Plus, the truth would come out—better sooner than later. She released a pent-up breath. "But then my parents died."

"I'm terribly sorry, Madison." The lines of unfiltered sympathy in his face hindered her from uttering a reply.

If only they'd go back to lighthearted chitchat, even the stilted kind—even if she had thought it best to get real. At least she wouldn't be losing it on network television. Nothing could be worse. But down deep, she knew her private affairs would surface. A certainty about reality TV was that people better not fear the skeletons in their closets.

"Do you want to talk about it?" he asked.

"A day doesn't pass that I don't think of my mom and dad." She was about to add more, but reality shows played up personal tragedies. Well, it wouldn't happen to her. She rose to her feet. "That's about it."

Her hands shook the dishes as she carried them to the sink. Talk about an emotional basket case! Anyone seeing this last film clip would think *Madison's about to have a meltdown.* Her falling apart wasn't acceptable. As an agent, she upheld a reputation. The iron butterfly, they called her behind her back. At least, she wanted to believe they did. True, she might seem hard-nosed given the right conditions, but a woman in power must appear invincible.

Brandon didn't speak. It was like he sensed she needed time to herself. The man was perceptive—she'd give him that. He scooted out a barstool for her, but she insisted on helping him clean up. They did the dishes without stacking them in the dishwasher, did them by hand like an old married couple bonded by routine. He washed, she dried.

****

Madison's interview caught on-the-fly...

"Those veggies threw out an aroma that made me famished. I was craving meat and potatoes. So I expected the worst. But the broccoli rated five stars. I couldn't believe it. Brandon explained I didn't need much food to be full.

"I have a mandatory weight-loss clause in my contract with the show. I feel positive about it since it was my idea. The reason I signed on is to learn to take better care of myself. But it's an ego thing too. I'm more likely to stay and to do my part because America is watching.

"The candlelight made our first dinner together intimate. Not in a romantic sense, mind you. More a get-it-off-your-chest confession. I told Guru Brandon things about me that may or may not air. Since then, I've been second guessing myself—if you must know."

After the interview, Madison wanted to get far away from the cast and crew of *Guru Brandon*. She needed to connect with her people. Her staff. Her clients. The persons who needed her as much as she needed them.

The producers had turned off her Internet access. That meant she must disengage herself from Facebook, Instagram, and Twitter, and that meant no texting or blogging—no communication with the outside world, period.

Only hours into production and Madison's chest felt like a rock was stuck there. Her hands and feet were all jittery. The pathetic truth, this going cold turkey from all she held dear was giving her fits.

Brandon was spraying the countertops with a vinegary liquid that burned her nostrils, which gave her an excuse to leave. Seconds later, she'd ascended to her upstairs bedroom. She shoved into her traffic jam of a closet and clicked on the throwaway cell phone she'd buried in a pocket in case of emergency. The phone lit, showing her messages, adrenaline kicking up inside her. She moaned with pleasure.

Minutes later, her body relaxed. Her eyelids at half-mast, she listened to her voicemail with the ecstasy of one eating dark chocolate or having great sex. Even though the dust inside her closet made her sneeze, she cleared a space on a bench and sat in the comfort of the dark, her chin on the silky fabric of her collar.

But then the light flashed on, and Brandon appeared. "Madison, what are you doing?"

She clutched her cell phone to her chest.

"Whatever do you mean?"

The cameras crowded in. Her walk-in closet was a catchall—a spot in the house so much like a warzone she often felt like entering waving a white flag. Now all of TV Land would know Maddie Gray was, in secret, a slob. This moment was hardly her finest.

The heat of Brandon examining her made her armpits damp.

"I'm sure you have a good excuse to have a phone in your hand." He appeared polite enough.

Her left eye spasmed. "I got a little homesick for the sound of my clients' voices. You understand how it is." The edge of his sleeve grazed her forehead, and she experienced a curious ting-a-ling deep inside. "You've had your share of clients."

"Come on, now." That fascinating cleft in his chin deepened. "Because you're a pro, you know not to break the rules."

"If I were allowed one call, it would get me through."

He gave a calm and collected shrug. "There's a stipulation, isn't there, in the contract? You wouldn't want to break it."

Her chest heaved. "Oh, what the hell can it hurt?"

"You don't have to curse." His voice had grown quieter than before.

She bit the inside of her mouth. He was right. She'd stumbled on this last scene unrehearsed and forgetting herself. Could things get any worse?

She gave him a smile sweet as peach pie. "I apologize, but I have a client who missed his connecting flight out of Dallas, so he will arrive in Hollywood four hours later than expected. He wants to know if he should still go to his audition. I need to take this."

"It's my understanding you were to turn your workload over to one or more of your colleagues."

Her eyelid felt like a devil moth was beating its wings against it. "So you won't grant me this pertinent exception?"

His erect carriage took on an ascetic aspect, his arms at his sides, palms turned upward—a holy shrine of masculine bravado. "It's your call."

"I need to stay connected." Her employees and her clients would survive, but what about her? Much of her time consisted of running theirs.

"Madison." The way he spoke her name was so gentle he could have been addressing a child. "You can't get in touch with your soul while checking your voicemail."

She dug her bare heels deep into the rug and glowered at him. Why didn't he bend? For one marvelous second, she thought she'd convinced him. She'd been wrong. The more she pushed him, the more serene he became. Time for another tactic.

"I wonder what the viewers will think? Odds are they'll agree with me." She moved her mouth into a determined line for the cameras. "I believe most of you will say this is a free country. We may own a phone unless we're in prison. Am I in prison, Officer Brandon?"

"There's nothing about this you haven't agreed to." His dogged self-assurance held no aggression. "The contract. Remember?"

She wilted. Out of the corner of her eye, she spotted Spencer Hugo, his hands on his hips. If she weren't careful, she'd get herself sued for breach of contract.

Her shoulders drooped even more. She'd already bungled things twice. What was wrong with her? Why get fixated on a meaningless stress like a cell phone?

She had underestimated Brandon Kennedy with his silent verve, and now she felt defeated, done-in. Madison inhaled so hard her lungs hurt. She hung her arm in the air, struggling to release her fingers from the object of her desire. Usually, when obstacles arose, she changed her direction to reach her goal. The least she could manage was leaving Brandon flat.

Let the footage show her ditching him. "I'm off to bed."

Too tired to think, she padded straight out of her bedroom and halfway down the stairs before she realized her mistake and turned back.

****

After returning to the first floor, the cameras circled Brandon. The faces of the TV crew in the shadows were mask-like. The air hot. *Snick, snick, snick. Whir.*

They were signaling his take on the previous scene. Perspiration trickled down his sides. He held back, thinking of what he owed his audience, of his privacy and his need to cut Madison some slack.

"It's difficult," he said, "to be on a reality show after suffering a concussion and learning you must change your lifestyle. Even the best of us would have trouble not showing a little raw emotion. Tomorrow, Madison will get up and begin a practice that will start her on a pathway to better health."

Spence barged in from the sidelines. "That's it for

now. Let's call it a night."

Brandon relaxed his shoulders and addressed the crew. "There wasn't much time to put this show together, and it's different from anything we've done. You're used to sprints. I've opted for a marathon. I want you to know how much I appreciate your cooperation."

The hot lights of the cameras faded, and the staff filed out the front door. Relieved, Brandon trailed behind them and hoisted equipment into a van idling with the other production vehicles in Madison's driveway.

After they'd gone, the gates swung shut with a metallic clang. He ambled back, peering through the trees out at the Pacific under a silver sky. He loved the sea and would have given a week's salary to sit on a cliff in the briny wind and meditate himself into a trance-like state. But Madison might need him tonight.

Never had he dealt with such a hard-headed woman, but the eyes that kept meeting his had been unflinchingly beautiful. The electricity each time she spoke had caught him unaware, making it difficult to get air into his lungs. He had won that last round only to feel like he lost. Who knew why? But he hadn't signed up to police Madison Gray. Or had he?

He went back inside to mull things over. Silence. The house was holding its breath. The soles of his flip-flops squeaked, and he took them off. In the echoing cathedral of a room, a motor rumbled from the kitchen. As he tramped barefoot over cool teakwood, he found the fridge door open and emitting light from its small appliance bulb.

He didn't want to scare her. "Madison?"

The refrigerator door hid her from view.

She must have gotten hungry and was trying to put together a snack. Brandon should have plopped his yoga mat down and guarded the kitchen like a watchdog. When he was around her, he'd turned into someone else. To Madison Gray, all rules were up for debate. "A badass." That's what she wanted everyone to believe. But he wasn't buying it. He remembered her desperation after she'd mentioned her parents at dinner. That pained look in her eyes, the unsteady gait after she'd revealed more.

A day doesn't pass that I don't think about my mom and dad...

Their death had left behind a scar that still bled. He didn't have a right to pry into her past. And yet. Maybe bringing it out would set her on the road to recovery.

Everyone had secrets, even him. An unexpected wave of nausea ripped through him. He saw himself as the boy who'd rushed home to cook meals for a mother so ill she couldn't manage it herself. Was it any wonder, at twelve, he'd decided he wanted to heal the sick?

Madison scraped the cartons along the shelf of the fridge.

"Madison, what are you—?"

He saw her then. Bent over, she was stark *naked*. He let out a sharp groan, yanked off his cardigan, and threw it over the back of her shoulders. She radiated with warmth from sleep and smelled of musky femininity. When she stood, he got a flash of her nude body before he fastened all the buttons and jerked his gaze to her face.

"Madison." He noticed her eyes. Unfocused and

vague. Was she asleep?

He tossed the dish towel on the remote camera. Now what? To wake her up would mortify her. He couldn't do that. If he steered her toward the stairs, she'd likely wander back to her bedroom. But what if she ended up outside? Holy Mother, he had to do something.

But wait! The top drawer screeched, and cellophane rattled.

What kind of game was she playing? Was she hitting him up for a package of Hostess Cupcakes? Of course, not. She was asleep, but he couldn't allow her to eat them. It would spoil all she'd accomplished. No rules existed for this. What should he do? Let her consume the plaque-building calories and turn a blind eye? His fist pounded the air. Not on his watch.

He gently nudged her shoulder. "Madison, wake up." No reaction. "Madison?"

Her eyes fluttered open. "What are you doing here?"

More than anything, he wanted her to feel safe with him. She might get the wrong idea, but he had to tell her the truth.

"I didn't mean to intrude."

"Intrude?" Her stare lowered. She peeked inside the sweater with its haphazard buttoning job. "What's this?" She uttered a startled cry, her eyebrows lifting. "I'm not wearing any clothes."

"You're wiped out. Sleepwalking's not that uncommon when—"

"Oh, go stand on your head." She bolted away, but not without first throwing the cupcakes at him. "You better destroy that film, or I'll track you down."

Chapter 5

At six thirty a.m., while waiting for the wooliness in her vision to fade, Madison shifted on her mattress. The divine scent that accompanied Brandon Kennedy drifted up from beneath the Egyptian sheets. Her forehead tightened. Had he slept with her last night? For a mere second, she smiled. Any man so, well, masculine, with his—

She sat up straight and tensed her fingers on the cardigan she wore. An absurd image wormed its way into her thoughts. Hadn't she found herself in the kitchen last night? She slapped her cheeks and shook her head. *Oh, my Lord!*

She'd experienced one of her sleepwalking episodes and set off downstairs naked as a centerfold. If she hadn't been so exhausted, she would have taken the time to at least grab a nightshirt before hitting the sack.

Nobody was to blame but her.

She rammed her back against the pillows. Shit, shit, shit! Brandon Kennedy had gotten an eyeful of her body. She'd rather die than face him now. If it weren't for the damned contract, she'd bail.

She nibbled the cuticle of her index finger. When it came down to it, she trusted Brandon, trusted him to act professionally. And hadn't he? She remembered seeing a dishtowel over the eye of the remote camera. She recalled he'd created a benign distance between them, his hands stuffed in the pockets of his jeans. When he spoke to her, it was with the tone someone would assume to calm a spooked filly.

And what had been her response? Madison cradled her head on her arms. She'd been like a wild thing, throwing cupcakes at him. Why did she keep getting herself in more hot water? Nothing about this reality TV business was easy. But then maybe her becoming fit, even with all her pitfalls and disgraces, would motivate others who struggled with being overweight. Or did she want to believe she could make a difference, needed to believe it?

Whatever the reason, it got her slipping out of Brandon's sweater and into a thick terrycloth robe. In the semi-darkness, as she descended the stairs, the house possessed a shifting quality, the ceiling beams and carved Italian mantel slightly out of focus. The dark mauve sky through the glass bore the beginnings of a bright new day.

The promise of coffee and maybe even a cigarette, if she were quick about it, had her tiptoeing into the kitchen where she opened a cabinet. She'd just fetch a cup to stick under her idol, the coffee maker.

Without warning, Brandon wove out of the shadows and stepped into the light. With his mussed hair and flushed face, it appeared he'd gotten up before dawn to jog down the coastline. Didn't it figure?

"Good morning, Madison." He set a steaming hot mug in her hands. "Thought you might appreciate a little help from a friend."

"Thanks." Wishing to dissolve into the floorboards, she raised her elbow so that he could retrieve his cardigan. "I had a bad night, but I'm well now."

Everything seemed fine between them. He had passed her the mug like it was a peace offering. He likely felt guilty about the cell phone ordeal. Seeing her in the altogether must have embarrassed him, and he was trying to make it up to her. She clutched the mug with both hands, feeling smug. He owed her this one little favor.

Coffee! Every cell inside her screamed. How some people fell out of bed and hobbled to jobs without a blast of caffeine was beyond her.

She laughed for joy. "Bless you, guru dear." The pure bliss associated with drinking a good roast depended on the warmth of the cup. No accident behind why folks cuddled up to enjoy their coffee. Nothing like it on a chilly morning. A warm mug was a warm heart.

She grinned as she took that very first sip.

What? Icky! Nasty!

She spat out the liquid and choked on what she'd swallowed.

"Madison?" Brandon pounded her back. "It's just hot water with a splash of lemon."

"I expected something leaded."

"You mean coffee?" He shot her an incredulous look, shaking his head. "Coffee's a hard wallop to your kidneys."

"My kidneys never complained." She thought they rather liked the abuse. How could she go without caffeine? Anything but that. "Come on, just give me a teeny, weeny bit of those precious wake-up beans." Every nerve in her body screamed and twitched. "I need my coffee—don't you get it? Without java, I turn into a zombie." A fix, she needed her fix. Why didn't he understand? "Please, just let me wean myself from the juice."

"It takes three weeks to break a habit," he said. "You may drink coffee, but in twenty-one days you won't remember needing caffeine." He pulled out a plate and handed it to her. "I thought it a good idea if you made breakfast this morning, if you're up to it."

With her mood as out of sorts, she couldn't help lashing out at him. "Only if me making breakfast means warming up a jelly doughnut in the microwave."

"A cardinal rule, Madison. It's not a good idea to use the microwave because it zaps nutrients from foods. Another thing, there's zero nutrition in doughnuts."

"I should have figured as much." She longed to take a jackhammer to the cameras. "You'll say doughnuts are like swallowing barbells."

"Now you're catching on. You can create a diet...not to excess." His lecturing had no end, just an endless chain of denial.

"I need a shower."

"You'll breathe easier after a little hot-water therapy."

Lucky for him, he ducked into the pantry because she'd been about to throw her coffee mug at him and shout, "How's that for hot-water therapy?"

The man was a total bohemian. No coffee, the very idea was countercultural. She spent an hour showering and styling her hair, exasperated when she noted a new rash had erupted near her temple. Brandon's spiel about makeup sprang to mind, and she refrained from troweling it on her face. Once dressed, she took to the stairs with such a fierce hunger she could have eaten every hotdog in Dodger Stadium.

Of all things, he placed a grass-colored smoothie in

front of her at the table.

Her mouth unhinged. He had to be kidding. "It's not St. Patrick's Day, is it?"

He handed her a plate. "There's more."

"What do we have here?" She laced her hands together and angled her head. "A ripe banana, a handful of berries, kale leaves, and some weird sprouts. Yippee."

He set a teapot before her. "Green tea and chai—enjoy."

Was he out of his mind? "This isn't exactly eggs Benedict." She meant to laugh but cackled instead. "It isn't even a blueberry pancake, but I suppose it will do."

"Do? Is that all you can say?"

"Don't push it." With both hands, she wolfed down the banana.

"Hold on there." He leaned around her shoulder. "Chew your food at least thirty-three times to digest it well. Savor and concentrate on each bite. Eating is a sacred act."

Brandon was watching her with his matinee-idol intensity. It was as if he believed worshiping this rabbit food was equal to kneeling before the Holy Grail. Still, she had trouble breaking her stare away from his.

"Well, Madison?"

She lifted her elbows and cradled her head in her hands. *Oh, shoot me!*

His crazy ideas grated on her nerves, but the steamy way he peered at her sent tremors rippling through to those weak places inside her. No denying he fostered the image of male virility. A walking, talking ad for the benefits of a habitual healthy lifestyle, and that reminded her how much she wanted to be well.

He whisked her empty plate off to the sink. "How about we start the day with a trip to the market in Sycamore Square?"

"Now you're talking!" Maybe she'd coax him into getting some real grub. Things were looking up. "That's wonderful. Absolutely fab."

A laugh rolled out of him, deep-throated and lush. "Try not to look so glum."

"Yes, well…" She batted her eyelashes. "Deprivation will do that to a person."

"Speaking of which." He flashed her his lady-killer grin. "I took the liberty while you were dressing of throwing out everything you shouldn't be eating from the cabinets and drawers. I knew you'd thank me."

With a flat hand, her warm, fuzzy feelings dissipating, she slapped the tabletop. "Oh, tell me you didn't toss out my chocolate?"

"Candy bars pack unhealthy substances such as sugars and fats."

"You don't understand. An occasional bite, now and again, will keep me satisfied. My body will keel over without a dose or so of sugar. I love—"

"You can't love something you're a slave to." He turned on the faucet, dipping the dishes under and scraping them clean with a brush. "Don't stress. You'll survive." His voice was condescending. "In fact, by the end of the month, you'll—"

"You're going to say I won't crave sweets. The same as you did the coffee and my cell phone and the champagne in my fridge." The nerve of him. She jumped to her feet, ready to strike him where it hurt. "On June 1st, I'll restock my supply."

His shoulders stooped. "Madison, I hoped—"

"You hoped what? That I'd stand by while you take, take, take."

She was tempted to tell him more, but she'd said enough. Instead, she disappeared into a bathroom and snagged her hair in a ponytail at the crown. She splashed icy water on her flushed face, then blotted her forehead with the towel. Her temples pulsated. She had lost control—again.

She returned and discovered her reappearance premature. Brandon was confiding to the studio cameras. She tiptoed closer to eavesdrop.

"Madison forgets she asked me to make her healthy. She doesn't seem aware of the truth. She's capable of healing herself. I can give her the tools, but if she doesn't have the desire to improve her health, it won't work."

Her previous fury faded. Brandon was writing her off like she did those prospective clients who didn't show up for an audition. If she didn't apply herself to his principles, she'd flunk out of the one thing more relevant than anything else. Staying alive.

She had rejected the inevitability of death, treated it like a taboo subject. In the middle of the night, though, reality woke her. At those times, she had no trouble sifting through the hoopla to the meaningful. In the light of day, even with her best intentions, she kept allowing her emotions to get the best of her. It had to stop.

Resigned, she whipped on her sweater while Brandon spoke to his virtual audience.

"I'm ready," she piped up when he'd finished, sounding unduly cheerful and accommodating. "I've got a hankering for herbs and seeds."

****

Madison had insisted on driving her car, telling him and the potential viewers she didn't trust his Chevy Volt, her hand curled on her hip. To Brandon, her refusal wasn't a problem. Being a passenger offered him a chance to go over a questionnaire she should have filled out before filming, but he hadn't seen.

"Do you recall the Dosha quiz you took?" he said, thumbing through her file.

"Whaaat?" She backed out her Mustang convertible, the sun blinking through the canopy of trees in dazzle and black shadow.

Her arm slung over the passenger seat all but touched him with a nearness that made him squirm. In fact, his blood was boiling since he had slid in next to her. Telling himself his discomfort had nothing to do with her close proximity, he opened the window.

In addition, he leaned forward. "Dosha is a Greek name, meaning gift of God. It's a science in India developed nearly five thousand years ago to bring balance to the body."

"It's all Greek to me." She threw her head back and laughed. "To be honest, I didn't take the test. I meant to, and I will. How about now? An oral exam. Are you game, guru?"

She sounded so upbeat he wondered what had changed. She'd been ready to bite his head off earlier. It amazed him that now she listened to him, her head tilted at a thoughtful angle, when he discussed Ayurveda, calling it "the science of life," and that she asked him questions when he explained food was medicine. As a result, she agreed what she needed most was a change in her diet.

She drove the Pacific Coast Highway with the top down, her body clad in an apple-green sweater and a matching scoop-necked blouse. Slim cylinders of gold danced at her ears when she spoke. She looked better this morning, sexier, he was forced to admit, with her freckles showing and those big green eyes subtly shaded with color. Her ponytail jostled around in the wind—a mad tango of flame.

"The Dosha quiz," he said, "I have it here." He thumbed through the papers in his binder until he found it. "Normally, oral testing isn't how we do it, but I'm in." Her risk-taking spunk was contagious. "Let's see. Number one, how would you describe your body?"

She shot him an appraising glance. "I don't know. How would you describe it, teach?"

Her voice, so irresistible, even the way she drove the sleek bullet with self-assurance, drew him, the combination lethal enough to undo any man. "Your body?"

"Yes, what do you think?" She darted a calculating look his way.

Her careful observation of him got him remembering the night before, the shot he'd had of her hourglass figure—her nipples large, dark, and swollen from sleep. A fact he'd been trying his damnedest to forget. The erotic image kept flicking to mind unbidden. Under these circumstances, giving her the test before a dashboard of concealed cameras might not be such a bright idea.

Her grin appeared forced. "Is there any hope for me?"

A tiny dimple appeared near her mouth. The sharp

angles of her cheekbones made him think of India and the heroines of which his mother had penned tales.

"Of course there's hope, Madison. Now let's get back to the question. How would you describe your body?"

"How?" She brought one hand to her throat as if feeling insecure. "I suppose I should be honest."

"Please do."

She let go of an endless sigh. "Some folks might identify with my experiences, and for that reason I've opted to be perfectly straight with you."

Her sudden candor straightened him in the seat. "Telling the truth sets us free."

"Yes, well, I guess." She eased up on the gas pedal a little. "When I was a girl, my weight fluctuated. Fad diets stripped me of weight, but soon I was back to scarfing down the carbs." Her hand stroked the back of her neck. "One day, I had my hair done in the beauty shop and thought I just might get a second glance. Near the overpass, a gang of jocks was checking me out, and my heart catapulted. Then one blocked my way. 'Hey, girl, you're kind of a tubby broad.' Another one joined in. 'She's an extra big mamma.' I plowed through them with my head lifted high so they wouldn't see me crying."

Her confession made him ache for her. It had taken guts to tell her story before an eventual audience. He longed to add something more than the standard, "I'm sorry."

She kept her eyes on the road. "Well, they were nothing but bullies."

He had a mad urge to zip back in time and rip the bastards to shreds. "We're already working on your eating habits."

She beat the steering wheel with her thumb. "I know." She sounded so lost.

"Soon, you'll experience a healthy weight."

"I'm glad for that."

"I'm glad too." He caught himself echoing her and shook his head to clear it. "Let's see."

To ask her the next question on the list would be hurling a grenade into the mix. *How would you describe your body frame?* He'd skip it and the following even harsher question. *How would you describe your chest?*

He skimmed to the safer inquiry. "How are your joints?"

She took her right hand from the steering wheel and yawned. "Sluggish."

He scanned to the following. "How do you describe your skin?"

"Bumpy, lumpy—take your pick."

"Yes, but—" He recalled her after she'd passed out, the feel of her cheek—velvet over a delicate bone structure. He shook his head to clear it again. "What about your hair?"

"I'm afraid it's rather oily."

As he checked the right box, he couldn't help but catch sight of her mane—a brilliant scarlet against the turquoise sky. "And your eyes?"

"The whites are a little red and discolored." She glanced at him as if to show him.

For those split seconds, her irises, flecked with gold and amber in the mid-morning sunlight, mesmerized him so that even after she looked away, he saw their fire.

He'd learned how to handle women, and he'd

learned how to ask all the right questions of them, even to superstars. Beautiful women. He'd had his share. He knew how to keep professionality at the forefront, but with Madison Gray, all bets were off.

"Are you done?" she asked, giving his arm a nudge.

He bolted out of his stupor. "How's your appetite?"

"I'm hungry right now. I'm used to snacking." She smacked her lips. "I don't think you fed me enough to get me through."

He didn't know whether to be offended or ashamed. "You told me you loved the breakfast I made you."

"Oh, it was nice, all those weeds and chimp food, but it didn't stay with me."

The arrow on the speedometer rose as if she couldn't wait to get to the market, the landscape zooming past, her blouse clinging to her and displaying her curves in a thoroughly eye-catching way. He tried not to stare. Hard to believe she suffered from a bad body image. How much of it had been erroneously formed in her youth? Clearly, her revelations bothered her.

He had to speak up. "Careful, ace. You're well over the speed limit. I don't think you want the CHP pulling you over." He cut his voice to a murmur. "The drama would give the audience something to talk about."

Her lead foot eased up on the gas pedal. "Sorry, I wasn't paying attention."

His cell phone picked then to ring. Forgetting to silence it bothered him. For half a decade, he had been doing reality TV and had never kept his phone on during a film shoot. He guessed he hadn't been paying attention either.

Chapter 6

As much as a few weeks ago, the last person Madison expected to be coupled with was Brandon Kennedy. Even in a crowd, the man stood out in his navy-blue and white striped polo shirt and tight jeans. Women were staring at him. They were stopping and nudging their friends, and then their friends were gawking at him too. Madison anchored her floppy, straw hat against the Santa Ana wind and preened across Sycamore Square. "Look at me!" was on her lips to say. "Look who I'm with. Bet you wish it was you."

So this was how the people of Santa Monica, aside from her, spent their Sundays. The aromas were to kill for. The Brazilian coffee and croissants, Belgium chocolate, the fine wine—everything Brandon had denied her. Talk about torture. While the eclectic sounds of Pink Martini drifted from a café and people milled in the shops, her appetite grew to mega proportions. The flower pots in cinnamon and saffron colors looked good enough to eat. Even the seabirds patrolling the square got their fair share of pickings. Life was not worth living without a good, hard, fast slug of caffeine and a sugary French dessert.

She spotted the ooh, la, la, strawberry savarin through the window of a bakery and pushed west toward the market Brandon had set as their destination.

Meanwhile, he strolled with that easy-goingness

she found both annoying and irresistible.

"Everyone's relaxed, living in the moment. Have you been here before?"

She shook her head. "On the weekends, I leave for work at six to avoid the tourists that pack the highway. By now, I'm on my fourth espresso and going strong."

He squeezed her elbow. "How are you holding up?"

"You mean, do I have a caffeine headache pounding behind my eyeballs?"

"Please tell me you don't."

Ah, but she did. She blinked to clear her vision. "Don't worry." Civility wasn't her strongest suit right now, but she'd promised herself, no matter what, she'd be a good sport. "I may fret, but I won't hurt you."

He nodded dubiously. "Good to know."

She couldn't resist a playful dig. "Unless you get too close."

He jerked away, putting his hands up in surrender. "The lady needs space."

"You betcha." She peered at him from under the brim of her hat. "I'm liable to wrap my hands around that hunky neck of yours."

He opened the door of the market. "I've got a better idea." He waved a hand with a flourish. "Welcome to my pharmacy."

She shimmied inside, delighting in the dark coolness whisking around her. The air smelled like the East Indian restaurant she favored on Hollywood and Vine. The stone floor chilled her sandaled feet, and the blades of a Casablanca fan circled lazily with a soft hum. Madison turned down an aisle. Maybe she'd find a package of soda crackers here among the brass incense burners and the porcelain tigers. Something to dim her hunger.

Thank the good Lord for small miracles.

A monster TV camera strapped to the shoulder of a cameraman burst out of nowhere and spotlighted her. Temporarily blinded, she stumbled. Brandon tripped over a pile of small wicker baskets, stumbling and sending them skittering around their feet.

He caught the cameraman by a sleeve. "Give us a second, would you?" Brandon asked.

The light faded to black. "Just doing my job," the camera guy said.

She tottered, a little disoriented, and Brandon steadied her with his arm. Frustrated, she shook him off. A hidden production crew? Seriously? She had grown tired of surprises, tired of his good humor amid her starvation. Her eyes narrowed, but then she caught the way he looked at her with brows arched in shock.

Heaven help her if she hadn't already forgotten to play nice.

She swallowed the hysteria rising inside her and scavenged through her tote for a yellow legal pad and one of her agency's pens. "I'm ready to learn all you have to teach me."

"First, I'll give you some background." Brandon motioned for the cameraman. "Can you get this clip? Just lower the lights a little. That's it. Thanks. How about a couple of mics for the two of us?" He took the pen from her and replaced it with one with no writing. "We can't have you flashing your company's logo. Now let's just walk while I give you a lecture."

Madison felt like an actress playing herself. "Go ahead, shoot." She removed her hat and swished her ponytail for a carefree effect. Let them call her a natural. And just how would she act if buying more broccoli and sprouts did nothing but excite her?

"Ayurveda is a system the ancient sages developed many centuries ago. The test I gave you in the car enabled me to know how to treat you."

He looked a little rough and rugged with his hair mussed and the dark stubble on his face. He was utterly appealing, even if he was speaking a lot of mumbo-jumbo. For some reason, she found herself willing to listen to him. He spoke so well she couldn't help but take note. It was her job, after all, to hunt down talent. And he had a voice as rich as crème brûlée.

But then he said, "Your primary Dosha is Kapha, and your secondary is Pitta."

"Like the bread?" She just couldn't seem to forget her fierce appetite.

"No, the bread is spelled p-i-t-a. P-i-t-t-a energy is what drives us to achieve our goals."

"Maybe it should be packaged."

"Yes, it's a good thing." He was getting carried away. "The energy is what makes you Madison Gray."

"No kidding." Tell that to her stomach. Did he hear it rumble? "A personality shaped by a specific energy? It sounds so out there."

"If your Pitta energy is erratic, it can cause you to heat up and feel angry, temperamental, and overwhelmed."

"Ah, geez, and all along I thought it was *you* making me bewitched, bothered, and bewildered." The amazing aroma of coffee beans drifted from someplace close. Wanting just then to shake the daylights out of him, she waggled the pen. "Get on with it, will you?"

"Your Kapha energy helps to keep you grounded and calm during stressful situations." He nodded toward the candy aisle. "But when it's out of balance you tend to eat the wrong foods, especially sweets and oils, and those can make you feel heavy and lethargic."

"So I can blame my love for chocolate on Kapha energy." She wrote this down, not buying into it but willing to go along with him. She didn't have much choice, now did she?

"You'll be stronger in a few days," Brandon said and twisted away from her. "You stay here and rest, and I'll be right back."

Now what? He had deserted her at a smelly herb counter. The man behind it looked like Dev Patel from the acclaimed movies *Slumdog Millionaire* and *Lion*.

"May I help you, ma'am?" Dev Patel asked with a gracious nod.

The cameraman zeroed in, focusing on Madison alone. The herbs in their glass drawers resembled small corpses. Brandon wasn't planning on feeding her any, was he? She caught her reflection in the mirror above them. Her face had turned an unbecoming shade of toad green. "I...I'm looking for my..."

As if on cue, Brandon rounded the corner. "I bring you gifts," he said, lifting translucent plastic bags holding powders—ah, precious Babylon spices. He nodded at Dev Patel.

"There's my guru." She gestured toward Brandon. In his striped shirt, his dark hair sun-bleached with coppery highlights, he looked as if he'd be more at home on a surfboard than practicing mindfulness and quoting ancient sages.

"You can use this ginger to cook or to make a tea,"

he said. "It's good for the stomach. It has an anti-inflammatory effect on the system, and it's tasty. Hold out your hand, and I'll give you a sample."

He poured a smidgen of gold powder into her curled palm. Thinking of gingersnaps and gingerbread and a little diner called The Ginger Monkey on the Sunset Strip, she tipped the entire amount on her tongue.

Ouch! She wildly fanned her face with her hand, tears coursing down her cheeks. Chili peppers and even Mama Maria's Salsa were never this hot!

He passed her bottled water, and she chugged it.

He grinned. "Lightweight."

She couldn't help but giggle, even if her laughter reached a discordant note and her stomach knotted. After all, what else could she do? She was on camera.

****

A half hour later, Brandon left the market with reusable shopping bags of groceries weighing him down and sweat dampening his brow.

His fans appeared from shopfronts to ask for autographs as the two made their way over the pavers. *Never say no. Give them their money's worth.* That had been drilled into him back when he was an extra at Pasadena Playhouse. Back when giving an autograph was a thrill equal to dining at the White House, which he'd done a year ago when the president wanted to incorporate yoga into his daily routine.

A journalist (That's what the horsey-looking lady called herself), and a parrot-eyed man along with a baby-faced guy (both supposedly from *The L.A. Times*) exited the café as if they'd been lying in wait, and fired off questions.

"Is it true, Madison, that you almost died from a blow to the head? Are you exhausted? Did you quit your job? Sell your agency? Are you two seeing each other? Were you married in Vegas? Are you pregnant?"

Could it get any crazier?

Brandon waved his hands. "You'll have to watch the show to find out."

"Yes," Madison said, "if we tell you now, what fun would that be? Suspense, it's the chili peppers in the cheese, the cheese atop the spaghetti…"

Was it his imagination, or did Madison keep talking about food? He rubbed his chin. All he wanted was for her to finish the month with her health fully restored and a sufficient weight loss. But they lived in this era that let people communicate firsthand with celebrities through the media via the World Wide Web. Madison appeared to get this and wanted to comply. But he saw the glazed look in her eyes as she wrestled up a comeback.

If he had his way, she'd be deep in a meditative lotus pose. Less than twenty-four hours ago, Madison had left her sister's house. The studio execs had pushed for the segment, and at the last minute, they had added the change to the storyline.

When it came down to it, he wouldn't put it past the producers to have unleashed these publicity hounds. Anything to create tension. Big drama, baby! Not ethical and to the expense of his student. This insensitivity made him doubt his place in reality TV, his discontent growing by the day.

Madison drew close to him. "I'm a little spent."

He felt for her. "I hear you."

But while leaving Sycamore Square, Madison

caught the paparazzi in her wake. They whisked along behind her, she the Pied Piper, they the rats. She posed at her Mustang parked on the curb and talked to the media about raising public awareness and embracing diversity. Giving her opinions and insights in spades. Strappy flat shoes, a skirt at mid-calf, a peasant blouse. Color, action, she had it all. No one could clone her.

Tourists stopped and took cell phone photos, amazed to find the reality show in progress. The Hollywood agent and the reality TV guy. Lights, camera. Only in Santa Monica. On a Sunday. While calypso music coasted from a speaker, a wiry-haired dude photographed the scene from a balcony, and the camera operators got pushed to the wayside. He couldn't help but grin at that. Served them right.

Brandon borrowed Madison's keys, opened the trunk, and handed them back to her. He loaded the groceries. Rising up was the yeasty smell of warm bread. On impulse, he grabbed two bottles of purified water. Cheers, baby!

Madison waved goodbye, blew kisses, and got into her car. Her swishy skirt rustled as she slid across the driver's seat and opened the door for him. "Let's roll."

Slipping on her sexy glam-on-the-go sunglasses and hitting the gas, she then pressed the button for the radio, but nothing happened. She frowned, tried again. Still nothing.

One of her hands tightened on the steering wheel; the other squeezed the neck of her bottled water. "Okay, my partner in crime, what gives?"

Chapter 7

Madison drove, following the twisted, tree-shaded ribbon of highway. "Are you saying the freaking field producers have highjacked my car?"

"It's standard procedure to place cameras in vehicles," he said. "You can't listen to the radio because the studio would have to pay royalties to Beyoncé if you listen to her, or to Coldplay. You name the band, it's all the same."

With the sound of bongos still thumping in her head, she resisted the urge to wring his neck. People were everywhere, eating and having a good ole time while she fumed. Just her luck, she'd gotten through the agony in Sycamore Square only to discover a lock on her radio. Was this the camel's straw, the breaking point on her resolve?

He wrapped his hand around her maimed water bottle rattling in the cup holder. "Hydrate. It's essential to good health, and you'll feel better."

She shoved him away with a little more finesse than she'd intended. "Right about now, I need to unwind by jamming to Maroon 5 or Pearl Jam." Nibbling on her lip, she lowered her brows. "Can't you do something?"

"I wish I could, but it's not an option."

She bit back the need for a snarky retort. How many casting directors had given her that line—*a model with cerebral palsy isn't an option.* As an agent, she prided herself in knowing how to fight for something she believed in.

She moistened her lips with her tongue. "Here's the deal. I'll fork out the money to Pink and Rihanna or anybody else who keeps me sane by way of radio waves." Even if she couldn't afford it. She'd do anything at this point.

His brows rose. "It's against the rules."

"You and your rules." She shook her head so hard the road blurred in front of her. She was arguing with him—yet again. For the life of her, although she knew it was wrong, she couldn't quell her need to ruffle him. "You're a drill sergeant posing as a pacifist."

"It's non-negotiable, Madison." It just might be exasperation she briefly spied in the set of his jaw. "We'll have to find another way for you to cope with stress."

"Maybe I should just stop the car, drop to the ground, and do pushups."

He tapped his chin with a long, lean finger. "It might be a better idea to do sun salutations instead." His lips twitched. "What do you think?"

Did he believe he was funny? She fired off an if-looks-could-kill glare. "You may be considered God's gift to reality TV yoga, but if I were a network exec, I'd pass on you."

If she didn't know better, she'd have thought she heard a muffled chuckle.

"And you'll dislike me more before this is over," he said.

The angrier she became the more she wanted to knock him down a peg. "How could I detest you more?"

He clapped his hands to his chest. "You do know how to hurt a guy."

"You copped everything I love, and now you nab my only vice, rocking out."

He turned his body toward her. "I'm sure you'll live, Madison."

Was he patronizing her? Was he settling in to figure out another defect in her personality so he could poke fun at her? She felt that cool blue stare of his. She'd seen women unable to manage anything but a sigh when his eyes met theirs. Not her. Never her!

She very casually flicked her tongue over her teeth. "Let me know when the cameras go down so I can tell you what I really think of you."

"No need. Mission accomplished."

"And the press thinks we ran off to Vegas." Fresh out of good will, her chin shot out. "The very idea of marrying you!"

He covered his mouth with the back of his hand. "You did agree to a short-term marriage, sort of, wouldn't you say?"

Oh, he was trying to bait her. The long-legged, sexy man, barefoot now, his profile shaded with a darker stubble than before—as if he'd just taken a long, exhilarating nap, his voice gravelly. He was teasing her, the arrogant so-and-so. *Don't look at him*, she told herself and kept her eyes focused on the winding road.

Still, she pictured what it would be like to sleep with him and hated herself for it. Thinking of him made her hot, and dare she admit it even to herself, bothered.

She wanted nothing more than to holler, "Brandon Kennedy, be damned!"

But to swear on syndicated TV? She'd slipped up last evening. Nothing irritated her more about reality shows than those beeps whenever a person uttered a cuss-bomb. Some shows bleeped from beginning to end. In her book, people should ban them for assaulting the ears.

A bicyclist swung out of the trees onto the road. Madison had enough time to cut the wheel sharply to the left to avoid the collision and just missed being broadsided by a Ford pickup in the opposite lane. The Mustang lurched off the highway, brakes screeching, dust flying. The car fishtailed and came to a stop facing a strip of the ocean where beach bums were carrying their surfboards into the water.

All color drained from Brandon's face as he grabbed her arm. "Are you okay?"

With her breath caught in the recesses of her gut, she couldn't answer. Motion had begun to crawl as she fought to collect herself. The surfers were a choreographed slow dance of simultaneous cuts through the powerful, undulating waves. Smoke billowed up from the tires, engulfing the metallic frame of her beloved car in black.

Brandon was pulling her around to face him. "Madison, breeeaaathe!"

Was he out of his mind? She couldn't get any oxygen into her lungs. Her ears buzzed. Her mouth felt like it was full of lamb's wool.

"I—" she began, but that was as far as she got.

Her heartbeat boomed against her chest and backbone. *Oh, no!*

He gripped her shoulders hard. "Inhale through your nose so that your abdomen begins to expand, and your lungs. Now exhale the air out of your lungs through your nose."

But her heart bucked against her ribs as if threatening to burst out. "It's not working."

The smell of burnt rubber made her feel like she was going to be sick. It had been her fault—she'd almost gotten them killed. She might have hit the guy on the bike. How would she have lived with herself if she had?

Dr. Buckley's warning slammed in her head. "I'm worried you won't see middle age."

She wiped her clammy hands on her skirt. "The heart attack…is this it?"

"Madison," he said, his tone hypnotic, and one look at his face told her he was her only hope. "I want you to say the words, *Sat Nam*."

To think, before she almost rubbed out the biker, her only troubles had been not being able to play her radio.

She moved her thick lips. "*S-a-t N-a-m*."

If anyone had told her she would be spewing a mantra…she wasn't a believer…no hocus pocus manuvers for her… *S-a-t N-a-m*.

"Concentrate on your breath," Brandon said. "There's nothing else."

"*Sat Nam*." She said it as slow as she was able. "*S-a-t N-a-m*."

"That's it. The beginning and the end. Yin and Yang. The alpha and the omega…"

His eyes bored into hers. Did he fear she was on her deathbed? Somehow, she didn't think so. He believed in her. That's what his expression stated loud and clear. He thought she could heal herself. He had said as much earlier. Maybe he was right.

She chanted, "*Sat Nam*." Chanted it like a genuine yogi. Meanwhile, she tipped her head up, and the cerulean sky opened to her—an endless span of serenity. She'd never seen it looking as beautiful, with clouds floating in a steady stream through azure.

Her heartbeat, she realized, had settled down.

He still had his hands on her shoulders, grounding her. He drew closer and peered at her like he could interpret the workings of her mind. Could he? Maybe the two of them shared a psychic connection after their near brush with death. Stranger things had happened. She wondered what it would be like to touch his lips with her own. Would he melt? Would she?

He was so near that his breath smelled of licorice. His toothpaste? Not at all bad. She liked it. There was that scar above his left eyebrow. She could picture him as a boy on a surfboard before he grew up and went off to India to study the wisdom of the gurus. Had he fallen while shooting the curve or crashed his skateboard? She'd have liked to know him when he was an ordinary guy. Not a TV star. And she was still a girl—before her world had shattered.

****

To the right of the road, the traffic rushed past the Mustang, expelling an aftermath of fierce hot wind. The bikers streamed by in a single thread; heads turned to rubberneck. Seagulls whimpered from above, and Brandon wanted to shout to Madison, "You're not going to die, not while in my care!"

He couldn't let her know he was worried. He took her pulse, his thumb on that tender blue vein in the white flesh of her wrist.

She shook her head. "I'm sorry I went ballistic."

"You have to learn to breathe," he said, thankful she couldn't see the sweat sliding down the sides of his torso. He thought of the terror of losing his mother during the end stages of her disease when taking a breath was nearly impossible. And of the dark figure of his uncle, Father Tim, who had hugged Brandon after giving his mother the last rights. Father Tim who was always around in times of trouble, and his biological father who wasn't.

Madison fixed him with her emerald gaze. "It was only a panic attack. I've had them before. You'd think I'd know by now not to flip out."

At first, he couldn't speak; he didn't want to show the strong emotion he felt. He inhaled a breath and let it out, following his own advice. "Start using your lungs to their full capacity. They'll get stronger."

"They will?"

"Your lungs are capable of sending more oxygen to the trillions of cells in your body. And you can expel all the toxic impurities from your system."

"Really, an honest to goodness miracle," she said as if she believed in such things.

He checked her face for cynicism. Not any he could find.

With a trembling hand, she wrote on her legal pad. "You have a voice, guru. I knew a broadcaster once from Milwaukie who talked like you. Makes me think of mountain streams and a big brass bed after dark. You won't reconsider me as your agent?"

She came closer as if inspecting him for flaws—a jeweler with a diamond—and he felt drunk on her scent. It was like voodoo. Illogically French, yet as natural as rain and sultry summer nights.

Simmer down!

His task now was to calm her, which would inevitably quiet his nerves. That's all there was to it. Still, he didn't trust himself.

He looked over her shoulder rather than into her eyes. "You've heard of the giant tortoises off the coast of Ecuador?"

"I've never had the pleasure. Giant tortoises, oh, my."

If she meant to be coy, he chose to ignore it. "The tortoises have a life span of more than one hundred and fifty years."

"How do turtles get to be that old?"

"They take only four breaths in a minute."

"Whoa, that can't be easy."

"Breath control is the practice that empowers us to move the mind into a new state of being." Although his eyes were still averted, he'd graduated to a heightened state. Drifting in lost horizons—she had that effect on him. "Have you ever worked on your breathing before?"

"I never thought of breathing as work. I thought it came naturally—like breathing."

He leaned his side against the seat, enjoying the hint of cleavage showing over the gathers in her blouse, full breasts raising and lowering, eyelids half closed. Very sensual.

As it was, he laid a hand on her stomach. "Breeeaaathe," he said over and over until it became a mantra.

All the while, he was gulping deep breaths himself, trying to ward off the crazy temptation he had to reach around to the back of her head and slowly work that rubber-band thingy loose. He wanted to see those deep burnished waves tumble down over her shoulders so that she'd look like she had the night before. Now her nearness made the sky flash with crimson and the pines overhead shoot upward like the tips of arrows. He could get hooked on the crazy effect she had on him.

Her eyes flickered like butterflies. "What are you doing?"

He was stunned by the raw passion and jerked away like he'd gotten too close to fire. "I was making sure you were breathing from your abdomen." He replaced his hand with hers. "You feel your breath, nice and slow? In and out, that's what you do."

"Is this all part of the yoga way?" Did he hear a mocking edge?

For a second, he didn't care. He needed to touch Madison. He'd forgotten what it was like to want. The conflict went against his need to keep things proficient, against samsara and the philosophies he believed. Hunger stronger than a need for food or even water got the best of him. His defenses crashed down as sensations shot through him like hundreds of electric currents.

A smidgeon of consciousness hit, making him aware of where he was, and he turned away from Madison and scanned the dashboard. All those prying cameras. Had his viewers caught a look or a piece of body language—a film clip that would reveal his lust? He found his bottle, half the liquid spilled. He drank when he'd have rather dumped the remaining water over his head. Snuff out that telltale fire.

He sank back and cleared his throat. "The yogic

life can give you peace if you work it." Hadn't he used those same words to her before? It sounded cornball even in his own ears.

****

By the time Madison sat down to lunch, she could have eaten the entire spread, even the sprigs of wildflowers placed on the table for effect by the behind-the-scenes crew.

Brandon lit a squat, plum-colored candle. "Let's eat without talking."

"What for?" Did he need space after the near-fatal accident? Or was it something else?

He shook out the match, smoke sailing. "Silence equals health."

More than anything, she wanted to drag him off to some unwatched nook—the back pantry or the alcove beneath the stairs. She thought she'd witnessed a spark of something like desire in his eyes, and she wanted to investigate it—in private.

Instead, she speared a carrot with her fork. With her other hand, she propped up the Sunday edition of *The New York Times*. Words, she had to have words, to keep her from blurting out something inappropriate before a possible audience.

"Ms. Gray..." Why did he sound so peeved with her? "You can't give your undivided attention to your food if you're reading the paper."

She balked at his authoritative manner. "Just so you know, in my business, I wouldn't get by without the ability to multitask."

"I can tell you about the benefits of eating mindfully, but the best way for you to experience it is to try it yourself."

There he was, the teacher again, an unlikely cross between Jesus and her late grandma's take on perfection, Tyrone Power. Madison noted a tightness in her chest and breathed in, and her abdomen expanded. She let out the breath through her nose and continued again as Brandon had taught her. In seconds, this way of breathing dissolved her discomfort.

She closed her eyes and inhaled the aroma of her meal. In time, she quit gulping down her food and tasted the tangy ginger, the burst of buttery flavor. Each bite of cauliflower was crisp and crackly in its yellow succulence. Even the carrots were a delicacy. She chewed slowly, meditatively, savoring each bite like it would be the last thing she'd ever taste. This deep appreciation of her food was unmapped territory for her, a discovery of new continents of pleasure and satisfaction. She allowed the newspaper to fall away, forgotten.

So this was eating with mindfulness. How had Madison lived for over three decades and missed it? Her encounter was enough for her to want to take up cooking and to master the art. Maybe she could open a restaurant, teach diners how to eat. What an uber-concept. Maybe, for the first time in her life, she would actually lose a few pounds without cursing her lot.

Brandon made her a cup of hot, gingery tea that proved calming this time around. She wanted to say thank you. But as the afterglow of a satisfying meal warmed and nurtured her, she thought of an adage she'd heard, *silence is golden*. Wasn't it a song title? Oh, who cared?

She laced her fingers together, stretched them toward the ceiling, and yawned.

"Tired?"

Startled, she glanced across the table at Brandon there, a smile on his face. Instantly she relaxed even more. He had broken the imposed silence, not her. Perhaps he had already forgotten those rapturous looks that had passed between them earlier. But she hadn't.

"You look peaceful," he said when she remained quiet. "I take it you enjoyed your veggies *à la vapour*?"

"So much so I could fall asleep."

He cleared the table. "Then do it."

"But sleeping during the day is a waste of precious time." She punched the air with her fists. "I have so much to do," she added half-heartedly.

"I'm sorry?" He set her plate in the sink. "Last I heard, no clients were waiting for you. You have no pressing engagements, no books to keep. No phones to answer, no deals to make."

"I don't have anything keeping me awake, now do I?"

"You're free as a bird. If your body's telling you to snooze, go with it. It's what you need." He gave her a friendly pat on the shoulder. "Doctor's orders."

How long had it been since she allowed her mind to rest? With no thought whatsoever. Except maybe one—*oh, hell, no*! She wasn't about to waste another grain of consideration on the man assigned to saving her life.

Chapter 8

Brandon faced the cameras in the kitchen with dread. "I think we don't take enough time to savor our food," he said over the swish of the dishwasher. He told himself he really would have enforced the silence, and that it had nothing to do with him not trusting himself to speak. "With our thoughts centered on each bite, eating is a gourmet feast."

Raising his hand, Spence signaled a break in filming. "The writers put together a hot sheet after the story writers cycled through this morning's footage on their monitors. I'd like you to go over it and let me know what you think."

Brandon didn't like the bad feeling he had but took the sheet of paper and read:

"Guru Brandon" Hot Sheet: Day Two, morning.
Summary

The trip to Sycamore Square went without incident today, except that reporters bombarded Brandon and Madison. Brandon was angry, and it showed. Expect blow ups whenever paparazzi appear on the scene.

Things heated up when Madison nearly struck a bicyclist and veered off the road. Afterward, she suffered a huge anxiety attack, and Brandon tried and succeeded in easing her nerves. Sparks fly between the two. They are either arguing or flirting, which has never been part of the show's script. But maybe it's time for a change.

The tightness in Brandon's neck grew painful, and he rolled his shoulders to loosen his muscles. "Somebody's got things all wrong here."

He hated hot sheets like this one, the conjecture about what would happen in the days to come, and all the wrong conclusions.

"I've never been inappropriate with the talent," he said.

Spence plucked an apple from the bowl, polishing it on his sleeve. "You're right. You're professional to the core. You don't crack under pressure. And you'd never sleep with a student."

"You've got it."

"Sorry. I know you don't want to hear this, but the show could use a little shakeup."

Brandon turned his head. "I have no idea what you're talking about."

"Sadly, you don't. I'm talking about tension—sexual or otherwise. If you want to please the viewers, maybe you should rethink things."

Feeling as if he were struggling to make his way above a current tugging him down, Brandon said, "Look at the big picture, why don't you? How would anyone put their faith in a guru who's not entirely on the up and up with his pupil? I sure didn't mean to come off like a Romeo, not in a million years."

"I know. That's what makes this morning's film worth its weight in gold."

Brandon hurled the paper wad and missed the trash bin. "I say we start all over. Either that or edit out all the..." What would he call it? "The mistakes. Yeah, that's it. Edit. And edit again until we get it right."

Lilly, her hair swept up like cotton candy, glided toward him with the candor of a good fairy, a small sponge in her hand. He knew the procedure, wanted to skip out. More of his special non-toxic face paint. She took his arm gently and sat him in the chair.

"I'll have you fixed up in no time, dear," she said as if she had special powers, which Madison might attest to but not him. If he had his way, there'd be no makeup. Then again, when did he ever get what he wanted? Not much lately.

Needing a breather, he slipped his hand under Lilly's round arm. "I'll be back."

He disappeared into his assigned room down the hall. Ten minutes later, he'd gone the five-minute distance and was cascading down the sandy embankment wearing nothing but his swimming trunks and carrying his yoga mat, towel, and his cell phone.

Whenever stressed to the max, he depended on the business manager who had been with him since he started. Jason Bennett had to juggle clients, which meant he spent much of his time traveling from set to set, but he favored Brandon over the others. That was why, when Brandon called, Jason answered on the first ring.

"Hey, buddy," Jason said, "good to hear from you. I just left the studio van. A group of producers and their assistants were videotaping Madison eating cauliflower."

Brandon blew out a sigh through clasped hands. "It didn't take the van crew long to plug in. I better warn Madison. Even when you think you're out of earshot, those guys will find you."

"Hey, man, it's on their dime. And you never know

when blood's gonna get to boiling. Those angry, reckless soundbites—that's what viewers want."

Jason munched chips, his go-to food. He could stand to lose fifty pounds, and Brandon never quit hounding him. Nobody could change Big J., but Brandon trusted his judgment. Truth? He loved the guy who was old enough to be his father, and so he kept trying to curtail Jason's overeating and general lack of interest in any form of exercise.

Brandon kicked at the sand near a concrete bench. "Have you seen the film?"

"Just the lunch scene a half hour ago. That enforced silence was a great move on your part. Uncomfortable silence always gets filled. It separates the meat from the cheese puffs."

"I don't know what you're talking about."

"The way Madison looked at you with her heart in her eyes." Jason all but purred. "The way you looked at her. Man alive, it was like one of those Turner Classics, those oldies but goodies where the lovers can't quit staring at one another."

Brandon rubbed the tight spot between his brows. "Excuse me?"

"Guru Brandon and Madison Gray have a thing going on."

"It isn't what it looks like," Brandon said with too much emphasis on the "isn't."

Besides, no one had to tell him that his business manager was a hopeless romantic. Brandon had spent many a night listening to him belt full-tilt-boogie blues in a smoky nightclub in East LA. Sometimes Jason drank too much and wept over his long-lost love while peering out through Coke-bottle lenses and strumming his guitar. That was always Brandon's cue to take Jason home and get him safely to bed.

Crunch, Crunch. "Listen, buddy. You can't worry about what gets edited and what doesn't. If the writers think some flirting is good for the show, it will make the final cut. On that note, maybe you should play it up. In the end, it's all about the ratings. You know that."

By the time they finished their conversation, Brandon's head pounded. Yes, he'd admit he felt something whenever he was around Madison. He didn't want to. It just seemed impossible to resist. But allowing feelings for her to show on film? No way. Some rules he had made with himself he couldn't break.

He shoved between the ficus hedges and tromped through the sea grass, the sharp breezes invigorating him. All around him, people were going about their lives in the endless summer that was Southern California. The air smelled of suntan lotion and the honeysuckle that shrouded the stone wall to the south where, caught in the wind, cattails nodded.

Brandon waded into the refreshing aquamarine water. He considered himself a reasonable sort of guy. Even the women he dated called him levelheaded and fair. His women were good-natured and grounded. There were no temperamental divas in his future. A date should like doing the same things he did. His motto was a bit clichéd. "The couple that meditates together stays together." But he believed in its merit.

Not that he wasn't just as red-blooded as the next guy, but burning the midnight oil had lost its appeal when he'd started taking care of himself. And if he ever settled down, the woman would be a soul seeker like himself.

And he wouldn't be goaded into another relationship for the sake of publicity. His so-called former girlfriend had warmed up to him for the camera. Being seen together had given her fame because of the publicity. Her fawning over him in public had been for nothing but show. He hadn't been happy. Dishonesty went against his principles, and he'd informed the producers he was done. The pretense had been over, for him, none too soon.

Brandon returned to the beach, toweled himself off, and dropped his mat in the sand. As he went through the yoga sequences designed to gain strength, balance, and grounding, he let his gaze drift to the cool blue surf and battled to clear his head.

The problem was, Madison had more passion than anybody he had ever met. She was so remarkably colorful and vivacious. If he dated her after filming the show, it wouldn't go well. It could never end with a shake of the hand. No, it would be as volatile as the beginning.

Right now, he had to accept the responsibility for his part in this mess. Most of this trouble was his fault. If he'd been smart, he wouldn't have let Madison talk him into taking an oral Dosha test. That had led to folly. If only she hadn't shown her vulnerable side, he wouldn't have turned into a sap. From now on, he'd have a blueprint and stick to it. No more ad-libbing as they went along. The weeks would fly. Then he'd resume his ordinary life, with Madison a distant memory. He'd return to his ordinary work. He was a man of routine, after all. A man who never got riled or miffed.

As he settled into warrior position, the rustling noise of movement in the high grass met his ears, and he turned to find Madison.

"Hey, guru, are you ready to show me what you've got?"

It was just his bad karma she had to have such a sexy voice. He twisted around. She was all quicksilver energy and tough-babe swagger—the total opposite of his dream girl. So why had his pulse spiked at the sight of her? And why had he gotten a dumbass grin?

Chapter 9

With the cameras surrounding her, Madison eyed Brandon Kennedy on the beach below. Sweet Almighty! With his hair blown back and his shoulders so erect and body so sculptured, he was a living, breathing myth. All other Greek gods need not apply. The late afternoon sun silhouetted him against the burning blue sea and the coral sky, inducing to mind the image of bigger-than-life, studly male.

He set his hands on his slender hips. "Ready to try a little yoga?"

She rubbed the last remaining sleep from her eyes. What dreams she'd had. In one, her tastebuds delighted again in that scrumptious lunch, its sweetness intense. Then she was sampling Brandon's kiss, equally sweet, a study in flavors, his tongue a flirty discovery of sensations. She awoke with the unsettling feeling that she could no longer trust herself.

Now she was down on the sparkling beach. The man was all sex and sunshine as he grinned at her. She stopped in front of the bench. With her hands in her pockets, she kept her distance. "I've never been much good at sports."

"Yoga's not a sport; it's a way of living—a path toward self-realization. Yoga is proactive techniques that must be applied every day. We don't want to mistake the physical benefits as being all there is. What we're doing is making the body strong enough to sit for hours on end in meditation. That's our goal."

"No offense, but I think idly sitting is a waste of time. Life is too short with no spare seconds for lollygagging."

He looked at her like she had slapped him. "Nothing could be further from the truth. If you're serious about good health, learn from the animals who strengthen their bodies by stretching after napping."

He seemed unaware that the sunbathers had turned their heads to ogle him as he imitated a rippling tiger stretching toward the sun. Whatever he called that posture, she didn't know, nor did she care. Watching him was better than a five-star movie, better too, than dripping hot fudge or pink champagne. She believed the ladies drooling from their beach towels and chairs under giant umbrellas would wholeheartedly agree.

And like any god coming down to earth, he lowered himself into a cross-legged sitting position on his magic carpet of a mat. "Namaste."

"Hello to you." Unsure of his lingo but aware of him then in every pore, she scooted in so that she faced him. "Take it away, guru dear."

He touched his thumbs and index fingers together. "Most people think of yoga as being done in a classy studio with quiet music playing. Frankly, you can practice yoga anywhere, but the main thing is to center on self-surrender."

She generated a playful smile. "Okay," she said to the TV reality people flocking around. "Give it up to Guru Brandon."

One of the crew members handed her a purple yoga mat, and she did her best to imitate Brandon reaching forward toward his toes and cupping the bottom of his feet with his hands. Her legs were not bendy, and her hamstrings screamed from the strain. She couldn't release her fear that anybody watching would think *why is that lady making such a fool out of herself?*

Her insecurities poured out of her. "I don't care for having the cameras on me."

"And yet you want exposure for your clients?"

"I do, but I am my best when I'm going about business as usual. And you know, my work is exciting because no deal is ever the same thing twice." God Almighty, she missed being in the place in the world where she excelled.

He eased into a yoga sit again. "What do you mean?"

She dropped down and faced him, squaring her shoulders. "It's those details that keep me hopping. If it's a movie, will there need to be a nurse on location? What additions need to be added to the trailer to make it wheelchair accessible? If it's a child actor, will there be a tutor?"

"Can't you delegate?" When had he taken hold of her wrist?

"I don't sluff off my responsibilities, and I didn't even tell you what I do on the business end to keep the doors open. Plus, I'm still working on creating a case as to why include disabled people in television advertisements."

"Ah, I get the picture." He added pressure with his thumb against her pulse. "The trick will be when you can talk about work without your blood pressure rising to kingdom come."

Resolutely, she pushed herself away from him and

got to her feet. "Why not demonstrate your moves, Yoga Man?"

"Okay," he said, stretching forward on his mat and lying on his six-pack of a belly.

She lay opposite him, turned her face, and rested it on her mat, shutting her eyes so she couldn't see him. "Maybe I'll just chill for a spell."

"Not so fast. Now lift the upper part of your body in cobra position."

"Say what? You want me to impersonate the national snake of India?"

He was opposite her on his mat so that they were facing one another. A little too close. Her heartbeat? So not at ease. He began to demonstrate, the show off with his spectacular pecs and deltoids oiled and coconut-scented. If someone snapped his picture, they could put it in a how-to book. A perfect pose, no less.

"You can do this, Madison." There it was, all that confidence he had in her—much more than she had in herself.

She edged forward off the mat and groaned as she lifted her upper body.

He gave her instructions. "Weave the spine back and forth. Straighten your arms. Breathe. Widen your chest. Breathe. Raise your collar bones and look at the sky. Breeeaaathe. That's it!" *Was he staring at her cleavage?* "You're getting the hang of it."

She didn't have the strength in her forearms to hold herself any longer and collapsed, her face buried in the beach. She came up spitting pebbles from her mouth. "Laugh at me, and I'll make you pay."

He brushed the sand from her cheeks with the balls of his fingers. "I wouldn't think of it."

But she couldn't help expelling a girlish giggle. How long had it been since she had laughed at herself?

His smile was from his teen-idol days. "Don't you feel good?"

She was so afraid of flirting with him that she pretended he was her tax accountant. "Not so bad," she admitted.

He ran his palms along her shoulders, straightening her back. "Breathe."

Her skin shivered, begging for more of his touch. She caught sight of his throat, the muscles moving beneath his bronzed flesh as he swallowed. The full force of his masculinity hit her like a punch to her solar plexus. He was watching her with a trace more than a casual interest in her mastering the posture.

The impact of his magic hands intoxicated her, her body seemingly floating as high as the kites sailing in the sky. "Do you think I'll ever be able to perfect yoga?"

He arched up again into the cobra pose, his muscles flexing and tensing, and she couldn't tear her gaze from his glistening body.

"Yes, if you follow my plan for you. I'm calling it 'The Madison Project.' All you have to do is work on it. You can do it, trouper."

If she didn't change the subject soon, she'd lose herself to the persuasion of his voice. "If there's one thing I possess, it's an excellent work ethic."

"I never doubted it." He was still arching backward on the mat, his gaze beatific. His mood lent the opportunity she needed.

"Do you have an agent, Brandon?" *Keep it light and breezy.*

Full account? She wanted to hide inside with the artificial air. She functioned better while working—and work she must! Her career kept her alive. Without it, she felt like the shells scattered on the beach. Emptied out and abandoned.

"I have a business manager, Jason Bennett." He sounded cautious.

"I know him," she sang out. "A good man. He keeps in touch with you every day?"

"He does."

Sweat seeped down her spine. "Wouldn't you feel lost if you didn't hear from Jason? I mean, seriously, ditching your client? Who does that?"

"Madison, we've been through this." He looked like he knew exactly how she felt, like he got her, the empathy in his eyes unmistakable.

"Don't worry, I'm getting used to being unplugged," she said, though the knot in her throat told her otherwise. "I don't even miss the daily media with all it's a distraction."

Her chest ached, and her nerves snapped like hot wires—withdrawals, probably, from all she held dear. The need to be connected to her agency—her tribe—burned fiercer than all the rest of her cravings. To deny her was like cutting off her reason for being.

"Madison, I can see your temple pulsating." He eased her into a "lotus" position, and it was a matter of seconds before her leg muscles strained painfully.

He covered his buff shoulders with a T-shirt, then knelt in front of her. "Pay attention to your breathing."

My, oh, my, if he wasn't as close to her face as an optometrist conducting an exam. Close enough to see the beads of sweat breaking out above her lips.

If only she could find a way to make herself relax, she would. The first day or so of beginning a healthier lifestyle was most likely always murder. She couldn't cave, or she'd never lick her addiction to work, a dependence nearly as strong as that of heroin. Not that her work wasn't important, but she was more than her job—wasn't she? Somehow it didn't ring true.

He took her palm and placed it against her heart. "Feel the beat?"

She nodded feverishly. "It's thumping like a bass drum."

"What are your senses telling you, Madison?"

She shook her head. "I can't hear over the roaring in my ears."

"What are you tasting?"

She ran her tongue over her lips. "Salt, naturally. Which makes me think of popcorn and potato chips. Maybe we don't want to go there. I'm ravenous again for junk food."

"That's perfectly normal. I promise it will get better. Just hang in there."

She needed to focus on something besides her lack and wished to center on anything other than his hand on hers.

"Describe all that you smell."

She turned her head and sniffed. "I'm getting a whiff like Fisherman's Wharf. Fancy fish dishes from the sea. Grilled wieners, burgers." She smacked her hand against the wet sand. "I don't think this is working."

"Realize how grateful you are that you're *alive* and that you can see, hear, smell, taste, and feel. Gratitude is the precursor of happiness. What are you thankful for?"

She knew why she felt grateful. She had almost made it through the first day, and she hadn't quit. There was something to be said for small victories.

They walked back up the hill, cameras following on their heels.

Then a woman stepped out from the woods, and Madison turned to Brandon. His smile instantly faded.

Chapter 10

Madison took stock of the newcomer. Her looks said Hallmark Channel with her high forehead, clear complexion, and polished honey-blonde hair. Just what brand of clothes promoted her tall, lithe body? And where had she gotten that statement clutch?

The fashionista called, "Hi, there, Madison. I'm Audrey Powell."

Madison's head whirled in disbelief. "*The* Audrey Powell?" Was this the same Audrey Powell who was being mentioned on social media?

"Well, I should hope so."

Audrey Powell had founded *Powell's Review.* She was known for landing stories about the up and coming people who staggered the world with their accomplishments. What was she even doing here? Did Madison dare to hope Ms. Powell might be contemplating a piece about Madison's experiences? Must be. Why else would she have staged such an entrance?

Madison couldn't believe her good fortune. "It's wonderful to meet you."

Audrey passed a smile that could only be described as artificial back to Madison. "I hope you don't think me pushy, but I wished to speak with you about a possible story for the newspaper." She said it as if the very sight of Madison turned her blood to snow slush.

Media hype, of course. Everyone had a gimmick these days.

Playing along, Madison sighed. "Well, I don't know."

Audrey grimaced, and for an absurd moment, Madison thought she was about to turn and leave. This asserting tension where there hadn't been any before was genius. Ms. Powell knew the art of show stopping. The two women would have to meet up for coffee after Madison's two-month hitch and compare notes.

Madison smoothed down her windblown hair. "Okay."

Such a brilliant move to rustle up Audrey Powell. Madison must applaud the casting department for their insight. Just how had they guessed she wanted to tell everyone who would listen about her agency? She started up the step but caught sight of Brandon and stopped dead as the question struck her. Did he know Ms. Powell?

He looked a little shell-shocked. "Can't Audrey give it a rest?" he muttered to Spencer.

"She got a release. Too bad, guy. My hands are tied."

"Yeah, sure." Brandon's tone had turned brisk. "Give me a moment," he said to the cameras bobbing up and down like dolphin tails. "There are some things I have to discuss with our guest." He gestured for the operators to take a break.

Madison didn't care for the warning bells going off in her head. "Brandon?"

"Please," he said, minus his usual warmth. "Stay down here. Give me some time to sort things out, would you?" He squeezed her arm encouragingly, then dodged past her as if she were a stage prop that had gotten in his way. "Audrey, hello. Production began yesterday afternoon…"

What were they saying? The two disappeared inside the trees and proceeded toward the house. *Don't overreact.* She'd do anything rather than be televised in a bad light for the umpteenth time. She stepped toward Spence who held a glazed doughnut she had an impulse to grab and devour. Unaware of her, he wore headphones while he grazed unabashedly. Was he listening in on Brandon and Audrey? Madison's stomach knotted. She didn't take well to being left out in the dark.

Her near blurt of "Let me hear or I'll scream," made her swoon. She caught herself in time. "I'd like to give an interview." She waved a couple stray camera guys toward her.

"Knock yourself out," Spence said to her with a mouthful of doughnut.

Too many people roamed the set, a lot of them Audrey Powell's entourage, others straggling beachcombers and sun worshipers that had followed the TV caravan. Madison did her best to strike a pose, but elbows stuck out everywhere as she floundered in a tide of spectators and worker bees.

Willie rescued her and positioned her beneath the shade of a vacant umbrella. His usual spiked hair hung in pale shards over his eyes. "How do you think you did today?"

She pulled a rueful smile for the camera. "Guess I could do with a few more lessons."

"Do you believe Audrey Powell wants your story?"

"We'll soon find out, won't we?"

"You seemed happy when Ms. Powell emerged on the scene." He cleared his throat. "What went through your head?"

"I'm a clotheshorse, and so is she. I may have found my soul sister." *Choose your words tactfully.* "I just can't wait to see why she's here."

"Did you know Brandon and Audrey were *a couple* several months back?"

"Huh?" Hadn't she done her research? Wasn't Brandon's name linked to some woman in an online article? "That's news to me."

She hoped the irritation didn't show on her face. Her feelings had nothing to do with jealousy and everything to do with ownership. She'd signed a contract—a short-term marriage of sorts. Wasn't that how Brandon had described their alliance?

Looking miserable, Willie said, "Sorry, Madison, I had to ask. It's my job."

"Thank you for telling me." Her words came out carefree and mild. "I think it's time to find my guru. But believe me, I'll look you up if I have anything else to say."

Under her breath, she swore a blue streak while pushing through the crowd, certain this little stunt was still another production setup. And Audrey Powell was smack dab in the middle of it.

****

Brandon didn't trust himself to speak as he led Audrey to the northwest side of the house where a wooden deck stood on stilts above the sea. His stomach rolled with annoyance. The slim thread of patience he had with the studio was about to snap. The crew had gone behind his back for the last time. He would have had it out with them if not for Madison. His dilemma stopped him from acting impulsively. If he walked off the set, he would fail her.

He observed the landscape from the deck with a sigh. He usually loved this part of the day, the light and shadows with their tricks on the eyes. But circumstance had paired him in the wrong place at the wrong moment. With the wrong woman.

At least there were no cameras around. "So what are you doing here, Audrey?"

"When I got wind of Madison Gray being on your show, I thought I'd stop by and check up on you."

"That's not why you crashed the scene, and we both know it."

She took a seat on a patio chair. "I had an idea that Ms. Gray might be interested in collaborating in an article about herself."

He frowned. "Madison's probably *dealing* with the aftermath of your surprise appearance to the press as we speak."

She dismissed his seriousness with a wave of her hand. "Oh, tell me you don't feel guilty? After all, reality TV is about surprises." She moistened her lips. "Besides, I'm doing a good deed, providing Madison with a chance of doubling her exposure in this venture. It's good for Madison's cause. Good for the show."

She wasn't fooling him. "You showed up here to get some PR for your paper."

"I'd like a little piece of the action, and why not? You owe me that, my love. You were the one who ended it with us right when everything was going along splendidly."

"There was no *us*. Our alleged relationship was just

a ploy for you to score more readers. When is it ever enough with you? If there's one thing that rubs me wrong, it's insincerity, especially when it hurts someone else. Your arrival will throw off Madison's schedule."

"Sorry, but I have employees who depend on me for a paycheck." She sounded a little discouraged, frantic even.

Still, he had to say, "Resorting to grandstanding isn't cool."

"Ouch." Without raising her head, she texted away on her phone. "After watching Madison doing yoga," she continued, thumbs flying over her keyboard, "I don't know if all the instruction in the world could help her."

"Slamming others doesn't do any good, and it's never called for."

Audrey lowered her phone, her expression softening. "I apologize, truly. I don't know what's wrong with me. I've been hitting my head against a brick wall lately. It's not easy to run a small business these days."

He took the chair next to hers. "That's the first honest thing you've said. Here's the deal. If you're not true to yourself, you'll never find out who you really were meant to be."

"That's what you used to tell me." A loud sigh. "Over and over."

"Maybe it's time you listened."

"I guess. It's just I heard you were working with her, and I wanted to do something to prevent you from getting in trouble."

"You making an entrance doesn't benefit anyone."

"Listen, Madison will leave you flat before completing this little fiasco."

"I doubt that," he said calmly enough. "We signed a contract."

"Right," she muttered. "While I was waiting, I snuck a look at some of the footage. She walks a thin line between altercation and dismissal."

Brandon resented Audrey for viewing tape he considered faulty. "You shouldn't have watched a storyline before the postproduction editing."

Her violet eyes glossed over, a columnist after juicy gossip. "Why? Is there something in it you don't want me to see?"

His temples pulsed with that headachy pain. "It's just the beginning of shooting. The crew and the players are all trying to get their bearings."

"Well, one thing is for sure—Madison won't make it."

"That's just your own insecurity talking. Of course, she'll see it through."

"She only cares about promoting her company."

"Because that's all you care about, Audrey?"

"I'm warning you she'll fold. It's just a matter of time—I bet you."

"Too bad I gave up betting along with booze, or I'd take you up on it."

****

"Well, I'm not above gambling." Madison hadn't meant to eavesdrop but thought it lucky she'd entered with the camera crew in tow. "You see, I'm a rather poor student, not having perfected yoga on day one."

Red-faced, Ms. Powell sprang from her chair. "Madison, I hope you're not mistaking my concern for

Brandon as hostility toward you."

Madison's hands curved around the back of the two-seater swing. "The only mistake I can see is that you've entered my home uninvited."

Audrey's face went as pale as milk. "But I thought you would be thrilled about my seeking you out for a story. I wouldn't have bothered to stay otherwise."

Madison had an urge to shove Audrey over the rail of the terrace, which was a little over the top even for her. Those blasted hunger pains made her not only light-headed but ready to brawl.

Brandon must have seen the lethal look in her eyes. "How long have you been standing there?"

His question did nothing more than ring in Madison's head. "Long enough to get the picture. But then, always having to have my way is the catalyst in the proposition I wish to discuss with you, Ms. Powell."

Audrey pressed a hand to her chest. "I didn't mean to horn in."

"Oh, but you did. You most sincerely did."

"I'm sorry you see it that way."

Holding Audrey accountable for her intrusion was the right thing to do. "Now tell me, are you woman enough to make a bet with me?"

Audrey's mouth had fallen open. "Perhaps." She seemed to calculate the aspects of doing so mentally. "Why, yes. I can't think of anything more tempting."

"How about if I see the two months through, which is what I plan, you leave Brandon alone and don't bother him again."

Audrey massaged his shoulder. "Oh, I think he's a big boy who can tell us what he wants. Isn't that right, Bran?"

"He's too nice," Madison said in a confidential tone. "But I'm not."

He raised a hand. "This has gone far enough."

"No," Audrey said. "I'll match Madison's bet with one of my own." Eyes bright with excitement, she gestured toward Madison. "If you lose, I get exclusive rights to your story."

Trepidation caught in Madison's throat. "Girl, you've got yourself a deal."

Audrey cracked open her briefcase and pushed a contract toward Madison. "As I promised, something to explore at your leisure."

"Thank you. I'll stop the door so it doesn't hit you on the way out." Madison poured a glass of water and drank until she felt rejuvenated. "Oh, and just so you know, I'll go claw to claw with you if you show up here again without an invitation."

Uttering a startled cry, Audrey then made her exit in one continuous motion. Watching from above, Madison spied the newshounds outside the house having a field day snapping pictures that would no doubt end up smeared across the media.

Madison could almost feel sorry for her. As angry as she'd been, she couldn't help but notice an underlying desperation in Audrey's words and actions. Being a founder of a fledging startup company, Madison identified with not making enough money each month to pay her staff. Earning no profits wore on a person. Hadn't she herself resorted to off the wall antics to promote InSight? Frankly, the reality show was no doubt her biggest publicity stunt to date. Because of this, she couldn't wholly condemn Ms. Powell. On the other hand, Madison had her own media attention to consider. She had to come off as a woman not to be trifled with. A must in this day and age.

****

Brandon opted to busy himself in the kitchen. "At ease," he said to the television troop marching behind him like soldiers ready to charge across hostile lines.

No, they wouldn't back down. Reality TV consisted of action/reaction. Brandon retrieved a peach from a basket on the counter. He heard the shower running upstairs. He needed to take advantage of his time without Madison to plan where they would go from here. First off, though, he'd deal with the questions hurled at him now like battle fire.

"What is your take on what happened?"

Brandon dropped a bag of green beans on the counter. "There was a slight confrontation. And a proposition made between the two women. Time will tell us which way it will go."

He'd satisfied the viewers without giving too much away. Mostly he supplied them with a mystery—a will-she-or-won't-she question. The show thrived on its mysteries. Besides, the outcome interested him. Not because of the show, not because of his loyalty to his student—although both played into it. He wanted Madison to succeed more now than before, wanted it a little too much for his own good.

He took a bite of the peach and chewed meditatively. If he had the time, he'd go outdoors to unwind. He rented a pad in Hollywood when he was working, but mostly crashed in a tent under the stars. Kicking back now wasn't an option for him. Not when he must change his clothes and prepare the evening meal.

112

"We'll talk more," he said to everyone buzzing around him.

Much later, after a dinner that Madison hardly touched, he suggested she look at the agenda he'd compiled for her. She propped her forearms on the table, most likely to keep from toppling into her peach pudding. "Dead on her feet." The expression fit her to a T. Of course, she'd been spurred on by the catfight that might have hit YouTube by now. Still, as one second clicked into another, she faded more and more.

He cleared off the dishes. "It's been a long day. Maybe we should call it a night."

"No, no, you go ahead." Her yawn stretched across the room. "I need to hear what I have to do to emerge a winner."

They didn't directly talk about the bet, but Madison had taken it to heart because that's who she was. And he rooted for her. Again, maybe a little too much.

He placed the schedule on the table. "Here's to your new life."

Awaken at 5:00 a.m.

Prayer, chanting, meditation, yoga positions set to get Madison's body moving.

A jog along the coastline or possibly doing laps in the swimming pool.

9:00 a.m. Breakfast—eating is preferred for a Kapha/pitta individual.

Morning activities: practice fourteen yoga posture sequence.

Read the Yoga Sutras or other spiritual material.

Lunch, eat in silence.

Life Lessons.

Practice more yoga more energetically than

before.

6:00 p.m. Dinner.

Meditation, the opening of the mental and emotional channels.

Lights out at 9:00 p.m.

Had she even looked?

"I guess this means we still have to meditate tonight."

He mouthed, "I think I'm losing you there, trouper."

Her lips quirked. "Go on."

"Did you know, everything you do is affected by your breathing? Your state of consciousness, your sleep. And get this, if you breathe faster or slower or hold your breath, your state of mind will alter, your mood changes and even your emotional state. So it's important when you..."

A soft whistling sounded. Was she mimicking him?

He spotted her asleep then with her head turned to the side on the table. Her face in the thin, dimmed light had lost all its recent tension. She lay, so delicate and defenseless, and so damned arousing. It was in her breath, in her breasts rising and falling like chiseled clay come to life. Oh, he wanted to turn away from her. Finish his lecture and be done.

Was it only the night before she'd wandered into the kitchen bare-chested and sexy as hell? Because he knew what her nipples looked like when disturbed from sleep, their tawny color, their smoothness, the sensuality between her long legs, he couldn't seem to turn his head back toward the camera lens.

His breathing hurt in his chest as if he'd been

running for hours.

Unsteadily, he reached over and jostled her shoulder. "It's time to get to bed."

Swatting at his hand, she murmured, "Go away and leave me alone."

He picked her up from the chair and carried her up to her room. She snuggled her head against his shoulder, and he couldn't help nestling his face in her sweet-smelling hair. Aroused but damned if he would let anyone know, he knocked open the door with his body weight. "Would some of you women help me?"

By the time he got back downstairs, a restlessness brewed insistently inside him. He'd put space between Madison and himself. Now he needed to turn his attention to something else, pull his wits together so that the scent she'd left behind wouldn't be such a turn on. Wouldn't make him irrational. He concealed a sigh, carefully focusing on the people around him.

He should lose himself to meditation. But where?

Slowly, he came up with an idea, one that would benefit Madison.

He took a swallow of filtered water and then addressed the crew. "How would all of you like to make the next eight weeks easier for Madison?"

Chapter 11

Halfway down the stairs the next morning, Madison paused to take a whiff. Pie crust, flaky and buttery as the pastry tormenting her yesterday at the café in Sycamore Square. The aroma, with its riot to the senses, lured her toward the kitchen like an enchanted vapor.

Hmmm, no meditation and jogging this morning. Brandon must have let her sleep, the dear. But did she suddenly hear chanting—oh, God, was it some Sanskrit mantra? The surround sound speakers began to thunder. *Om bhur bhuvas svaha. Thath savithur varaynyam.*

The noise echoed in her ears so jarringly she imagined the ceiling plaster raining down around her. The floors and walls vibrated, and below the mantelpiece, cinders fell inside the white brick fireplace.

Didn't the man have any boundaries? He had invaded her turf. She preferred a little Reggae or cha-cha. Lighthearted. Zingy. Not low, droning chants dripping with the meaning of life. She marched into the kitchen, her hands on the hips of her black-pleated trousers, prepared for a showdown—a this-is-*my*-house routine.

"Good morning." Brandon greeted her with a pot filled with aromatic tea and the carousel of camera operators. He turned the stereo system down, but not

116

off. "I let you sleep in a little today. It gave me time to bike to that stand tucked in the grove where they sell the best raspberries known to man. I threw together a gluten-free tart I think you'll go for."

What could she say? "Brandon, we have to talk."

"Would you like honey in your tea?"

"No—yes." She'd take all the sweet stuff she could get. "About last night—"

"Don't give it another thought. There's no need to apologize."

In a fluid motion, he whipped egg whites. His brows arched over his eyes so it seemed he looked at the world in a constant state of wonder. Was it the mystic in him? Or did everything he see jazz him? Oh, the life of a guru. She should be so absurdly happy.

He wiped his hands on a towel. "It's lucky you slept through your meditation practice last night and this morning because I hadn't given you any instruction." He moved in a blur, chopped, stirred, sautéed, and tasted. "How are you feeling?"

"Fine." Fiending for coffee, she clutched her teacup between her hands.

"My guru used to say during yoga meditation our bodily temple heals itself. It's worked for me. Would you like more honey?"

"No." She sipped her tea and looked at it, stunned. The best she'd ever tasted!

"It's a special blend," he said as if in tune to her. He flipped the zucchini omelet with a practiced hand. "The tea is composed of organic carob, barley, chicory, dates, almonds, and figs. I've never had it, but I think it's important you have something that you enjoy. Ready for this?" He dished up the omelet, slid it next to a wedge of raspberry tart, and set the plate on the bar. "You've got a spectacular view from here."

Just to appease him, she forced herself to sit and look out the window. "Whoa, not half bad."

The opalescence of the morning slanted through the plantation shutters and shaded the kitchen in soft hues of blue. It was calming. Reflective. She reached for the fork. After she ate, she'd be able to discuss the wager she'd made with his ex. She'd been too exhausted last evening to say boo.

After a good night's sleep, her head clear, she recalled everything about dinner and his lesson afterward. He'd worn black, that dominating color, as he presented her with his vision. Shrewd on his part, his choosing a thin cashmere sweater—so casual she could feel herself unwind just looking at him. She'd relaxed too much and conked out. He had no trouble swooping her up and toting her upstairs like Rhett flippin' Butler. Her tired eyes had barely registered his presence. Thinking of it, she took a swallow of juice and sighed. Talk about hot moves and missed opportunities. Welcome to her world.

With practiced manners, she spread a muslin napkin across her lap. "I suppose your guru taught you how to take care of people."

"Yeah, he was a wandering monk. I wandered with him. How's your breakfast?"

"Better than anything you've made yet. Aren't you eating?"

"I already ate." It didn't stop him from plucking some grapes from a cluster on the bar. He chewed forever, swallowed, then rewarded the cameras with a grin. "You honestly don't cook, Madison?"

"I did when Andrew lived here, but after he moved out, I got accustomed to ordering out." Why did her brother's departure still grate on her? More than anything she wanted him to move back home.

To keep her mind off her troubles, she watched Brandon navigate around the kitchen. He scrubbed and wiped as if doing it gave him pleasure. What a man. He seemed free of complication, unlike anyone she'd ever met. She liked sitting here with the fragrance of natural peppermint soap, wet wooden cabinets, and his unique mix of cooking spices.

The atmosphere of simple delights struck her as strangely foreign. At the same time, it hit her as right—like Guru Brandon, with all his idiosyncrasies, belonged in her kitchen.

Her gaze met his, and her stomach teetered down to her toes.

He slipped behind her and placed a hand over her eyes. "I have a surprise for you, Madison. If you come upstairs with me right now, that is."

Now, how hot was that? She should have been warned by the heavy-lidded way he'd looked at her. Thank the baby Jesus, she hadn't humiliated herself by spilling salsa on her tunic. He cupped the back of her neck with his other hand, his fingers intertwined in the hair at her nape. A steamy move. She forced herself to let him hold the reins. Before this, she'd always taken the lead. How must his pushing her out of the kitchen and up the stairs look to the marauding camera crew? Her breath was increasing by the second. She couldn't remember when she'd been so turned on by a man's foreplay—a man so unimaginably handsome.

His lips vibrated against her ear. "You must be

excited."

"You don't know the half of it." Did he hear her panting?

"Your breathing is nice and deep. The benefits of filling your lungs are many. You're going to feel excellent. You'll get answers to life, answers to bigger questions. It will become something you can't live without."

He was driving her wild in front of a future audience. Had she shoved him into the place where nothing else mattered? She should stop now while she still had the presence of mind, but she was quivering with unsated desire, the cameras only adding to her arousal. He escorted her into a room, and she let out a little murmur of protest when she expected pleasure.

"Are you ready for it, Madison?"

She held her breath. Did she dare? Only a moment left to do the right thing.

"Here it is, our hidden valley of the moon."

He let go of her, and she lost her balance and frantically searched to find a familiar piece of furniture to grasp. She blinked, trying to see in the dimness. He reached out to help her, and she wrestled him as her glance sped in every direction.

Pillar candles barely lit a room darkened by blackout shades and draped with wine-colored taffeta. The place would be a love-nest of the first order if that brass gong didn't take up half the space. The pair of paisley pillows tossed on the floor made it dawn with appalling certainty—she'd gotten the wrong idea.

Holy Mother of fools! May I get a do-over?

He nudged her arm. "Your very own meditation room."

Madison wanted to slap him, slap him silly, the idiot. His eyes were so hopeful, so intent on pleasing her, that she just nodded mutely.

"We moved everything out of this guest room and stored them in another. Now you have your very own part of the world. Think of it; you can meditate whenever you want." He clipped a tiny microphone to her collar. "I knew you'd want to thank me, but thank the staff too. They all worked their tails off last night after you went to bed. You had a rough first day. I wanted—we wanted—to surprise you with something you'd love."

No way could she kick his butt, verbally or physically. *Mask your feelings.* She'd kept her cool with VIPs, after all. If she couldn't deal with an earthnut, she might as well give up.

He clapped his hands. *Chop, Chop!* "Let's take our positions."

With the TV crew, he discussed light angles and camera angles and the use of a brand-new floodlight to help in the dark, and other variables that would bring the scene together. Finished with them, done it seemed with her, he hoisted the mallet, triceps and biceps flexed, and *wham*! The *crash, p-o-n-g* clanged, scrambling her brains.

He said, "Hidden in each breath is a source of transformation."

She flipped off her ballet flats, rolled up her trousers, and sank onto the pillow. "Give it to me straight, guru. No drunk-with-bliss talk. Be forewarned; you can kill a flower by overwatering it."

****

Brandon could swear Madison's sarcasm meant

she wasn't happy. What had he done wrong? From when he had vowed to stay focused, he'd struggled to get Madison well—and nothing else.

Maybe he'd gotten a little carried away by wanting to improve her second day, letting her sleep in, searching out the best berries in town. He'd picked one of his mother's recipes, though he changed it a little to make it healthy.

Last night her early bedtime had given him time to assemble this haven—his stroke of genius—but she acted put-off when he uncovered her eyes. He'd have to convince her there was nothing oddball about meditation.

"I'm going to take you through some preliminaries," he said. "Close your eyes and observe your breathing, but don't try and control it."

She combed her fingers through the pillow tassels. "You mean you're not going to close my eyes for me?" Her eyebrows raised and lowered mischievously. "And here I thought you wanted to be the boss."

Just what was that supposed to mean? "Now start to deepen your breath by expanding your chest, your ribcage, and stomach."

She complied, and a vision of her naked breasts and long torso flashed to thought.

He sighed. "Exhale very, very slowly, and the air should exit so that there is no forcing it. Observe how your mind is."

"You don't want to know." She sounded like she wanted to strangle him.

His stomach muscles tensed. "Observe how your nerves are."

Her cheeks were scarlet. "They're tight as stretched

slingshots."

"Observe how grounded you feel."

"I could kick somebody," she mouthed, and he startled. Why was the woman so damned complicated? Happy one minute. Mean as sin the next. The ungrateful wretch. She should come with a book of instructions.

His breath faltered, and he inhaled as if from a stuffy nose. "Focus on the people that you are grateful for in your life. Now send love to them."

"That's awfully sappy, isn't it?"

He tried to ignore her. "Now you want to visualize your perfect day. Visualize how you would like it to unfold. See yourself making the right choices, whether it's what food to eat, the way you interact with others, or just feeling good about yourself."

"My perfect day?" Her eyes brightened. "Do you really want me to go there?"

"Yes, Madison, I do."

"My perfect day starts with coffee. It includes the moment I convince a director that casting someone who actually has a disability in a part about someone with a disability always makes for a better story. It's when I'm able to be a part of a movie that's nominated for an award. But my day should include landing a new client. There's nothing like discovering talent. It's a huge rush…"

He could think of only one way to derail her, and it wasn't pretty. "Now visualize how you want your life to look in the long term."

"Long term?"

He opened his eyes halfway to see her twisting the many bright-colored bangles on her wrists.

"If I keep up my hectic schedule—" She cleared her throat. "There'll be no future for me."

"I'm sorry," he said, sorry that he must remind her she couldn't go on the way she had been. "The things you do are meaningful and admirable, but when you push so hard and for such a long time without rest, it... Let's try again. See what your intentions are and how they need to change to reach your goal."

She scowled, then touched her index fingers to her thumbs in *gyan mudra* and breathed. "I want to live past the age of forty."

"You of all people should know any goal is possible if you make it important enough."

Her lips trembled. "Guru, you're more than a pretty face."

It would be so easy to fall for her. Lose himself to the heat he had begun to recognize and expect whenever they were together. Sitting this close to her, he couldn't help noticing the candlelight reflected in her eyes. Honestly? He loved listening to her talk about her ideal day. He loved her spirit, her giving nature. She could dazzle the daylights out of a guy.

He plunked one of the candles on the floor between them. Another round down, with much more left to fight—that's how he saw it. Could he hang in there while making sure Madison got the best of his instruction? He had to. He would get tougher on her while he stayed clear of his crazy growing need to take her to bed.

Chapter 12

Just because Brandon had bumped Madison's pride down a peg didn't mean she wanted to give up. No incentive rose higher than her bet with Audrey, except her life being at stake as he had just reminded her. As well he should have. She deemed the most important thing, the only thing that mattered, was Guru Brandon dictating from his swami pillow.

"Now start focusing on an object," he said. "Gaze at the candle flame, if it suits you, but don't have any opinion about it..."

See, that's where things got complex. How could she not have an opinion? To lose her opinion would be to disappear. To flitter into oblivion, for God's sake.

After a second, he said, "You may have noticed that the surroundings of the candle flame have faded."

No, she hadn't noticed. But in the brass candlestick, she saw herself slumped over and immediately straightened for the cameras.

Without a break, he kept instructing. "This means you are focusing very well. Now as the candle flame becomes the only thing in your mind, close your eyes."

Hold up, go back, please!

But Guru Brandon didn't stop. "If you can, see the image of the flame with your eyes closed, keep visualizing it while it stays with you. Try to see it with your mind and with your heart. Feel the experience."

"I've lost it." She crumpled forward in a heap of discouragement. "I think I've just flunked out of Candle-flame Gazing."

"Madison," he called as if through a tunnel. "The only way you can fail meditation is to quit trying." He lifted her gently by the shoulders until she sat in a semi-lotus position. "Remember consistency is the key factor here. Do you want to pass with flying colors?" He raised his eyes and caught her in his translucent blue gaze. "You get up in the morning and practice meditation every day. You'll become better at it, I promise you."

"Will do," she said and hoped she'd managed to sound encouraged.

Brandon got to his feet and rubbed the muscled stomach beneath his shirt. "Maybe we'll try something else now. You've jogged before?"

She slugged her forehead with the heel of her hand. "Me?"

As they emerged from the meditation room, amid the camera people eager to catch Madison at her worst, her sister, Harper, waved her arms over her head like a cheerleader.

Never had Madison seen such a welcome sight. "Give me a few minutes alone with my sister, would you?"

She scurried off with Harper to one of the few camera-free zones, the office which had been converted into a workspace. In respect to their privacy, the television staff started to vacate. Sounds came of their chairs rolling and squeaking. A cabinet drawer sliding closed. The garble of voices as the workers rallied in the hall until they were out of earshot.

Oddly, the stench of old coffee turned Madison's stomach, and she collapsed in a swivel chair. "Brandon's about to make me run, and you know how that will turn out."

"You don't sweat." Harper sat behind a crowded desk and pushed aside some files and an enormous purse. "You're just going to have to get over it. A little perspiration won't hurt you." She raked her fingers through her slick, walnut-colored hair. "Get up from your chair; it's killing you! Or haven't you heard? There's even a book written about it. Sitting is the new smoking; it's that dangerous." She leaped to her feet. "Now get a grip."

All Madison needed on top of everything else was a Harper Lee pep talk. Why couldn't her sister just be her friend for once? Madison didn't bother going on about the traumas and the dramas of the last couple of days. Too many to mention.

She began to pace and tripped over the computer cords. "I've just never been very coordinated, not to mention athletic."

"You were too busy maintaining a 4.0 grade point average. Between school and taking care of Andrew and your job, you didn't have time for anything else. That's why I kept house. You couldn't do it all, who could?"

There was no sarcasm in Harper's tone. And to be frank, back then, Harper had been Madison's savior.

"I couldn't have done it without you. I've never told you, but there it is."

"What?" Harper sounded disbelieving. "That's not true."

"Earlier Brandon asked me to think of reasons to

be grateful. Right off the bat, your name came to me. After Mom and Dad—" Madison couldn't continue. "What a surprise when you gave up everything as a kid to stick around the house doing the laundry and baking chocolate chip cookies."

"Yes, Maddie, and you wanted to be a singer and an actress like Grandma, but you ditched your dream and started working for the talent agency."

Madison thought of that awful winter after Mom and Dad disappeared, when she had to clear out their clothes and pack them into boxes and store them in the attic. Her throat tightened. She still couldn't get rid of their belongings. They might return. Lost at sea meant there was a chance of them surviving on some lifeboat. For nine straight days, Madison had worn Mom's robe and had not gone to school but stayed by the phone waiting for the call that never came.

Harper got Madison through that first Christmas— Harper who discovered Mom's dog-eared copy of *The Better Homes and Garden Cookbook* and threw herself, heart and soul, into learning recipes and how to set a proper table. Harper very generously spent all the money she'd saved up for church camp to shop for gifts for Santa to give Andrew. She even bought chocolate mints for Madison.

It was Madison whom Harper, years afterward, confided when Darrin proposed, when her water broke with Tyler, and when Chloe took her first step. What had happened to the two of them? How had they drifted so far apart?

Chapter 13

Interviews...
Brandon Kennedy:

"Madison's truly a fighter. I haven't seen a student struggle as hard to master yoga. Her body, unused to stretching, rebels. In the beginning, it was impossible for her to touch her toes. Even after a month, she still has about three inches to go. We never finish a session without me having to hand her an ice pack. No, I haven't given her a rubdown. I—

"I believe swimming helps people of all ages. It relaxes, massages, and invigorates punished bodies. I've seen students with arthritis move easier after a session in a pool. It also is great therapy for anxious people, boosting endorphins. I hoped Madison would benefit from the healing power of water, but so far, she seems to drive herself without any results other than leg and toe cramps.

"As for running, she adapted slowly to the stress of it and has started pacing herself faster. Maybe she won't ever win a marathon, but she won't finish last either. I got her writing out her goals. Safe to say, I don't know where she'll be in another month, next year, or even a decade. But today, she conquered three miles—maybe not joyfully but determinedly. And that's all I ask.

"My initial goal was for her to master the proper

execution of each yoga pose, and that, by running, she'd get her cardiovascular system working. It has paid off. Her breath control has improved, and her clothes are looser than before. She—um, uh—has taken her first real step toward being kick-ass healthy. I'm proud of her, though I don't tell her. With her saucy attitude and her high-octane get-up-and-go, she'll soon be a reality-show viewer's favorite. The Kardashians better watch out.

"This is off the subject, but it depicts a side to Madison worth noting. Weeks ago, while she was out jogging, she found a baby sea turtle tangled in a net and rescued it. Another time, she came back to the house with a gull, cleaned it of the oil from a spill, and turned it loose.

"I told her, 'I wrongly assumed it was just people you took under wing.' Her comeback? Typical Madison. 'You know what they say about assuming things.'"

Madison Gray:

"I don't know how I endured the past month. If I'd been training for the Olympics, I couldn't have pushed myself any harder. To avoid injury, Brandon had me stretching before a run, and he taught me strength training with yoga routines. He trained me to jog into the wind when I started out and to return with the wind behind me on the way back. I learned not to overdress even though it's chilly and to wear clothes that aren't layered. On warm days, he assigned lap swimming in the pool, which I hadn't done for the last few years. I hadn't had the time.

"Since the camera crew thought me taxed to the limit, they adhered to my every move. Running along the wet sand made my lungs feel as if they were on fire. My legs shook with the strain, and my stomach muscles ached. I wasn't born with the genetic makeup and physical traits to become an athlete, and nothing can change the fact. Brandon could give me all the positive reinforcement in the world, but it wouldn't change my natural gawkiness. I've acquired so many cuts and bruises I stopped counting them. And I almost always show up on camera with an ice pack attached to a leg or an arm or slung around my neck.

"I don't make the best representation. My nose got sunburned and then peeled. My elbows are scabbed from a nasty fall while jogging, and I live in my cutoffs and T-shirts. My workouts make me so sweaty I stopped bothering with makeup. I have just enough time to yank my hair up into a ponytail. Wisps escape the rubber band and are constantly hanging in my line of vision. I quit recognizing my reflection in the mirror.

"And I'm always worn out. Every night in the meditation room, I nod off, but after Brandon rouses me and I fall into my bed, I can't sleep. Leg cramps plague me and make me jump out of bed and stand on the cold floor for relief. Sleep afterward eludes me for hours. I drift off only to be awakened by the clattering alarm clock. I'm drained, burnt out, and I miss seeing people other than a TV staff that seems only interested in my every screw-up."

Chapter 14

Before the dawning of day number thirty-three, Madison's fingers fumbled with the matches. After trial and error, she lit a candle. In the dimness of her bedroom, her eyes were grainy like they were filled with sand. Her breathing rasped. After an hour of many intakes and outtakes of breath, her legs grew numb.

For the life of her, she couldn't concentrate. Her mind wandered like a balloon in the wind. *Whatever happened to that new hire? There was something a little off about him. What if he was embezzling money? And I'm not there to put a stop to it? What was the name of the girl in the elevator each morning who always looked tired? What were the names of the people in the breakroom—those employees I hardly ever spoke to? And why do they seem important now? I could die and never get the chance to apologize to them.*

A look at that big-brother-is-watching activity tracker Brandon had strapped on her wrist showed her heart rate at 110. *Turn off your destructive thoughts, why don't you?*

Her eyes ached because of the daylight slinking through the edges of the window shades. And if only the wood doves would quit cooing from their lovefest under the eaves, she'd be better able to concentrate.

She counted, begging herself to relax, but her back

ached as if she'd been shoveling cement. A shiver coursed down her spine, and a foghorn out in the ocean bellowed. Frustrated, she tried to get to her feet, but her limbs were needles and pins. Her legs buckled, and she hit the floor with a thud.

She swore, hugged her bruised knees to her chest, and rocked. Torment was all she got for working like a maniac. One day older and deeper in defeat. And to think she used to believe meditation was as easy as sitting under a shady tree. For her, clearing her thoughts happened only when in the presence of Brandon Kennedy.

In their special room, his voice affected her like a shot of tequila, the bones in her body turning to mush. The more he spoke, the more serene she became. But he wouldn't always be around. If she didn't learn to meditate on her own, she'd never succeed at being destressed.

That morning, during a breakfast of mangos and sassafras tea, Madison lamented, "I don't like sitting in the dark, trying to meditate. I just start thinking that I'm not supposed to be thinking, and then I keep thinking that I'm thinking—if that makes any sense."

Brandon shut the squeaky pantry door. "What you're describing is called monkey mind." He dropped several hearty sweet potatoes on the counter. "Everyone who meditates experiences it, but you just keep going. By practicing it, you'll be able to reduce your blood pressure, diminish frustration, and soothe your troubled emotions."

She started peeling the potatoes. "Promises, promises."

He went to work, chopping and dicing. "You'll

catch on." He paused, the knife in his hand midair. "Maybe you need a change." His throaty voice made him sound like he'd been up all night partying. Fat chance of that, unless the party included green kale smoothies and enough yoga for a month of Sundays.

But she'd give anything for a break in their daily grind. "Couldn't we take in a movie? Fill up on buttered popcorn and soda?"

He had gotten that spark in his eyes that usually meant trouble. "That's not quite what I had in mind." He wiped his hands on a towel and left a white sauce bubbling on the stove. "I thought we could tackle some of the clutter hidden in your closets and drawers."

He'd hit a nerve. "What does my stuff have to do with my inability to zone out?"

"In Eastern philosophy, your house is a reflection of you."

"You've got to be kidding." She heaved a sigh. "No wonder I ended up in the hospital."

"The simple act of clearing clutter can transform your life, Madison."

It still spooked her when he got all metaphysical. "You think my thought-littered brain might have something to do with the state of my closet?" She'd never heard of such a thing.

He twisted the knob to simmer on the stove and leaned against the counter, his arms folded in front of him. "I'm not sure." He looked like a study in bronze.

"I don't think I've ever cleaned out my closet." Seriously, had she just admitted this to every man, woman, and child in range of a television?

Everyone seemed to ignore her outburst. She would have tossed a retraction, but the staff was already skirting around Brandon. He might only be giving his future viewers a mini-course on feng shui, but there wasn't a camera that missed a gesture or a motion. All focus was riveted on him, as he said, "Clear the way for good things to start happening to you..."

Oriental music floated atmospherically from speakers as he lectured. The spotlight slanted and accented Brandon's burnished hair and princely bone structure. Excitement deepened the starry lights in his eyes as he dashed by her on his way up the stairs.

"Releasing these inner blockages is like a rebirth."

In exasperation, Madison mentally stomped her foot, tempted to say, "Oh, gag me." What had she gotten herself into? She fought a bout of meanness. After all, she was bone-tired. The last thing she wanted was to clean her closet, especially in front of the eyes of the world. For goodness' sake, what was the point? Minutes later, though, the entire production team was setting things up in her bedroom.

The square footage of her closet that used to be her parents' equaled that of the downstairs bathroom. The architect had designed built-in storage units to keep things neatly organized. With walls painted pearl gray and a vanity area for perfumes and jewelry tucked inside drawers, it was quite classy. A dusty chandelier dangled from the ceiling. The height of the rod was five-foot-three for dresses and forty-five inches for pants and blouses. It included a full-length mirror to see the total effect of an outfit before leaving the house. A small built-in bench stood front and center.

"My mom and dad's closet, when it was designed, was meant for glamour as well as efficiency," she said. "But as you can see—"

"A hurricane hit it," Brandon finished with an uncalled-for snort.

"Hurricane Madison." Heat spread across her cheeks.

When had she piled her shoes on top of the vanity? And why on earth had she bought so many pairs? Or they must have been pairs at one time. No wonder it took her so long to get out the door every morning. Whether it was metallic strappy sandals or knee-high boots, she had to grapple up a match. *Eau de Parfum*, did she own any? If she did, it was buried under the array of hair dryers—what were hair dryers even doing in her closet? And good Lord, there they were, the Christmas gifts she'd stashed last December and could never find.

Brandon snapped open a scented garbage bag. "Lady, can you spare a handout?"

"Well, I guess I should part with a couple of items." She tossed two faded pillows in crimson and peach into the gaping mouth of forest-green plastic.

He shook the bag. "But, lady, I'm still hungry."

Oh, brother, she didn't even respond to this. *Imagine him raising a pack of kids.* She rolled her eyes, then got busy because the image was somehow strangely appealing. Before she knew it, her hands found a squashed box of tissues, a broken visor, and a shopping list.

The obnoxious bag crinkled and yawned. "We've only just begun."

She shot a frigid look over her shoulder. "Quit messing with me."

She rebelled against his humor and his not-so-secret agenda of throwing out her stuff. She kicked at a tangle of high heels that had toppled to the floor, caught her foot, tripped, and sprawled in the quicksand of discarded clothes.

"For crying out loud." She reached up. "Lend me a hand, would you?"

He easily yanked her to her feet. "You can't always get what you want, but sometimes you can get what you need."

"You're not funny, Jagger," she snapped back. "I got along fine all these years without a closet Gestapo, thank you very much."

Brandon hung several wayward dresses over the crook of his arm. "When what you own starts to own you, it's time to let go."

"Maybe I should let go of you."

"I'm sorry," he said, nodding. "I know you're hurting. People—"

"I'm not hurting. I'm mad, and I'm going to use my anger to get things done." She smoothed her hand over the netting on a ballet tutu that she'd worn when she was six. With a sniff, she tugged it from the hanger and dropped it to her side.

"Good going," he said. "If you work hard at it, you'll experience faster results. Rid yourself of your old life and begin anew."

She scowled at his choice of words. "Maybe I don't care to rid myself of my past. Did you ever think of that?"

His pecs rounded and firmed as he lifted the avocado-green blender from the top shelf. "Does this tell a story? Or are you thinking the color will come back in style?"

"It was in our breakfast nook when I was growing

up."

"And it's in your closet because?"

Her fingernails dug crescents into her palms. "I can't throw it out." He didn't need any more explanation than that.

He set the blender on a table outside the closet. "Tell you what. We'll take this '80s classic to the kitchen where it belongs." He held out his hand. "Is it a deal?"

"Guess so," she snapped, and he moved in as if studying her. They shook, and she mouthed an ouch, rubbing her throbbing flesh.

"Sorry, lady."

He bent over so close to her that she found herself counting the bristles on his chin, most onyx colored, some auburn with a couple of stragglers of silver. Close enough that she noticed his bottom teeth had grown in a little crooked. Close enough that his scent, like an aphrodisiac, fueled her with sexual fantasies she'd rather die than reveal.

"Are you okay?" he asked softly.

She wasn't sure. She felt an inner quickening. "Yes. Thank. You."

Fighting for control, she plunged deeper into the maze and began pulling things off the shelves and throwing them on the floor. Where the mess would go from there, she couldn't say. But for better or worse, she vowed to take charge of her own loot.

He caught her gaze. "Madison, are you familiar with the word hoarder?"

Even though he gave voice to what she suspected, his accusation nearly knocked her over. "You think that's what I am?"

"Maybe."

She swallowed. "And all along I thought of myself as a collector."

He gave her a bittersweet smile. "Collector is a much better word choice, but most times there are reasons why people refuse to part with things."

She froze up inside. "You can stop right there." She disliked it when Brandon added psychoanalyzing her to the mix. She had a sudden desire to kick everyone assembled out of her bedroom and slam the door.

****

Brandon couldn't help noticing the resentment that surfaced in Madison as they spent the morning bickering. No, she wouldn't toss out her elementary school report cards. She'd transfer them to the cedar chest, and how could he ask her to part with her twenty or more handbags?

"It would be like giving away some of my children," she said. "If I had offspring, that is. I never want to. Not really. I'd teach them to squirrel things away. A bad influence that's—"

"Breathe, Madison, breathe," he instructed, but she just glowered at him.

If he weren't careful, he'd ignite a panic attack, and they still had the entire house to bomb-blast through. Years of accumulation. What was he going to do with a woman who believed he was out to get her? He decided to appeal to her giving nature.

He waved a hand at the heap of clothes. "A lot of these you can donate."

"What?"

"Give them to the poor. To the needy, you know?"

"You don't realize the sacrifice you're asking of me. Clothes and shoes are my Shangri-La." She narrowed her eyes in concentration. "I can't figure out what to part with."

"The general rule is to get rid of anything you haven't worn in the last year."

She bit her pouty bottom lip so hard that it left behind an impression of her two front teeth. "Is there not some clothes-horse support group I could join?"

He had to build up the positive aspects. "With a tidy closet, you'll experience a sense of freedom. You'll be a clean slate on the road leading to the rest of your life."

"How do you know what I'll feel? I'm tired of your fortune-cookie proverbs." She dug into the pile of shoes. "You're not me."

He eyed her scrimmaging through straps and heels. She was bent over now, all legs with tan lines separating her thighs from her shapely white butt. He laughed huskily. "No, I am certainly not you, babe."

She straightened and pivoted around to face him. Evidently alerted by the sexual undertones in his voice, her eyes filled with a hot, irresistible flirtation he didn't want to acknowledge. He inhaled a deep calming breath. A fat lot of good it did.

She raised a seductive finger to his lips. "You better watch out, buster. You don't want to go and start something you might be sorry for later."

She was mocking him, her sultry tone at odds with her agitation. One moment she acted as if he were out to hurt her, the next her "lover please come home." The sexy mama was well on her way to becoming a total knockout. Aware then of the camera lens, he lowered his eyes. His arms hung rigidly at his sides. His sudden consciousness of her body throbbed inside him, begging for release.

He puffed up his cheeks and blew out. "How about we stop for lunch?"

Madison ducked out of the camera range and snuck a wink at him. She had him pegged all right. She dangled a carrot, and he reacted—the snarky babe in her short shorts.

"I'd eat the state of Texas if you set it in front of me." Those sexy legs of hers broke into a gallop down the stairs. "I deserve a hot fudge sundae for all my work."

He gave chase. "The craving will pass," he said, but his need for her wouldn't.

In the kitchen, she stirred honey into her tea and settled on a barstool, crossing her ankles. "Do you mean in three weeks, six days, and four hours when I can give in to any craving I still have?"

Now, what did she mean by *any craving she still had*? Didn't she realize she was pushing him into a corner, making it almost impossible for him to do his job?

He had to put an end to her coming on to him. After all, they'd made it through the last four weeks without an incident. Not that he hadn't had to bite back his need for her with every yoga posture he demonstrated and she accomplished. He'd signed on to fix her. If he couldn't, he might as well join a hermitage, grow a pointed beard and long hair down to his ass.

"I think we both need a little time outdoors." He threw food into a picnic basket he found in the pantry.

"What do you say we eat on the beach?"

She spurted from the stool in a flourish. "Now you're talking."

Soon they were in the salty air with the fog rolling in with tentacles like some creature from a Stephen King novel. The waves hit with a wallop, and the frothy foam fizzed like a fancy expresso mixture—not that he drank them anymore. The tide was coming in, so he settled with Madison on a blanket near the house. Out of the basket, he took the thermal containers of sweet potato and leek soup. With the cooler temperatures and the coastline deserted, things looked a little nightmarish. Hard to make out anything three feet away.

She squinted as if striving to see. "I'd like to get beyond this black lagoon. Beyond the cameras and far across the world."

"Well, you know what they say. You can dig a hole to China, but you can't leave yourself behind."

"Oh, yeah?" She uttered a sarcastic laugh. "And just who are those forever-unclear 'they' to claim 'they' know everything? Don't you ever wonder?" She grinned. "I say, take off for the Far East, and 'I' ditch the clutter in my closets and drawers."

"Not so, Madison." He handed her a napkin the color of the sand. "Not until you discover what caused you to be a packrat. Did an event trigger your habit?"

She opened the lid of her soup, and the vapor rose as if she'd let out a genie. "Tsk, I don't know." She shrugged. "What's the big deal?"

He broke off a piece of piping-hot bread. "We could be on to something. Have you always *collected* things? Do you remember?"

"I can't think of a year or a month exactly." Her index finger scooped along the sand, making a small gully.

"Go ahead," he urged.

"Well, I—" She stared up into a camera lens protruding from the fog like some deep-sea monster. She shrank back a little. "Guess the 'when' isn't important, is it?"

"If you pinpoint the first occurrence…"

She heaved a crust of bread at him. "I'm tired of always talking about myself. Especially to…" She raised her fingers in quotation marks. "Mr. Perfect."

Blown away, he rocked backward and fell on his rear in the sand. "Are you kidding? You honestly believe nothing bad has ever happened to me?"

"I'm thinking of an adolescent who girls worshiped."

"Do you think being famous makes you happy?"

"No, of course not." She shook her head. "But you know how to live."

"I didn't always." He still didn't, not always anyway, but because he sensed she was feeling defeated, he thought it best to confide a little of his childhood. If he did, she might open up herself. It was worth a try, even though it would cost him his privacy. "When I was a kid, my mother…" He cleared his throat. "She got sick with a brain tumor."

Madison's mouth dropped open, and she shifted toward him. "Brandon, how horrible for you both."

"Her illness happened a long time ago. Dad was gone a lot. Mom kept slipping further, getting weaker. I took over the cooking. She was sick, so the quality of the meals she ate interested me. Even back in the 1990s, people started believing food was medicine. While other guys were playing baseball, I hung out at the Whole Foods Market. Convinced the right diet would save my mom, I became absorbed in the study of natural ingredients."

The empathic look she gave him warmed his cheeks.

"How old were you?" she asked.

"Ten, eleven. Trouble was I experimented a little too much and ended up overweight."

"You sure as heck slimmed down for the part of Matt in the soap."

"I did." He laughed, easing the knot in his chest. "After Mom passed, I went into a funk and got away from eating right. What good had eating right done anyway?"

Her hand covered his. "I'm sorry you lost your mother that way."

"Years filtered by." He forced himself to keep talking. "I discovered I enjoyed cooking. The motions of chopping and stirring calmed me. I started eating better after I entered the yoga institute. When I began preparing meals for others, something clicked. A shrink might say I'm subconsciously back in the kitchen I knew as a kid."

She moistened her lips. "I get that."

"I'm telling you all this because I believe we do things for reasons we aren't always aware of. If we can figure out why, we're on the stretch to self-knowledge and possible recovery."

"Uh-hum, I think you're leading up to something."

He had stepped out on a landmine. "You have a rough time parting with your belongings." He waited for her to look at him, then lowered his voice. "Let's explore the subject, find out where the thread leads."

"I had a fit over that avocado-green blender," she admitted. "I don't know what I'd have done if you hadn't saved it from the junkyard."

"Because it was part of your childhood?"

"Yeah." She fumbled with the lid of her soup container and dropped it.

Brandon clamped a hand on her shoulder. "It's okay."

She nodded. "When I was all of eight, my father took off work to take care of me when I had a cold. I still remember him slicing an orange and a banana and dropping them into that blender. I felt better after I drank it."

Her lower lip quivered, and she twisted herself free from his grip. She headed west, and he traipsed behind her as she scooted down the sandy slope to the water. She slid into a perfect warrior position, her feet grounded as he had instructed her. The surf covered her canvas Espadrilles, and the waves thrashed at her legs.

Her arm raised, and she shook her fist at the fog-ridden surf. She turned and pressed her body against his so that the warmth from her seeped into him. It felt good. It felt right.

"I kept praying my mother and father would show up here. I even dreamed about it. I kept waiting for them, but a lot of good it did."

He said nothing as he lifted her chin and studied her. Her face had paled, except for a few bewitching freckles, and the mist had given her hair a come-hither look. To comfort her, he ran his fingers through her tangled waves. Though he'd hated making her relive the tragedy, he felt it for the best. They had made progress.

He needed to reassure her, to reassure himself. "You just took the first step toward freeing yourself."

"Oh, just shut up and hold me for a damned second."

And fortunately—or not—he did just that.

Chapter 15

As expected, the camera team tagged behind Madison as she wandered back into her closet. She shoved a nest of belts off the bench and took a seat, recalling that first night on the air when Brandon had found her with a cell phone. Now that same TV crew awaited her reaction to the last emotionally charged scene.

Willie, bless him, asked if she was up to granting an Off-the-Cuff.

A surprise interview was the sort of thing that tested her mettle. She could use a nap. After this morning, her reserves were on empty. But if she were to help anyone who would watch this program after production, turning Willie down wasn't an option.

"This morning, Brandon took on my closet, and I wanted to punch him for invading my personal space. I learned, though, we're accomplishing more than clearing clutter. I faced some issues with my parents' death. I have to admit I feel somewhat better for having done so.

"Oh, and just so you know, now and then a girl needs a hug, even when she's all grown up. I feel so stoked now I'd like to try again to tackle meditation, which if you were listening earlier, you'd know I'm not mastering as quickly as I'd imagined. But then sages have been doing this practice for thousands of years.

147

I'm a virtual newcomer, so I'm not going to beat myself up over it."

Harper's voice boomed from the bedroom doorway. "Who is this lady, and what have you done with my sister?"

Madison spotted Harper, hair gelled in a spiky ponytail at her crown, a fringe of bangs accenting her eager blue-gray eyes.

Madison tilted her head to the side. "How much did you hear?"

"Enough to make me believe somebody hijacked my sister and set this prize student in her place."

Madison had to smile. Visiting with Harper each day had become an indulgence, replacing her smartphone and even social media. She'd forgotten how entertaining Harper could be, but she never felt completely free to confide in her sister without the threat of that silent sense of panic. Still, better to talk of the little irritants in their daily lives than nothing at all.

"I need a break from Operation Feng Shui," she said to the TV crew as she slipped out the door with Harper.

Brandon ambled down the hall, lugging more plastic bags, a broom, and a dustpan. Just looking at his enthusiasm made her feel guilty about ditching him.

"See you," she said. "I need a little sister time."

He nodded amiably. "When will you be back?"

She rolled her eyes. "Don't worry. I can't very well walk out on you, can I?" She waited until they had settled into the camera-free zone in the office before adding, "My norm doesn't include having a man under my feet every second of the day."

"I know what you mean," Harper said. "When

Darrin is on vacation, and we stick around making household improvements, I could just tear out what little hair he has left."

"Well, I'm not hitched to Brandon, thank my lucky stars. I don't even want to imagine. Pity the poor girl who winds up with him."

Hugging herself, Harper leaned back against the wall. "At least a thousand women from sea to shining sea would trade places with you."

"Do I have any offers? Going once, going twice...sold to the fool in yoga pants."

"Maddie, he can't be that bad."

"Oh, yeah? What would you say if a man dumped the contents of your closet in the garbage?"

"You weren't talking like this a couple minutes ago."

"Of course not." She rubbed a hand absently over a chocolate bar on the desk in front of her. "How would bashing the guru to all of America go over?"

In a snap, Harper had removed the temptation of Hershey and replaced it with an apple. "Well, it seems to me, your closet needed cleaning and revamping ages ago, but the last time I saw it was on my wedding day after I'd spent the night here."

"And we talked until dawn." They had been close back then. "Harper, you were so worried about tying the knot I was afraid you wouldn't go through with it."

Harper lowered herself into a chair. "I remember."

Madison noted the nostalgia in her sister's voice and asked the question she'd been wondering about. "Are you happy you married Darrin, I mean after all these years?"

"I thought I would lose my identity and be nothing

but Mrs. McGregor. Instead, I became a better me than before. Darrin has all the qualities I lack. He's truly impulsive and kindhearted. He never ceases to surprise me with his altruism."

Never seeing this side her sister's husband, Madison was curious. "Tell me about it."

"Well," Harper said in a meditative tone. "Take the other night. We were standing in line at Walmart. The mother in front of us came up short on cash and told the clerk to put back the Elsa lunchbox she was buying for her daughter. Darrin didn't hesitate to insist the mother allow him to pay the bill."

"He's a good egg." She'd always liked her brother-in-law. "But I don't know if I agree with searching for the character traits we don't have. Take Brandon."

"I'd like to take Brandon," Harper said dreamily.

"Not when he smacks you bright and early with, 'Morning, sunshine.' Sounds like some ol' country song, doesn't it?" Madison rolled the apple back and forth on the desk. "You know me, Harper. I never rise and shine. I stumble and fall on my way to coffee, which, by the way, I'm no longer allowed." She bit off a chunk of apple, chewed, swallowed, but it didn't satisfy. "I would give anything for a slice of bacon or a charbroiled burger."

"Hmm, aren't you midway through the two months? Don't most people start feeling a little crazy about then?"

"Maybe. Yes." Madison found herself taking a cookbook from a shelf and thumbing through the pages and drooling over a picture of linguine with shrimp scampi. "I've lost fifteen pounds," she said, wishing her weight loss were enough to lighten her mood.

"Maddie, that's wonderful."

"I'm not at all sure." She spied the sun burning through the fog outside the window and drew up the blinds to watch. "A TV program I saw once still haunts me. This woman wanted to be thin more than anything. Low and behold, she becomes as skinny as a supermodel, but like all magic, it comes with a price. The poor soul can't order the fizzy pink cocktail she thinks is so nifty because alcohol could cause tiny lines on her cheeks and dark circles under her eyes. She isn't allowed to eat barbequed ribs like everybody else, but instead, is given a stalk of celery. The ultimate dis comes when she is forbidden to lie on a lounge chair because she has to exercise to keep her 'perfect' body."

Harper's brows lowered. "It just goes to show you can't change from the outside without first changing on the inside."

"The chaser?" She lifted her shoulders for dramatic effect. "In the end, the girl wanted to go back to being herself."

"You don't feel that way, do you?" Harper sounded horrified. "You can't want to go back. I'm rooting for you, Madison. I want you to hang around, so you can be at Chloe's wedding."

"Is she planning on getting married anytime soon?" She sent her sister a teasing smile. "Last I knew, she had just started preschool."

"You know what I mean. Quit being such a wiseass. I wish Mom and Dad were still with us so that they could cheer you on."

"Uh-huh," Madison said flatly. The dreaded subject surfaced, inducing in her that familiar fright-or-flight response.

Harper was already off and running. "I contacted the producers of the TV program *Ghost Hunters*." She got all starry-eyed. "I think they might have better luck than the—"

"The last quacks," Madison supplied, restlessly moving her shoulders. "When are you going to learn, Harper? You can't put your trust in showbiz people."

"It's not like you haven't represented a couple of them."

"Okay, that's enough. We're not getting anywhere by arguing with each other. Do what you want. Investigate all the paranormal activity you can round up. It's not going to change anything."

"I'm hoping it will bring closure. That's what I need. It's what we both need."

"All right, go for it." Madison held back a sigh. She was tired of resisting, even more tired of debating when nothing was ever settled. "I've got to find Brandon so we can finish up the closet. I'll talk to you later."

Madison kissed her sister's forehead and hurried away. These disagreements were mostly why she'd given up contact before she collapsed in her office. Harper put all her faith in ghostbusters. They'd had their fair share of psychics through the years. People had to make a living, but why did some prey on the sorrows and grief of others? It was wrong. She couldn't stop Harper from consulting these so-called mediums, but she could prevent her own involvement. On a deeper level, Madison distrusted anything that had to do with clairvoyance. It was better not to ask for help than to be disappointed yet again.

Irritable, she found no one in her bedroom any

longer. She entered the comforting darkness of the meditation room and spotted Brandon in his signature lotus position.

Opposites attract, or so Harper had implied. With his tight buns, Brandon could stay planted for hours on end. A month ago, she would have said he wasted a whole lot of precious moments doing nothing. And now? Darn it all if she didn't envy him. Still, it was dangerous to sneak up behind him and spy like a—well, like a spy.

The sight of his body in athletic pants and a tank top, exposing dark honey-colored shoulders, made her swoony. His eyes that seemed to see things inside her no one else did, things she didn't even know about herself, were closed. The mixture of sounds and textures and smells of this exotic place with its candles and smoky burgundies delighted her. It was a slice of deep, dark India, a piece of his mother's world before he had lost her.

Purposely, she closed the door with a jolt so that he twisted around. Lordy, if the man didn't look as if he'd just spent time napping in a hammock on a lazy afternoon. Lucky him.

"Ah, Madison," he said as if glad to see her. He stacked his pillow on top of hers, such an endearing act, and lifted himself as effortlessly as a cat. "Are you ready to go back to work?"

Three hours later, the closet looked the same as it had when it was new. Madison strolled inside her walk-in, flapping her elbows up and down. "Roomy," she said with pride. "No 'my stuff runneth over.' "

Brandon followed her inside. "Yep." He nodded at the near-empty shelves. "Now there's a place for everything and everything in its place."

The presentation was primary. She'd sorted her handbags by type—tote, clutch, bijoux, etc.—her dresses by category and then color. Footwear hung in clear plastic bags, and jewelry sprawled on velvet in skinny drawers designed for that purpose. Bakelite bangles filled a boot box, and colorful perfume bottles stood on the vanity according to night and day use. Gone was anything that didn't make her smile.

With a satisfied sigh, she lounged on the bench and took in the polished chandelier's shimmering glow. "I think I'm starting to love where I live."

"Good. Maybe you'll come home from work instead of spending your nights in your office. What do you think?"

Confused, she turned her head to observe him. "Huh?"

"You don't recall the lady who lived her life on the fast track?"

She got a mental picture of a woman running around in circles. Had that crazy bee been her? Annoyed, she hugged her shoulders. "My, oh, my, don't I sound pathetic?"

"It's all about balance, Madison." Then, as if he thought she'd had enough lecturing for the day, he broke into one of his guaranteed-to-make-a-girl-swoon grins. "I'd say you deserve a reward."

Was her dream about to come true? "Does this mean there's an ice cream sundae with my name on it?"

"What I have in mind is a health food restaurant. In a week, after we've attacked the rest of the house. A little shopping for yoga clothes beforehand, practice on the beach afterward—what do you say?"

She sighed with pleasure. "I'd say you've got yourself a date."

Chapter 16

Lights, cameras. Bloomingdales. After a week of painstaking clutter clearing.

The hangers click-clacked, rubbing together on a rail, as Madison Gray chose a cashmere pencil skirt, an off-the-shoulder romper, and a keyhole printed dress. She spied Brandon flagging her down. Being in the store she could never afford on her own, she'd forgotten his existence.

"Hey," he said, puffing up next to her and shepherding in the cameras. "Don't you remember your motto, 'Only splurge if you can't live without it?' "

That catchphrase, coming from the king of catchphrases, had slipped her mind. Shopping without interference—a tribe of salesgirls on hand to supply her with all the latest fashion trends—meant a turf this side of paradise.

Brandon tapped the clerk who had been trailing behind on her shoulder. "What can you show Ms. Gray in the way of yoga wear?"

The girl took off. "We just got a new shipment. Wait till you see."

Who cared about yoga? Madison whooped at gowns too gorgeous for words, chiffon, georgette, silk charmeuse—Givenchy galore. She was browsing through them, fingering the ruffles and tucks, when someone tapped her on the shoulder.

Brandon wrinkled his handsome brow. "Did you forget why we're here?"

Well, of course, she hadn't. "No, how could I with the guru and his camera yahoos?" She'd be darn if he would make her feel guilty. After all, didn't she deserve a reward for fulfilling all his demands for reform?

The salesgirl awaited them with hands clasped at her waist. "Right around the bend," she prompted with a slight turn in the opposite direction.

Madison tried not to sound like a woman who had been locked away and denied shopping. "I'm right behind you."

Less than thirty seconds later, they were surrounded by racks of sports attire. A regular jock's paradise. Madison preferred the altered state she got being near *Parfum* and red-carpet apparel but composed herself as the girl handed her an armful of possibilities.

Brandon moved in. "How do we dress for a yogic practice?"

Tired of him going all "we" on her, she glowered at him. "I'll take a wild guess it's not in cut-offs and a baggy T-shirt."

"No, ma'am." He fastened his fists to his narrow hips, biceps like bricks, looking for all to see like he had a monopoly on the fitness market. "We're going to make certain the items we choose fit and feel good while we are performing postures."

Her teeth ground together. "Are *we* now?"

"Of course, we should always carry bottled water, especially in warm temperatures. In cold or wet conditions, we may require additional clothing if we decide to work outdoors."

He'd started this "we" business shortly after she

told him to hug her that day on the beach. She suspected it was his way of maintaining a genderless relationship while on the air.

"About yoga pants," he prattled on, oblivious to her irritation, "we should be able to move freely, but..."

He was watching her as he lectured with his matinee-idol allure while indirectly speaking to his audience in the forward motion of a soon-to-be postproduction. The potential he had for market appeal never ceased to amaze her. But this "we" thing he had developed had to go.

She caught sight of a rack that sparked an idea. Going for varied sizes and makes, she said, "Brandon, what about these sports bras?"

He squinted at Spencer for a script change, but of course, Spence only shrugged. And Brandon squirmed deliciously. Taking the plastic hangers, he cleared his throat. "These are available in a range of colors, sizes, and support, and can be worn with or without a top."

"So we can go topless?" What a kick in the rear, Brandon Kennedy blushing. "And how do we know that a brassiere will fit?"

"Will fit?" His eyebrows angled in perplexity. "It must fit snugly without slipping up, binding, or restricting movement."

She couldn't resist teasing the man who rode her almost every waking moment. A man who needed a shakeup, in her estimation. "*We* will just mosey into the dressing room," she said, "run in place and jump around. Test the bras for stability and comfort."

The salesgirl had been turning back and forth between Madison and Brandon, observing them as intently as a tennis match at Wimbledon.

Brandon's mouth suddenly quirked at the corners. "*You* do that, trouper."

Aha, score a point for her. He finally got that she'd been making fun of him. Game over.

But in case he hadn't quite gotten it, she wrapped her arms around herself. "There is no we unless you're talking about the bossa nova."

He moved toward her. "Gotcha," he said, holding back a laugh. "Blame it on the bossa nova."

His foolish attempt at dancing, stepping on his own feet, missing all the right beats as she sang, made her giddy, made her melt. She loved a man who knew how to clown around, thought it hot. Right about now, she would give her left earlobe to yank him with her behind the privacy of that dressing room curtain, kiss him until he begged for more.

Still, just for fun, she carried their banter a step further. "I suppose such lingerie should feel smooth and soft to the touch."

He feigned a solemn look. "If not, chafing may result."

"You've studied your product, guru. I can tell."

"Speaking of which…" His voice came out hoarse, making her realize he'd forgotten where they were. "Cotton kills," he announced, slinging the subject away from the suggestive. "Workout gear should always be synthetic to absorb moisture. If *you* must wear a natural fiber, I recommend either silk or wool."

"Enough already!" She tore open the fitting-room drape so that it shrieked along the bar. "I'll check out the labels," she called, "and let you know."

Once inside, she came face to face with herself. It wouldn't do to try and fool the cameras. If she didn't measure up, the footage would show her failure to reach her goal. Reluctantly, she tugged on a crop top and star-patterned leggings and whirled to the mirror. With joyful awareness, her hand pressed against her flat stomach. When had her obliques become this firm? Before now, she wouldn't have dared bare her midriff.

Even so, her pulse fluttered as she crept out and awkwardly pivoted. "Well, what do you think, my favorite guru?" Did her apprehension show?

"What do I think?" The strain in Brandon's voice alerted her. "That top has potential." He directed his stare to the wall above her left shoulder. "But won't you be cold?"

"Southern California is hardly the North Pole." Her spirits took a nosedive. He was making excuses, being tactful. "Never you mind. I'll go change into something else."

"No, no, your current outfit is a keeper," he said a little too fast.

Was he afraid she wouldn't buy it? Or was his patience already maxed out? Oh, men! A woman should never depend on the opposite sex when it came to shopping. She wished she had included Harper because she never hedged but told the truth, no matter how brutal.

Back inside her dressing room, Madison yanked on some lace-up yoga pants and a shockingly tight pink shirt. "Well?" she said, poking her head from the drape before stepping in front of the cameras and an audience that now crowded the entrance to the fitting rooms.

"Well, what?" Brandon said, shaking his head like he needed to clear it. "That fits."

What was he keeping from her? "That fits, but

you're a *mess*," he didn't say, but she guessed it lingered on the tip of his tongue. Just her luck, she had almost reached her goal only to discover she hadn't tried hard enough.

Hey, girl, you're kind of a tubby broad; the boy's voice echoed back. But what did she expect? In the dumps, she clomped back to try on more clothes.

She sighed as she selected a pair of lustrous Capri leggings and a neon halter-top. "Here I am." Her head lowered, she appeared again. "I don't suppose—"

"Yes," Brandon said, his face lighting up. He applauded her choice, then obviously caught his reflection in a mirror. Visible dread rearranged his enthusiasm. He froze, dropped to his chair, and assumed an expressionless Zen gaze. "Not bad," he added.

All at once, she understood why he had been offhandedly dismissing each of her outfits. Everyone and his neighbor watched *Guru Brandon*. God forbid he show any emotion. Such favoritism might be easy to misconstrue, but his lapse in control delighted the heck out of her, and her mood lifted to the zenith.

****

Later, Brandon kicked off his shoes and slid with Madison down the hill toward the sea endlessly sprawling out on both sides. Few people had surfaced yet, so they had the strip all to themselves. The warmth of the sun heated a guy whose temperature had spiked back at Bloomingdales. Those cut-offs Ms. Gray always wore were a tease, but her new skin-tight outfits? If he had his way, the network would ban them for making a man smolder. He hadn't dreamed her weight loss was as prevalent or as hot.

But it was only fair for him to give her a chance to try out her new clothes. Wouldn't he do the same if the woman were any other student? He could be neutral. The reality TV show deserved his impartiality. He had to believe that.

Her hips this morning swayed as she walked, still humming that catchy tune "Blame It on the Bossa Nova." They'd sung it in a duet on their drive. Blame it on having no radio and needing to improvise. Blame it on the wildflowers blowing around her ankles in the sand along the footpath, the blooms of yellow and fuchsia. The dragonflies, their wings multicolored, looped through the backdrop of sky. A bird hovered near her shoulder. Unaffected, she strolled, tall, tan, and lovely. A woman seemingly without any other care than to enjoy the day.

As the sand on the beach squeezed through his toes, massaging them, he gave her the cue. "Mountain pose."

They both began in unison, and Madison appeared powerful, invincible. Maybe it was her new workout gear, her pants slinky and shiny, her top a neon flash of green. The spandex displayed her newfound angles and curves in a blazing hot way. He found the long arch of her hip beyond fascinating. Wonder Woman had nothing over her.

They sat in hero pose, like a king with his queen, he thought, glancing out into the vast blue day.

Without a word, they did their warming posture, cat/cow. He nearly moaned out loud watching her. Then she started to gather energy, so that when they went into downward-facing dog, he discovered, with her well-earned agility, she didn't bend her knees as usual.

"Madison, you're touching the ground!"

She beamed up at him. "I am!"

She was unimaginably beautiful. The way the sun seized the golden streaks in her red hair, the way the natural wave framed her angular face, distracted him. He had his fantasies about her, and this was one of them. The two of them by themselves on the beach, doing yoga—Kundalini yoga with its fire breath, hot yoga with its heat. The only problem? The usual. They were *not* alone.

Warrior pose brought with it an expression of victory on her part, and child's pose caused her to fold up within herself like a flower after sunset. No woman had ever done the positions with as much raw sensuality. Being with her made him, the yogic practitioner, forget how to move and how to breathe.

This day she stood taller and bent farther. The muscles in her arms supported her with effortlessness. Even her hands seemed stronger than before. She balanced herself with greater ease, like a goddess surveying her kingdom by the sea. Brandon closed his eyes against the gush of erotic pictures she evoked in him. He had been with her too long, yet not long enough.

When they finished, she purred, "I just might learn to love this."

"You did well."

"Do you think it was the fancy yoga outfit?"

He shook his head. "Nah, I think it was the woman." He couldn't prevent the throatiness from his voice any more than he could keep his arousal from showing. Desire tightened all his muscles. Oh, God, he wanted her, needed her, and that was why his next words were "What do you say we go to breakfast?"

Did he really want to split the scene? Hell, no. He longed to take her behind those rocks to that secluded beach no one knew about, rip what little she had of her clothes off. Ever since he witnessed Madison in her first yoga number, he'd been jonesing to get her by herself. Right about now, he could easily destroy every last camera. He would pay the crew thousands of dollars to disappear, but how would that look?

It was just as well there were boundaries. He couldn't relax even for a second. If he did, all he'd worked so hard to accomplish would be for nothing.

"I am famished, even more than usual," she was saying in a cheery voice. "Am I excused from eating produce? How about a waffle?"

Good question. Brandon was on it, on the job. "It doesn't work like that, Madison. You must learn how to make nutritious choices when you eat out. Call it a learning experience."

"There you go again," she said, pinching his arm. "You're such a stuffed shirt."

Was he? He wished she weren't as close. She smelled of mandarins from the essential oil she had bought at the health food store. And her hair had an orange blossom fragrance. Her lips most likely held the salt from the sea. He loved sweet and salty, craved it this morning. Somehow the thought of breakfast in a diner didn't interest him in the slightest.

****

Before today, Madison had driven past the Harbor Inn but never stopped. All that natural grub hadn't been on her radar. Now she felt full of vitality, rollicking into the foyer with Brandon Kennedy and the TV people.

Decorated in blue paisley wallpaper and furnished with wrought iron tables and French antiques, the restaurant gave off a European vibe. The wraparound windows offered views of the profusion of poppies draping the rolling hills and spilling down to the glittering beach.

Steam shot from a stove. Sweet, spicy aroma filled the air. People, out for another Santa Monica Sunday, chatted and laughed. The cash register dinged as coins clinked into a tip jar. A hostess led them around tables where folks sipped organic coffee and ate muffins and pancakes that teased Madison's nostrils with their aromas of blueberries and maple syrup. They sat on padded seats and scanned a menu while the TV troop boogied around them.

Minutes later, their waitress, a lean, tall girl, her hair an up-sweep of loose dark curls, pulled a pencil from behind her ear. "Are you ready?" she asked in a chirpy soprano.

"I would like to start with..." Oh, man, what Madison wouldn't give for coffee. She could almost taste the rich dark flavor of Columbian. "Apple-spice Infusion," she relented.

"Excellent choice," said the girl. "And you, sir?" She shielded her eyes from the glare of the cameras. "Could y'all move back some?"

Yes, like off the cliff, Madison wanted to add. Brandon mumbled something about the crew taking a break, and thank the Lord for small favors, they complied, heading out the side door.

The waitress blinked at Brandon, then pointed with her pencil. "Hey, aren't you that television guy on the cable station? That yogi somebody or other?"

"Not quite," he said, sounding mildly amused.

"I remember now. You're Guru Brandon." She poured water and ice into Madison's empty glass. "You're a lucky lady."

Madison rubbed a thumb. "If you only knew." Being with Brandon Kennedy was an Argentine tango of push and pull—a dance of utter frustration.

"Well, I could sure use me some yoga lessons, let me tell you, but y'all aren't here to listen to me carry on. Now, what can I get you?"

Brandon said, "I'll start with a glass of water."

"Coming right up." She tipped her pitcher and retrieved her pad. "Now what else sounds good?"

Madison needed to pass the test. "I'll take a gluten-free waffle—if there is such a thing."

"Of course there is, darlin'. You came to the right place. Lenny will whip you up the best waffle you ever tasted. You got a hankering for blueberries?"

Madison's mouth salivated. "That would be terrific."

"On top of that, he throws in a dollop of good-for-you topping you would swear was the real McCoy." The waitress lowered darkly mascaraed lashes. "And what does the guru choose? Something to get the blood pumping, I'll bet."

"I'll take what the lady's having."

"You've got it, sweetheart."

After she took their orders, Madison relaxed against the chair. She could at least make conversation. "This place is intriguing. It's somehow Old World and nautical and I don't know...I keep expecting a pirate to swagger out from the back."

"You mean Jack Sparrow?"

A hand flew to her chest. "You know him?"

"Know him?" he asked in surprise, then winked. "I hang out with him."

She leaned forward, elbows on the table. "Are you good with a sword?"

"You better believe it."

"Too bad you can't show me." She looked at him for a few seconds, not blinking. "Or are you afraid?"

"I'm not able to act on my impulses." He glanced at his hands, then back at her. "It doesn't mean I'm not just as human as the next guy."

****

He drank his water, but it didn't satisfy him. He was thirsty for Madison, couldn't say so. If she had her way, he would forget who he was, who he had to be. Keeping a distance between his feelings and his obligations was imperative. Some things were taboo, no matter how much it killed him at times, like now.

She accessed him with an accusatory glare. "The cameras are nowhere in sight, but you're still on."

"Point taken." He shifted in his chair but couldn't think of a thing to say.

The silence between them lingered so long he couldn't stand it. The noon light through the window touched her eyes and tinted them a glittery teal. Her face, still dewy from their workout, radiated with health, and her skin had a luscious satin sheen. If she only knew how much he longed for her or what temptation was doing to him, all the crazy things, she wouldn't think him a stick in the mud.

Soon, the waitress appeared with two plates filled with steaming waffles and eggs. Madison's hands sprang to the hollows of her cheeks, eyes widening in apparent joy. The TV group returned, muttering shoptalk back and forth between themselves. All went quiet when Madison took that first bite of her omelet.

She chewed and chewed more, the intensity of the moment hanging thickly in air. The camera crew could have taken a break, gone home for dinner, and come back again in the time it took her to chomp her food. The woman knew how and when to create tension.

Eons later, she swallowed and blew out a sigh. "Mmm, I can taste tarragon, basil, thyme, and a bit of sharp rosemary."

Brandon's pride in her surfaced. "You're becoming food savvy; you know that?" He couldn't have been more pleased with her.

She arched a brow. "Maybe I had a good teacher."

"Whoa, I think I'm going to fall off the chair."

"Why?"

"I can't believe it. You just gave me a compliment." Her praise caught him off guard with a squeeze of his chest.

But she shot him a withering glance. "Get over yourself, guru."

Instinctively, his hand crept toward hers. Stopped. His fingers drummed the spot beside his glass. *Lonely.* She sat across from him, such a short distance, but she might as well exist on a solitary shore or inside a moon crater. No one guessed how out of control he was with lust for her, and it must remain that way. He had to think of her career along with his—not the entreaty in her eyes.

Still, he wanted to do something nice for her. He watched her eating with relish and came up with an idea. "What would you say to my building you an herb garden?"

"Would you?" She brought her hands to her chest like she just won an Oscar.

"Think of it, Madison, fresh-picked herbs with every meal."

Her grin lit all the empty places in him. "I'd rather own a little rosemary, parsley, and thyme than a shipload of diamonds."

"Your wish is my command," he said with a Johnny Depp flair.

The waitress paused at the table. "Is there anything else I can get you two lovebirds?"

Brandon had tried to keep his growing attraction to Madison secret. How would the postproduction editors handle a screw-up like the waitress linking them together as *lovebirds*? But he believed he knew the answer, and it wasn't to his liking.

Chapter 17

Madison spotted her brother's flatbed pickup in the driveway. A surprise like this made all the rest of the red-letter things this morning a tad less bright in comparison. His coming home warranted a welcoming party. Bring on the Spirit of Troy University Marching Band—banners, flags, and all. The prodigal son returns and yadda, yadda.

The producers, seizing the opportunity when it hit them, jumped on her for an interview. Handing her Bloomingdale bags to crew members to take to the house, she then let Lilly spruce up her makeup. There was no use fussing with her hair since the wind was gusting in from the Pacific. Okay, the weather sometimes added a thrill factor to reality TV. Stirred things up. Predicting the next scene would go in her favor, she moved into the spotlight.

"The last time I saw my brother was in the hospital. Between the interruption of the medical staff—not to mention my sister being there—I didn't have a moment alone with him. Then came the three-way phone call where I relayed I'd decided to hand my life over to Guru Brandon to reinvent. After that, well, you know the rest.

"But there has been so much to learn. Shaping up required more work than I had been prepared to give. Now everything is falling into place, so I think Andrew will come around.

"He left home straight out of high school, and so I dealt with my nerves the only way I knew how. Work, food, and shopping. The latter I still fight with, God knows. Still, my coping mechanisms are taking a new direction with the calming skills I picked up from the guru.

"Just so you know, I raised my baby brother, and he's the most important thing in my world. Providing the best for him is still my supreme goal. College is what he needs. I suspect, by now, given time and his inability to secure a good job, he'll see I'm right."

Madison rounded the path, trying to empty her mind. But his showing up at the house was major. She couldn't wait to talk to him. Who knew? By the time they resolved their differences, he might move back and be in her debt for letting him. She wouldn't rub in how wrong he had been. Making a stink might make things awkward when he tried to apologize.

They had parted after a falling out. Andrew had been turning into a beach bum. She'd told him as much. None of the colleges were beating down the door, he'd argued. Why couldn't he hang out with his surfboard until he made up his mind about what he wanted to do? She'd told him no, then had given him an ultimatum. Either sign up for classes at the community college or move out. She had said a lot of things that day she was sorry for.

As she passed the oak tree near the house, she avoided looking at the rope still strung there. A tire used to be attached to it. She shouldn't recall her brother when he was just a boy. Not now. Not when the adult Andrew had some crawling to do.

There he was on the front porch, shrugging his shoulders before the cameras like he felt unsure of himself. But what was that mistake of a dog doing at his side?

"Hey!" he called to her with his disarming grin. "Sis, this is Harley."

Andrew loved dogs. But after their last one got old and had to be put down, she'd sworn never another. Having an animal meant making a huge commitment to provide companionship and love, and her agency required all her time. Plus, when they had lost their beloved four-legged family member, she had discovered emotions that brought back painful memories of her parents' disappearance.

She crossed her arms in front of her and frowned. "For the love of God, Harley's no pedigree. He looks like a cross between a mountain lion and a timber wolf."

"Huh-ha, that he does. He was lost and scrounging through the garbage can. My living arrangements then didn't pan out, but he's been my best bud ever since."

"Imagine that." How could she break their bond? Relenting, she sighed. "I bet you're starving, Andrew."

"Don't you know it." He was born able to wolf down a stack of pancakes, a half a pound of bacon, followed by a quart of milk.

Carefully, she slipped past the dog who was lifting his snout, no doubt savoring delicacies only identifiable to canine nostrils. "Let's go in." Was she actually going to grant the monster dog entrance? Ah, so what if she did? If he got rambunctious, the TV crew would be on him in a flash. Still, nothing like complicating matters.

Brandon dropped his hand into Harley's line of

vision. A sniff, then a tail wag, and soon the hunky guru was scratching the mongrel's head.

"I'll leave you alone to visit with your brother." He slid backward, his hands in the pockets of his jeans. "I'm going to rustle up some supplies to build your herb garden."

Infatuation, like a drug, shot through Madison from head to toe. What a love, her intuitive health aficionado. She all but kissed him. Part of her wanted to say, "Bye-bye, hubby. Be sure to take the TV folks with you."

But the camera lenses were already sniffing out dirty laundry like schnauzers for a bone. She'd have no luck ridding herself of them.

"Sorry I can't hand you a soda," she said as her brother and The Tramp padded behind her into the born-again immaculate kitchen. "Soft drinks aren't on my list of acceptable beverages."

Par for the course, Andrew headed straight for the snack food. "What happened to the pantry?" He ripped open a bag of twice-baked, apricot ginger crisps. "It's so clean I feel like I should take off my shoes."

Pleasure flooded through her. "The space clearing is called feng shui. Brandon and I threw all my old stuff into a rented dumpster and hauled it off." Her shoulders lifted to her ears. "Clutter free is the new me."

"Clutter free looks good on you, Mads."

His praise lifted her higher. "Thanks, Drew." She picked up two tumblers and set them on the counter. "I won't kid you. The last month and a half have been challenging. Some days I didn't think I could haul my body another step." She poured some water into a bowl for the dog. "So what brings you by for a visit?"

"Do I need a reason?" He scooped up the glass she

offered. "I tried to come before this, but I…you know how it is."

"If there is one thing I learned through Brandon's lectures, it's to be up front. You left on bad terms. Are you feeling any different now?"

He nibbled at his knuckle. "In some ways." He seated himself at the island and checked his phone. "You took over after Mom and Dad passed," he said without looking at her. "I mean, we could have gone to live with Aunt Susan, but you said no. I didn't realize how cool you were until I got older and thought things out."

"Older, huh? Ah, to be twenty-one again."

"Yeah, old enough to buy booze."

"You don't have to tell me. I remember being able to order a cocktail for the first time."

"You didn't drink back then."

"Oh, I had my moments." Too many as she recalled.

With a troubled frown, he stretched his gangly legs. "You know how it is. You start off having a beer after work, and before long, you're leaving the bar when it closes."

God, if only she hadn't brought up his being twenty-one. "Are you telling me you have a problem?"

He gave a solemn nod, and she winced. Now everyone in the country would know.

"Why didn't you come to me before?" Her underarms were quickly becoming wet with moisture. "You know you can tell me anything."

"I didn't want to bother you." He pointed his finger at her. "You're a busy lady."

Well, that was a direct hit. "I should have been

there for you, Drew." It shamed her to admit it. "I'm so very sorry. Things are different now." Without thinking, she wove her fingers in Harley's warm chest fur. "If you have anything to tell me, anything at all, feel free to unload."

A big part of her yearned to ask him to wait till the cameras shut down for the day.

"Okay," he went and said, staring at his Converse shoes then at her. "I'm going to level with you. You've been a mom to me, and I appreciate it, but things are about to change."

Her hopes rose a notch. "You signed up for a semester at a community college?"

"That would thrill you, wouldn't it?" He shook his head. "No, sorry to disappoint you."

She kept stroking the dog's soft coat, a little desperately now. "Hmmm, I'm fine with whatever you do. No one takes the same road."

"That's for sure."

"Do you want me to help you get into a recovery home?"

"No, no, it's nothing like that." He looked down into his glass. "It's just I—" He lifted his head toward the ceiling. Was he looking for guidance from a higher power?

"You're not going to jail?" As soon as the question slipped out of her mouth, she wished she could snap it back.

His face flushed red, nearly matching his hair. "Maybe I got close to getting myself locked up, but no."

Whatever the calamity, she wanted to help him through, the same as she had when he was little. "Talk to me. Things can't be that bad."

"I joined the marines."

"What?" She gulped for air. "You're telling me you signed up for the military? When?"

"A while back, around April I guess it was." He lifted his glass. "Cheers."

"Andrew, what the hell?" The anxiety in her face reflected in the toaster on the counter. "This is something I can't get you out of."

His body stiffened in that defiant way it had when he was seventeen, and she'd tried to get him a job at the agency. "I'm not asking you to. I want to serve my country. I figure I'll be able to make something of myself."

"I'm not surprised, not really." She wasn't when it came down to it, given a moment to think. "When you were little, you were always playing with toy soldiers."

"And guns," he interjected.

"I didn't like the guns." A thought brought her to a halt over the dog. "So what are you going to do with him?"

"I came here...I was hoping...I was going to ask you to take him."

Astonishment knocked the rest of the wind out of her. "When?"

"I leave tomorrow."

Her jaw unfastened. "Tomorrow. So you're dropping King Kong off with me at this late date? Couldn't you find anyone else?"

"I wanted you to take him."

"But I go back to the agency in two weeks. What will happen if I work late and Harley needs to eat? What will he do when my job carries through to the weekend? He requires exercise and grooming and vet visits." When he remained silent, she crumpled over the butcher block. "Damn, I've been putting my all into getting myself well. Still, I can't be sure if everything I accomplished is enough. I can't risk failure of any kind."

There was nothing on his face but a sad, enigmatic smile. "I wanted you to take Harley because you need him. He's terrific at helping people. I was hoping he'd mend the part of you that's broken."

"You think I'm broken because I work hard?" Her eyes were wet. "What's wrong with loving what you do? Isn't it called having a purpose? Since when did passion become a bad trait? I just don't get it."

He shook his head. "Oh, man, I didn't mean to make you upset. Forget I asked. I'll give him to Harper or one of my buddies."

Had she ever actually meant to change? Telling herself her life was on a new course, believing it— why? The dawning that she'd been fooling herself all along caused her eye to twitch like it had all those weeks ago.

"I'm letting you down, Andrew. I—"

"No worries," he said and headed out with Harley behind him. "I'll get out of your hair."

The dog's toenails clicked on the slate entry, and the camera guys made loud stomping sounds as they stumbled wildly, hoping to get the finale. She followed them outside. Through the trees, the sea had gone as still as glass. If she could just weather these tense moments, hold tight to her resolve, everything would be okay. She struggled to breathe, taking her breaths, in, out, in, out, as Brandon had taught her. Let Andrew's words go. *I was hoping he could mend the part of you that is broken*. The hurtful remark was a balloon floating away. Nearly gone. Another few seconds, both her brother and his big lug of a dog would be gone out of her life. Maybe forever.

Lost. It had been Andrew that she'd lost, and she'd suffered the dismal feeling of it that day in her office. Losing those she loved had become unbearable, and there seemed nothing she could do about it. Or was there?

Brushing the hot tears from her cheeks, she started to run. Daily jogging gave her more stamina. Still, she never guessed the trail away from the house was as long, or that pain would strike like hot coals in her gut.

"Hold on," she cried when she got to the driveway. "Don't go, Andrew! Don't you go!"

How could she let him leave for boot camp without kissing him, hugging him? He was her baby, after all, the boy who had grown into such a fine man he made her proud. She had to tell him before it was too late.

Please, God, let me reach him in time!

The truck screeched to a stop a foot short of the highway. "Maddie?"

She leaned inside his open window. "I'll take Harley. I want him, and I'll come home to him just like I did to you." She swallowed back sobs. "I promise."

If his smile got any bigger, his face would split in two. "You mean it? I can't tell you how glad I am. I didn't want to leave him with just anyone." Now it seemed his turn to tear up. "He's *the* dog, remember? You always used to say that everyone has *the* dog, the one that's better than any other, the dog of a lifetime."

"He's a keeper all right, and I'm happy to have

him."

Andrew took Harley's bed out of the jeep and grabbed the bag of kibble, and Madison carried in his bowl and his toys. Her heart beat like mad against her chest—no panic attack this time around. She'd almost lost her brother all over again, and that might not have been something she'd have been able to come to terms with.

Chapter 18

Brandon found Madison sitting on the carpet in front of the fireplace, running her hand over the length of Andrew's dog. She had been crying. He didn't know why, but he wanted to slug something. What had her brother done to make her so upset?

"Did you and Andrew have a tiff?"

She put a shushing finger to her lips. "You'll wake the whirlwind on four paws. I spent the last half hour calming him down after my brother left. I needed you here—you with your togetherness. You don't even have to work at it. Serenity just falls in your lap."

She was prattling, which she hadn't done lately.

He didn't know what to do. Should he tell her to breathe? Family squabbles baffled him. He'd been an only child. Whatever had happened, that nuisance of a camera gang still unabashedly loitering around had most likely filmed everything.

He whispered, "Where's your brother?"

"I don't know, but I'd wager he's packing his bags. He'd better be. He's got to report tomorrow at Camp Pendleton."

"I see," he said, stepping on a rubber squeak toy. "Marine bootcamp's tough, but by the looks of Andrew, I'll bet he'll do fine." He sat down next to her on the floor. "Did Harley get left behind?"

"Andrew asked me to take him in. I said no. Then I

changed my mind. I never could say no to my brother, but I almost did." She looked like she had been about to add more but turned her head away from him.

"Well, Harley's fortunate to have you."

"You think so? A dog's a big responsibility. I have to feed him twice a day and run him and make certain he gets to the vet and the groomer."

"And you want to make sure you'll be the best dog owner on the planet?"

"I do. Naturally, I do."

"It must get exhausting being you."

"It's just that I haven't had anybody to care for at home in a long time."

Brandon rubbed the sweet spots around Harley's ears. "I have a feeling he's just what you need, and he will thrive with you. Just you wait and see."

For the rest of the evening, he tried to help Madison out with her new live-in. He sprinkled some feta cheese into the kibble. "It's good for his coat."

Thankfully she didn't argue, but then she had other things on her mind. After he finished the dishes, he eased into the steamy bathroom to find Harley in a tub full of piña colada bubble bath. Madison was scrubbing his coat with a brush while rap blasted from a speaker. God, if she didn't look sexy in her tight pants and traffic-stopping halter top.

She saw him and blew wisps of red hair from her damp forehead. "Close the door. We don't want him to bolt."

"Okay," he said, but it was hard to hear. "Does your brother play Dr. Dre?"

"Yep, he cranks it up, he told me. That's what Harley's accustomed to."

It wasn't as if Harley needed anything to make him feel at home. Being a large percent retriever, he dunked his huge body under the water and came up shaking himself with ecstatic delight, water slashing out everywhere.

All this fuss over a dog. What Brandon really would love to see was Madison in that bathtub, minus Harley of course. His feelings for her had gotten out of hand today, especially after being with her at the beach this morning, but thankfully his needs would have to take a backseat thanks to the arrival of one colossal pooch.

Well, okay, having Harley around would keep him centered on his original aim, which was to teach Madison to live better. He wondered how caring for a canine would affect their schedule. Her daily practice had been moving along smoothly. He had been more and more hopeful that she would succeed. Would Harley's presence on the scene throw a wrench in their routine? Brandon became determined to see it didn't.

And so he brushed Harley while Madison used her girlie-pink hairdryer. The dog arched his back and uttered his appreciation in deep contented groans. By the time they got the bathroom back to normal, both Madison and Brandon were exhausted.

"Come on, Harley," she coaxed with a slap to her gorgeously firm thigh. "I've got you all situated. You're sleeping in my room tonight."

"Lucky dog," Brandon said under his breath and headed out to the beach for a cold dip in the surf.

Chapter 19

Madison rolled out of bed at six the next morning. All that expelled emotion yesterday, plus taking care of Harley, had worn her out. She'd overslept. Rubbing her eyes, thankful for the dark, she settled down to meditate before the sun rose over Santa Monica. She'd just begun her chant when Harley licked her face.

"Come on, big guy, go lie down."

It didn't work. She could see Harley standing in the semi-darkness. His tail wagged, and he growled in that endearing way he had the night before. Was the dog talking? What was he saying? Did he like it here? Did he miss Andrew?

"Of course, you do," she said aloud, to which Harley danced closer, whimpering.

Geez, had he read her mind? "Are you an old soul?" she asked, cuddling her head against his. "Or do you just have to go outside and do your chores?"

His tail charged into fast gear, thump-thumping the carpet like a drumstick. He moaned with urgency.

"What's wrong with me? You have to go out." She yanked on a pair of shorts and a T-shirt and hit the hall running. "All right, boy, let's go."

He whisked past her. With his snout, he shoved open the door to the meditation room and galloped toward Brandon, who was in his usual morning trance state.

"Harley, no," she cried. "Stop!"

Plow! The hundred-pound bundle of mischief pounced on top of Brandon's shoulders, knocking him back off his pillow.

"Hey, boy," Brandon said, good-naturedly rolling around to play with Harley.

"I'm sorry," she said but couldn't help laughing. "I guess we're going to have to teach him some manners."

"Looks that way." He shot to his bare feet. "First, though, we better get him outside."

There were no real fences around the property, just bushes, so Madison and Brandon had to stay with Harley. The sun had risen, flaming up the sky like a scarlet battalion, and they were still taking turns throwing the ball for Harley. Did the dog ever wind down?

"How old is he?" Brandon asked.

"Not old enough to know his strength."

"He does have boundless energy, doesn't he?"

"I'll say. Do you think we could package it and sell it on eBay?"

"We're going to have to get him under control." But whooping and laughing, Brandon continued to roughhouse with the dog, running one way and then the other while Harley chased him. Brandon was enjoying himself in a way Madison had never seen before.

Somehow, he'd never looked as handsome to her. Gone was any conception of him being an Apollo or Adonis. Greek gods hovered somewhere above the rest of humanity, untouchable and inaccessible. She had placed Guru Brandon in the same category. This morning, playing with Harley, he was the man most likely to succeed at winning her heart. She could learn to care for this fun-loving guy—genuinely and not just in an I'm-hot-for-you sort of way. What was it Harper had said? She had fallen in love with Darrin's heart. Holy moly, sometimes Harper Lee McGregor uttered something downright profound.

An hour slipped by before they ended up sitting around a hastily thrown together breakfast. Gluten-free toast and more toast. Dry bread was not what Madison ate nowadays. The platters full of veggies were missing in action along with the kiwi and kale smoothies.

"Don't beg," Madison said into Harley's longing eyes.

"I bet your brother gave him table scraps." Brandon shook his head. "They say that's not good for a dog."

"I've heard the same," she said and reached a hand behind her to slyly drop a tiny piece of crust.

"Harley, go lie down," he said firmly as he crossed to the sink.

Hey, wasn't that a bit of toast on the floor beside Harley? Brandon wasn't pulling the wool over her eyes. She dropped her plate in the sink.

"Pushover," she added, jabbing Brandon with her elbow.

He cocked his head in her direction. "What?"

"I saw you sneaking food to the canine."

"And you didn't?"

She put her hands on her hips with mock seriousness. "We're going to have to have a meeting of the minds. We both need to be on the same page when it comes to the way we plan to discipline Harley."

"*We*? Madison, I won't be here after another couple of weeks." He sounded sad, a little sorry even.

185

"Oh, that's right." Better be careful, or she'd say something stupid like *don't go*. Didn't she want her house back? She had been looking forward to sleeping in, just once or twice. She'd been counting days and hours until coffee. "We'd better get a game plan now."

"I say we go about our day as usual. Let's start our yoga practice."

"Of course," she said and carried her mat into the great room.

It was like any other day. Their mats unrolled and facing the open window that let in the clean ocean air. Only niggling at the back of her thoughts were those dishes piled in the kitchen sink. That couldn't be called commonplace. Neither could the dog be called usual who wandered between them, sniffing them, and doing his weirdo doggy talk.

Brandon unwound from baby cradle pose. "We have to do something with him. Things aren't going according to plan."

Madison paced back and forth, her hand massaging the back of her neck. "We can't put him outside without a fence. I suppose I need to call some carpenters to remedy the situation. We could try putting him in a room."

"An excellent idea." Brandon led Harley into the screened-in back porch. "There you go, fellow. We won't be long. Here's ball." He returned wiping his slobbery hands briskly on his workout pants. "Everything is under control." He took his position on his mat. "Let's go into downward-facing dog," he said with a grin. "No pun intended."

The groans came first and grew into discontented growls, followed by yowls, and then the barking, sharp penetrating yelps that made Madison lose her footing.

Folding into a ball, she plugged her ears. "Make it stop."

"We often have to cope with outside noises," Brandon said. "The trick is to block it out. Try to center your thoughts. Go within yourself to a place of eternal stillness. All is—oh, hell, forget it. Nothing is working."

"No, it's not," she cried through Harley's howling. "Maybe we should give him a day to get adjusted."

"I agree." He released the dog who happily greeted them by licking their hands. "Why don't you round up the carpenters, and I'll do the breakfast dishes."

"Sounds like a winner." She glanced at her Fitbit. "After all, it's almost time for lunch."

She bent down to pet Harley who rolled over on his back, his bear paws kicking the air. "Oh, buster, what are we going to do with you?"

Minutes later, she wandered into the office with every intention of retrieving her laptop. "Wait, I took a vow not to use computers," she called out.

She could hear him scraping the dishes. "Don't you have the Yellow Pages?"

"Who uses Yellow Pages anymore?"

"Well, I guess this is an emergency." He dried his hands on the towel slung over his shoulder. "All right, but we can't make a habit out of any of the extreme measures we had to resort to on day number forty-seven of your makeover."

She set her laptop on the coffee table and blew off the dust. She happened to catch sight of the camera operators. "You're getting an eyeful, but I don't suppose any of these doggie antics make for good reality TV."

She copied down a number from a company called Mr. Handyman and plugged in the discarded landline phone.

When a polite female voice answered, Madison said, "How fast can Mr. Handyman build a fence around a property?"

"Well, since there have been no fires, earthquakes, or floods today, I think we could send a man out today to take a look. Say around four this afternoon?"

"Great, fantastic, thank you. Four it is."

Really? This fence would set her back even more. The house was already mortgaged to the hilt, but what else could she do?

Before she could stress about it too much, Brandon met her in the hall with Harley's dog leash. "I have to go to the hardware store for some supplies. I don't have everything I need to build the herb garden. I thought maybe we could take the dog out for a walk. You know, teach him to behave while he hopefully wears himself out."

"And takes a nap?" It sounded like they were talking about a baby. *Let's take a stroll with Junior, give him that fresh ocean air, so he will sleep and maybe we can too.* She grabbed her purse. "I'd like to buy some flowers while we're at it for the upstairs window box."

The TV herd didn't seem to faze Harley as they started out. But accustomed to Andrew's run each day, he sprinted ahead. Harley dragged Madison who couldn't dig in her heels as he tugged her across the highway. By the time Brandon caught up with them and took over, she'd lost her breath along with her dignity.

"He's got to learn to heel when you tell him." He tromped with the dog up a walkway that led to an elementary school. "We'll work with him for a few minutes here on the soccer field."

Disconcerted, she watched as Brandon used the same voice he had used when he gave her a lesson. By the time she'd gotten a drink from a fountain, Harley had begun catching on. This impressed her. Even more so when Brandon passed the leash to her, and the dog trotted right beside her like he'd done so all his life.

"Brandon Kennedy, are you really The Dog Whisperer?" She smoothed back the hair she hadn't had the time to brush this morning. "Maybe you should rename your show."

"I'd probably get better ratings," he mumbled, and he sounded discouraged.

****

Since Harley came aboard, all Brandon's demanding work had been thrown out the window. Not one thing today had gone right. Madison had skipped her morning meditation practice, and so had he. Their breakfast had broken all the rules, and their yoga practice had gone south with the dog. If Brandon didn't get a handle on the situation, Madison wouldn't finish out the month the way he'd envisioned. He wanted her to succeed, not just for his show but because she had already come so far. And he loved all the changes he saw in her.

That said, he had gotten such a kick out of playing with Harley and listening to Madison's warm laughter earlier in the yard that he'd started showing off. It must have stemmed from looking at her in that Dodgers T-shirt she was wearing. He didn't know where she got it, but the word Dodgers had never done such crazy things to him. *See what a terrific pitcher I am? I'll bet you never thought Guru Brandon could play baseball. Watch me. See how I do it?* His ego, that's what had caused him to derail. How long had it been since he'd tried to wow a woman with his athletic ability?

He was enjoying himself, though. It seemed forever since he'd had any real fun. Lately, he centered solely on getting Madison well, so much so he'd forgotten what it was to horse around. And chase a dog. Or chase a girl.

Madison pointed now, her fingernails painted a bright blue. "Look, there it is."

Pete's Hardware stretched across the corner lot—a parking lot that equaled the size of a football field and held vehicles with people going and coming. Nice neighborhood, friendly customers. Picturesque and safe, Brandon decided.

Madison must have drawn the same conclusion. "Why don't we connect Harley's leash to the recyclable can? That way he'll see us through that window, and we'll see him."

A twinge of doubt rippled through him. "You think he'll be all right?"

"He's smart. Look how fast he learned how to heel."

Harley was angling his head first at Madison then at Brandon as if he knew what they were saying. A longing look dominated his eyes as if he had a desire to speak. There was something about the dog. He was a furry person with his own personality and total devotion. Since Brandon had never had a pet aside from a goldfish named Tilly, he wasn't sure if all dogs weren't alike.

He might as well put Madison completely at ease. "How much time can it take to buy the bolts I forgot yesterday?" He peered through the window. "No one's in line at the register. I'll pay and get back out here while you pick out your flowers."

Did he hear a cameraman mumbling, "What are you thinking?" when he secured the leash around the can?

Before he could respond, Madison knelt and stroked Harley's thick coat. "You're my good boy," she gushed, then held up a palm. "You stay."

Brandon had just made it through the sliding doors with Madison when he heard the *woof* and turned to see a squirrel not more than five feet away from an airborne Harley. The cameramen scrambled to capture the dog, but no one could stop him as he dragged an empty recyclable barrel behind him, barking frantically.

Madison called out, "Harley, come back!"

Brandon took off as fast as he could across the parking lot. The runaway hound dodged the cars, miraculously not colliding into any, the metal cylinder clattering on the asphalt where the heat rose in a vapor.

"Stop him!" Madison cried, sounding not far behind Brandon.

People scattered, shopping carts rattled away, and vehicles idled. Brandon's foot smacked a Styrofoam cup, and he slid, almost losing his balance. A mother hollered for her child to wait. Rubbernecking, some man drove the wrong direction and dinged a parked car.

Utterly spooked, Harley drew closer and closer to the busy intersection. Brandon's tennis shoes made loud slapping noises as he raced wildly after the dog pulling the can behind him.

Stop, crazy dog! No, it isn't his fault. You're the dumbass, Brandon!

Helplessly, he watched as Harley darted into the busy street, a BMW and a Passat lurching to a stop, the air filling with the odor of burnt rubber. Gaining on the dog, near to conquering him, Brandon spotted a girl, no more than eleven or twelve, on the other side of the road. Her arms parted, and she successfully captured the renegade dog before toppling backward and to the side so that the can rolled beside them and crashed into a tree. By the time Brandon caught up, Harley was licking the heroine's cheek.

"Stay. That a boy." Freeing the leash from the can, he plopped down next to Harley on the hill of clover, his temples thudding, sweat running into his eyes.

Madison and he humbly thanked the girl and rewarded her with a twenty-dollar bill. She then headed down the street toward the stoplight. Panting, Madison collapsed next to Brandon. Her trembling body was so close to his that it filled him with a crazy need to hold her. But he didn't want her to know he was none too steady either.

She hung her head. "We're rotten dog owners."

She had included him, as he well deserved.

"I shouldn't have tied him to the trash can." He wiped the perspiration from his brow with the back of his hand. "I didn't know it was empty. I should have checked."

"My brother isn't even gone a day, and we almost got his dog killed."

"It's my fault," he croaked, miserable. "I should know better."

As if sensing Brandon's mood, Harley nudged his hand with his cold, wet nose. "I'm so sorry, buddy," Brandon said, rubbing his fingers on the dog's big, silky head.

The camera crew resurfaced along with bystanders. Willie jumped in and carried the receptacle back across the street to the hardware store. A guy with a wiry beard and hooded black eyes was filming the scene on his cell phone.

Infuriated, Brandon grabbed the punk by the shoulder. "You either knock it off, or I'll cut your head off and roll it down the sidewalk."

"Listen, man, this will go viral," the guy said.

Brandon cursed, which he couldn't remember ever doing before—well, frankly, he'd just broken a record for things he never did or said, not even in all the years of being chased by the paparazzi. He wrestled the man for the cell phone and hurled it into traffic.

Then he gathered up Harley, put his hand through the leash loop, and took Madison's arm. "Let's get the lead out."

"My hero," she gushed in his ear.

"Yeah, right," he said, somehow vindicated. But he didn't even recognize himself.

Chapter 20

The fence went up in three days around the perimeter of the property, and things began to return to normal. The canine, bribed with a treat for compliance, let the humans meditate. As the newness wore off, he seemed to tire of following their every move. He romped in the backyard and chased the ball. To keep him blissful, they walked him along the ocean.

Madison crossed the days off on her calendar. Her former mindset had been *twenty-five days until I can awaken again to coffee. Twenty days and I'll have a bacon and tomato sandwich. Fifteen days and I'll sleep in until nine o'clock—no snooze buttons. Ten days until I take my first bite of chocolate. Six days until I go back to work.* Somehow, all of it had stopped thrilling her as much.

She started to relish being at home with Brandon and Big Stuff, as they had taken to calling the dog. The moments ticked by too quickly: that Tuesday at the park, the picnic, Harley running alongside them as they flew a kite shaped like a dragon. The sunsets over the iron-colored sea, each seemingly trying to outdo the previous masterpiece. Snipping herbs in the garden Brandon had created for her, the tantalizing fragrance of them in jars on the windowsill.

Life, the way it was now, how could it end?

In five days, ten hours, and twenty minutes,

Brandon would be packing his bag and walking out the front door. Would they ever see each other again? Would they meet each other in passing and say, "I remember when. Do you?" Would he go on to help another gal find her way out of a dangerous lifestyle? Madison had never been the jealous sort, but the thought of him with another woman, even if it was business as usual, made her hair stand on end.

The other night, when they were strolling back after watching another top-notch sunset, she had teasingly nudged him in the ribs. "So what are your big plans following June first?"

"You mean what will I do 'after the Madison Project?' " he'd asked. "I don't know. Do you think the Dodgers would hire me?"

On one of their shopping excursions, she had bought him a Dodger cap, and he wore it nonstop ever since. "It suits you," she'd said. And it certainly did.

Brandon had changed, possibly more than she had, for the better—at least in her opinion. He had once been so strict about her diet, exercise, and how long she sat during meditation. Not that he still didn't practice and *eat right*, but he seemed to have become flexible, rounded, a better version of himself.

She suspected Harley's influence had a lot to do with his new motivational maxims. "We would all be happier if we lived in a dog's state of wonder with the world." Or "We could learn to celebrate the hours by imitating Big Stuff." And "Dogs are the truly enlightened ones."

She appreciated his dog-spun ideologies. She thought when he ran along the beach with Harley, both man and dog looked positively rapturous. What would the dog do without Brandon and vice versa? Lately, she couldn't picture herself not being with either of her guys—didn't want to, wished she could hold back time.

On Friday, four days before her time with Brandon was up, the landline phone rang.

It was Harper. "Darrin's boss wants him to go to Hawaii for business, and Darrin is insisting that I come along with him. He refers to it as 'The honeymoon we never had.' He's been pushing us to get away, says we need to fall in love all over again. It's not happening with Chloe and Tyler always around. Honestly, those kids keep me hopping. If it's not soccer, it's baseball for Tyler, ballet and tap for Chloe, and swim team practice for them both. Some days I feel like all I do is bus them from one activity to another. By the time I get in bed at night, I'm dead to the world. It's not a situation conducive to lovemaking. I can't even remember the last time Darrin and I got together or even shared a dinner by ourselves."

"If it's a night out you want, I guess I could..." Madison froze up.

"Would you? I was telling Darrin I thought you'd volunteer to take the kids, so I could go with him to Maui. He said, 'Good because it just might save our marriage.' "

"What?" This news slammed into Madison unexpectedly and brutally. "Your marriage is really in jeopardy?"

Harper started to sob, and that clutched Madison's heartstrings.

"It's not anyone's fault," Harper lamented. "But I'm afraid if I don't go with him, he'll find somebody else."

"Darrin wouldn't do that. He loves you." He'd better be good to her sister, or Madison would knock him flat.

"We're both so run-ragged we don't know what we're saying half the time." Another hesitation surfaced in Harper's rant. "Will you do me this favor, Madison?"

What else could Madison say? "When do you leave?" she asked, dread clasping her stomach and weakening her knees.

"Tonight, at six o'clock. I know it's short notice, and I am sorry for it, but I can't leave Chloe and Tyler with just anybody."

She couldn't believe what Harper was asking. "The kids don't even like me."

"Maddie, they don't know you."

"You're right, you're right, but dropping them off with Aunt Who-is-That-Lady is not the way to encourage their endearing feelings for me."

"Well, when do you suggest introducing yourself to them? How about at your funeral? Then you won't have to worry. I'm sure you'll make a good impression on them."

"Stop it, Harper." She shut her eyes. "There's no need to be theatrical."

"Isn't there? Have you ever heard that old saying Mom used to say now and again? How did it go? Something like, 'In the end, the love you take is equal to the love you make.' Well, if the shoe fits, Maddie."

Truth hung in Harper's words, even if she had gone a little Beatlemania on her.

Madison held her breath and shook her head like she was jumping into a cold, murky swamp without any hope of resurfacing. "All right, I'll see you in a while."

Quaking all over, she hung up the phone. What had she gotten herself into?

Chapter 21

Brandon had to hand it to Madison for being so cool about babysitting her sister's children. She only went out in the garage and screamed once, then returned, asking, "Do you think the kids will want veggies for supper?"

"Well, why not?" He was trying to sound optimistic for her sake. Inside, he resented the idea of anything else taking Madison away from her goal—his goal, for crying out loud.

She paced like she was arranging an aspiring actor's screen test. "Most kids don't like vegetables. I didn't like them. What kid says, 'Hooray for broccoli?' "

What were they going to feed them? "We'll worry about it when the time comes."

She separated her fingers. "Where are they going to sleep?"

A no-brainer. "It's not like you live in a tepee. You have three bedrooms."

At three o'clock, the little girl who Brandon thought must be Chloe clomped up the walkway in a plastic pair of Cinderella heels. In her small hand, she carried a girly pink suitcase. He'd seen her delicate looks on girls in Victorian greeting cards: Cupid's bow lips, a pointed fairy-like chin, and her hair was three shades lighter than the rest of the Gray clan, making it a strawberry blonde. Her honest to goodness liquid blue eyes grew even wider when she took in the sight of the cathedral ceilings. "Mommy, are we in church?"

Chloe's brother, Tyler, pushed himself against his mother's other leg. He appeared three years older than his sister, about seven. He had a side part in his white-blond hair. His eyes too, were the color of the sea as he gazed up at Brandon from beneath his fair brows and the bill of his New York Yankees hat. He had a baseball glove covering his left hand and a duffle bag in the other.

"The kids are going to be fine," Harper said and at the same time frowned as if she had applied an "It's going to be smooth sailing" to the prediction of a hurricane.

Harley circled the new arrivals, snout extended. Obviously, he couldn't get enough of the scents now invading what he already considered his territory.

Brandon took the Little Pony sleeping bag from Harper. "We've been looking forward to having the kids, haven't we, Madison?"

Why did she seem unable to move? Could fear truly petrify a person?

"I've been counting the seconds." She bit her bottom lip, likely regretting her fib.

Harper handed Madison a folded piece of paper. "Here's their schedule. I thought I'd jot it down. Tyler has a little league game tomorrow, but you two don't have to go. I can arrange to have one of the parents from the team pick him up. I know you are both busy with your agenda, and I'm sorry to butt in like this."

Brandon cleared his throat, intending to sound upbeat. "No trouble. We don't mind baseball, do we,

Madison? We even play ball with the dog." Somehow that hadn't come out the way he'd intended. "I mean, we're fans of the Dodgers." He nodded at Tyler. "Not that there's anything wrong with the Yankees."

"That's right," Madison put in. "I bought Brandon his baseball hat."

"Sounds like you have everything under control, then," Harper said. "I'll just get going." She kissed Chloe and Tyler who both looked at her as if she'd said, "Goodbye, I'm leaving you stranded with The Wicked Witch of the West and her sidekick, Fenrir Greyback."

Chloe dropped her suitcase on the floor and hugged Harper's leg like a koala, wailing for dear life, while Tyler shoved against her other leg and punched his baseball mitt with his fist.

"Don't go, Mommy!" Chloe cried.

Harper opened the front door and edged backward through the opening. "You'll have fun, and Sunday will be here before you know it."

"Mommy?" Chloe hollered, banging her hands on the closed front door. "You can't leave us. No, no, no. Bad Mommy."

Tyler blinked back a tear. Then he ran to the window to watch his mother driving away. Brandon recognized a boy who was trying to keep up a brave front.

"Well," Madison said shakily, "were off to a good start, aren't we?"

Chloe sat on the floor and yowled, kicking her feet, her Cinderella slippers flying off. Madison jerked away like her niece had become lethal, and maybe she had. Brandon wasn't sure how to proceed either, but it was obvious the little girl needed comforting, and Tyler teared up like he was about to lose it as well.

Not knowing what else to do, Brandon navigated over suitcases, sleeping bags, and toys to switch on the TV, a habit he rarely practiced. Television threw out harmful radiation. By no means should kids watch it.

"Do you have the cartoon network?" he said over the chaos as he flopped on a recliner.

"I'm not sure." Madison snatched up the remote. "Is it on cable?"

"Don't you know what kids like?" Tyler stuck his hands on his hips. "I heard Mommy telling Daddy that you were afraid of getting close to us."

Didn't Madison's nephew have a social filter? Brandon wondered if he'd ever been as oblivious to another person's feelings. Madison held the remote in a death grip as she channel-surfed through home improvement shows and the food network.

Brandon rested a hand on her shoulder. "Do you have a card that shows all your stations? You usually get it when the cable guys set up your service."

"I suppose so," she said, her face becoming red and moist. "I don't know. I'm hardly ever home. Oh, to be anywhere but here."

****

Tyler stepped between Brandon and Madison and said, "You two are pretty lame. You want a kid's channel. Here I can do it."

Bewildered, Madison handed over the remote. "Okay."

Tyler's judgment didn't seem fair. After all, the public called Madison Eagle Eye because she had such an uncanny gift for knowing who had star quality. And yet she hadn't been able to spot a kid's program when it flashed before her.

She desperately wanted to shout, "Turn off those cameras for once." She should be used to defeat, but no, things just kept getting deeper into Pitsville.

Cartoons burst upon the screen in all its blessed technicolor, and Tyler, Chloe, and Harley settled on the sofa, watching. By the time the second show came on, Madison had grown curious and asked if there was anything besides animation. No one answered, but the network did provide much-needed entertainment. She signaled Brandon, gathering with him in the corner for a powwow.

"Strategically, what should we do next?" she asked. "I'm asking you this as Brandon, not as a health guru."

"Well…" Even Brandon had his weaknesses, and as he hesitated, she doubted he'd had much experience with children. "If the TV holds them for the next hour or so, I suggest dinner."

"Do you think it would be beneficial to go out to eat? Maybe we could go to that nice restaurant you took me to."

Brandon scratched his head, looking baffled. "Harbor Inn is only open for breakfast and lunch. I don't know any places to take them. Maybe we should just get in the car and drive."

"Yeah, that would incorporate some time." She wanted to plan their next phase as she would a major decision at her agency. She excelled at organizing and being creative, for goodness' sake. Dining out with children should not be this difficult.

At six thirty-five, Madison said, "How would you kids like to go to a restaurant?"

Tyler inclined his head. "You two don't know how to cook?"

"We've been known to use the stove now and then," she said defensively. She should let her niece and nephew taste some of Brandon's veggies, but he hadn't signed up to perform for a brood of kids. "We thought it would be a treat for you both to go out to eat."

Chloe sucked her thumb and nuzzled a tattered rag against the tip of her nose. "I have to take my Mokie."

"Mokie is what she calls what's left of her baby blanket," Tyler clarified.

"Okay," Madison said, "but Chloe you shouldn't suck your thumb. You're going to have buck teeth."

Tyler raised his blond brows. "What are buck teeth?"

Madison stuck out her upper teeth in a beaver-like sneer.

Chloe popped her wet, red thumb out of her mouth. "I'm not going to look like that." She began to whimper again, rubbing her eyes. "You're a dumbbell."

Madison shot a shrug Brandon's way. "Help, I just got verbally abused by a four-year-old."

They ended up at a fast food restaurant called Goodtime Charlie's. Madison and Brandon, worn to a frazzle, collapsed into red plastic chairs while a shrieking and shouting Tyler and Chloe chased each other up and down a bright-colored jungle gym.

Brandon handed Madison ice water in a paper cup. "They've got that energy thing down pat. We're going to have to make sure they hang out with Harley when we get back home."

"Why didn't we think of it before?" She winked at him. "We'll have to hand them over to Big Stuff. After

204

a workout session with him, they'll be *begging* to go to bed."

Being a good sport made a guy even hotter. She recalled how Brandon had agreed to drive her dad's 1960 Ferrari. This model had a backseat, even if the kids were cramped. They had squealed with glee, thrilled to be riding in such a cool old set of wheels.

She loved the way Brandon looked now, a regular guy with a boyish grin, gathering up packets of ketchup, napkins, and plastic cutlery. None of the yahoos she'd dated could compare. While burgers and fries sizzled, she tore the tip of the paper off her straw and blew. It smacked him in the head.

He held his hands up in the air. "You got me."

"Thanks for not throwing in the towel and running for the hills, yoga mat and all, when you found out I agreed to take my niece and nephew."

"Do I look like the type of guy who bails at the first sign of the kiddy patrol? Give me a break, woman."

He didn't even sound like the man who'd come into her life telling her that sugary drinks were as nutritional as newspaper and even more toxic. Not that the two of them were downing anything but water, but he had stopped preaching. When had it happened, and when had she, out of habit, gone for the cob salad instead of the cheeseburger?

The kids argued and called each other names throughout their Goodtime meal. Madison soothed Chloe because her brother had teased her, while Brandon distracted Tyler by asking him about his little league team. All and all, dinner went well with only a few casualties. Tyler's Goodtime meal prize fell down the toilet, and Chloe unintentionally dropped her french fries on the floor so that Brandon had to buy her another bag full.

Madison had thought they had survived their first round of feeding the kids and felt almost smug about it. *I got this down. This babysitting thing isn't difficult. All it took was a little imagination and a fair amount of patience. Now to tackle the drive home, should be a snap.*

Even when the car backfired and the muffler sputtered smoke, Brandon didn't once hint that they should be driving another car—bless him. Because the producers didn't consider this vehicle on the list of useable transportation, there were no cameras. Thus, the eight-track cassette player blared Barbara Lewis' "Hello Stanger." Afterward, everyone sang along to "Purple People Eater." Madison leaned back, her head on the cracked, leather bucket seat, glad she hadn't gotten rid of her father's cherished Ferrari. Even if the car did need a little TLC, singing and laughing with her niece and nephew, she remembered being a little girl with her dad.

Certain things couldn't be price-tagged.

Then all at once, Chloe let out a terrified wail. "I can't find Mokie!"

Madison stiffened. "Would you pull over, Brandon?" When he did, she got the kids out and searched the tuna can of a backseat. "No, it's not here."

"It's no big deal," Brandon said. "Well just return to the scene of the crime."

On the endless drive back, Chloe screamed, "I want my Mokie!"

Brandon picked her up out of the backseat, raced

into Goodtime Charlie's, avoiding the cones marking a spilled soda, and pushed on to where they had been sitting.

"I don't see it," Madison heard him say.

And then Chloe shouted, "Somebody took my Mokie!"

Madison flew to the girl at the cash register. "Did anyone turn in a tiny piece of a blanket?"

The girl talked into a headset. "Aiden, I need you up here, stat."

A tall, skinny boy, carrying a mop, met them at the counter near the stacks of food trays. "There was an old rag on the chair. I threw it away."

Madison's throat constricted. "You threw it…you threw it—where's your trash?"

The boy shook his head gravely. "The can in the cabinet was full, so I just tossed the bag in the dumpster out back."

Chapter 22

If a couple of months ago someone had told
Brandon he'd be crawling around in mashed-up food
and God knew what else, he'd have said, "Oh, heck,
no." Never had he done anything that wasn't considered
healthy—well, at least not for years. But emergency
maneuvers were necessary when a man wished to
restore peace to an utterly distraught little girl.

Plus, Madison couldn't take much more drama
tonight.

And so he climbed to the top of the dumpster and
sat on the ledge. Below him a sea of bacteria swirled
like a bad dream. Did he have what it took to make that
leap of insanity? A glance at the group totally focused
on him told him he did. But what he wouldn't give for
plastic gloves. Maybe the crew at Goodtime Charlie's
had a pair? No time for that.

He plugged his nostrils with two fingers and
jumped. *Squish, squish, crackle*! His feet in flip-flops
took the brunt of the abuse. The snap of plastic forks
and spoons against his flesh had him hopping this way
and that. He sank and sloshed on the occasional dirty
diaper and whatever else lay in wait for him. He tried to
block out the gory details as he searched through the
refuse. The dumpster proved enormous and echoed his
every move. If he'd been swallowed by a whale, things
couldn't have been as wild. Or as dire.

He grew desperate when after digging inside one bag after another he came up with zilch. Oh, where, oh, where, in this iron gut had little Chloe's blanket gone? He longed to give up.

But Madison's voice drifted into his ears. "Go, Brandon. You got this."

She believed in him. And that kept his gag reflex in check, kept him going through the motions. In the next to the last bag, he spied the missing culprit. It was stuck to a wad of gum that had landed right underneath. The way his luck was running, the germs would do him in.

Madison, offering positive reinforcement from below, sounded garbled. "If anyone can find Chloe's Mokie, you can. You're one in a million, Brandon Kennedy."

Her confidence fueled him into using his bare hands to rip off the gum and free the blanket from the trash. His heart sang as he creaked slowly upward and popped over the top of the dumpster.

"Mission accomplished," he shouted, waving the filthy scrap like a flag.

Madison sprang into a cheer. "You did it!"

Chloe said adoringly, "My Mokie."

But Chloe's Mokie needed to be thoroughly sanitized if she was ever going to be able to cuddle with it again. He dropped it in a bag until Madison could wash it.

"Oh, brother," Tyler said when he looked. "That's a goner."

It wasn't that Madison didn't give it her best shot when they got home. She tried scrubbing it in the sink, but it remained stained and gray instead of pink, so she soaked it in bleach while they watched more kiddy programs. Two hours later, after popcorn and honey-dribbled rice cakes, Madison disappeared to check on her project.

"Oh, no!" she cried.

Brandon shot to his feet. "What's wrong?"

"I did it now." She didn't sound happy.

His feet were as heavy as cement slabs as he and the kids headed toward the laundry room. Everyone clustered around the washing machine to see. The blanket had disintegrated. She held up a strip, and like spider webs, it pulled apart in her hands.

"I'm sorry, Chloe," she said, testing another piece and getting the same results.

Chloe's face distorted in horror, tears flooding her eyes.

Madison's landline picked then to ring, and she ran upstairs with Chloe following behind her.

****

"Hi, how are things going?" Harper's voice came in loud and clear.

"Not so well," Madison said, wishing Harper was still here and not clear across the ocean. "Something very terrible happened to Chloe's Mokie."

"Oh, dear."

Chloe howled, "That lady killed my Mokie!"

Madison relayed the details to her sister, who kept up her chorus of "oh, dear" with each added increment. Harper wanted to speak to her daughter, while Madison wrung her hands together. What had she been thinking, using bleach on an already traumatized fabric? A former mom like herself should have had more sense. She should have said no when Harper asked her to babysit. She'd been away from kids for too many years.

She no longer knew anything about them. Dealing with children wasn't her strong point. It never had been.

Chloe handed back the phone. Her eyes were dry now, no thanks to Madison. She raced off downstairs.

Harper said, "I'm sorry, I should have taken that blanket away from Chloe ages ago. I was trying to wean her by cutting it into small squares." She sighed. "You see, I remembered how awful it was to part with my own Mr. Tibbs."

"Are you talking about your teddy bear? I thought you'd take it to college with you. Poor old Mr. Tibbs, he had no eyes, no nose, half of a mouth, and one ear. Whatever happened to him?"

"He fell off the boat, and you swam out to rescue him."

Madison felt a bolt to her heart. "I did that?"

"Then you put Mr. Tibbs in a shoebox, and you gave him a eulogy and called on Mom to say a few words. We buried him in back of the house."

"I'd forgotten about all the pomp and circumstance in honor of your teddy bear."

"Frankly, I was ready to move on but hadn't known how to say goodbye to my babyhood pal. You gave me the tools to do it."

Madison felt amazed. "I did that, huh?"

"You did."

How come she had forgotten? It was like she'd been another person. How had that imaginative part of herself gotten away? Somehow, she longed to retrieve that girl who would give a teddy bear a funeral.

After getting off the phone, she found Chloe sitting in a chair by herself with the remains of Mokie on her lap.

She slid in next to her niece. "You know, Chloe, I have been working hard on giving up things that I no longer need. I didn't like it at first. I got angry because I was afraid."

Chloe rubbed her cheek. "Why were you scared?"

"I thought I might suddenly need something I gave away, but I've discovered giving what I don't use anymore to someone else made me feel like I had wings on my feet."

"Who should I give Mokie to?" Chloe's voice was whispery and serious.

Madison was tempted to say the garbage, but that would never do. "Well, what is your favorite place?"

"The ocean," Chloe answered without hesitation.

"The ocean," Madison repeated solemnly. She measured what she had to say against her growing need to deal with her past. "Maybe we could give Mokie a proper send off."

Tyler, who had been listening, said, "She means we bury Mokie at sea."

Chloe's eyes widened adorably. "You do?"

"I think I have a shoebox," Madison said, holding off the shudder. "We could put your Mokie inside with some magic dust and anything else you can think of."

"What about a peanut butter and jelly sandwich?"

"I think we can arrange it." Madison nodded at Brandon for the okay.

"PB&J it is," he said.

Madison needed time to work up the courage to allow her niece to go near the ocean. After all, when it came down to it, her fear had been what made her rebel during Andrew's surfing days. The idea of losing anyone again to the sea was a pain that caught her between the ribs. Still, she had to work through her terror to get to the side where wellness existed.

With a shrug, she said, "How about a Sunday funeral? That way it will give us time to get ready."

Chapter 23

Madison thought Tyler and Chloe would be content to sleep in the two guestrooms. She fluffed the pretty pink pillows in the frilly bed, and she folded down the corner of the plaid spread on the daybed in the study.

"I want to sleep with you," Chloe said to her.

Tyler slid in next to Brandon on the couch. "I want to bunk with Brandon."

Since Chloe had suffered such a calamity, and being that the two were no doubt missing their parents, Madison gave in.

"All right," she said to Tyler, "but you know Brandon mostly crashes on the floor."

Tyler slapped his cheeks in apparent surprise. "I want to sleep there too," he said like it meant he was about to fly off to Neverland. "Wait until I tell Mom."

They set Madison's mat next to Brandon's, and she brought down some blankets. Brandon had already gotten into the spirit of the sleepover and was building a tent with sheets from the linen closet. Before she knew it, she couldn't see them but heard Brandon laugh. It was a campout inside the house, complete with flashlights and ghost stories. Andrew would have loved this sort of thing when he was a little guy.

Lately, Andrew jumped to the forefront of her thoughts more times than she could count. She was worried about him and hoped he'd send her a line. If only there were a way for her to have done things differently in the last decade. She'd have been braver about him wanting to be a surfer. He loved the ocean, and she had discouraged him, afraid of his drowning. If only she had a second chance, but he had grown up when she'd hardly been aware. Now he was learning how to fight for his country. She'd never been as proud but hadn't had a chance to tell him.

Madison brought the covers up over Chloe who was already asleep. How quick kids grew. Tired of being the aunt who occasionally dropped in for Christmas and birthdays, she promised to change. She tenderly kissed her niece on the forehead, and her stomach fluttered when Chloe's lips turned up at the corners.

Madison slept in the next morning, missing both her meditation and her yoga practice. She must have been tired. Raising herself up on her stomach, she found Chloe lifting her head at the same time. Madison slammed herself down and then glanced at her niece again. This little game of peekaboo got them giggling, and Madison recalled how much her brother and sister loved a good tickling.

She walked her fingers across the sheet. "The tickle bug's coming to get you."

Chloe giggled, then fell against the pillow to catch her breath. "My mommy makes us waffles on Saturdays."

Uh-oh! Madison didn't think she owned a waffle iron. "We just might have to go out to breakfast."

They wound up breakfasting at Harbor Inn. Tyler wore his baseball uniform in preparation for the big game at eleven a.m. They barely made it on time.

Madison couldn't believe what a big production Little League games were these days. Sitting shoulder to shoulder, fans (mostly parents) laughed, cheered, booed, jumped up and down, their drinks splashing. When was the last time she'd smelled mustard or heard peanut shells crunching underfoot? Nothing like being fired up when the team scored. Got the blood pumping, that was for darn sure.

Madison leaned toward Brandon. "Did you get any yoga in?"

"Only if you count doing handstands," he said. "As far as meditating, I got one *Sat Nam* in before I fell into a dead sleep last night. No problem. We'll catch up."

"We only have two days after the kids leave."

****

He did know. That's all he thought about—when he got time to think. Soon he'd be walking out of Madison's life, and it was driving him to count the minutes and seconds. He couldn't picture his exit. Would he raise a hand and say goodbye to the audience while she blew him a kiss along with a fond farewell? To be truthful, he had never worked with a student for this long. He had formed a bond with Madison. That was to be expected. But the tight knot he got in his chest whenever his leaving came to mind wasn't anticipated. He wasn't prepared.

And when had he, a guy whose life had revolved around quiet Zen moments, got caught up in the disarray of dogs and kids? His entire existence had been about teaching people how to live. But in the past few weeks, he felt like he hadn't been genuinely alive until now. It made no sense. Things would go back to the way they were before, but did he really want them to?

216

He'd become reckless because of her. Chasing a dog into traffic. Leaping into a dumpster. Changing his diet. He didn't even know himself anymore. No other time in his life had he felt like this. He'd been charging forward without keeping his head up, and the strangest part? He didn't care. He didn't care that the only turmoil inside him came from knowing his time with Madison was coming to a close.

He couldn't take his eyes off her this morning. Oh, she'd looked sexy as hell before in her yoga outfits, but there was something about this different side of her that hit him like an arrow straight to the heart. She was back to wearing her cutoffs, which fit better than ever, and she'd added a ruffled shirt and a pair of white-framed sunglasses that matched Chloe's. She smelled of that citrusy body lotion, and she was whooping and hollering because Tyler slammed the ball past the third basemen and had made it to second.

"That's my boy!" she shouted. "That's Auntie M's boy!"

And that was how she christened herself Auntie M, which fit her. She bit into a cherry snow cone, leaving its imprint on her mouth, making her lips an alluring rain-slicker red. Where was the Madison he'd known even a week ago? Any trace of the overachiever gave way to this light-hearted, sock-it-to-'em gal—a new and improved version that had nothing to do with his makeover of Ms. Gray.

Auntie M was happy, truly so. First Harley had come along to change her, and afterward, Chloe and Tyler. Here he'd been going about his business thinking he knew best. Who would have believed family ties had been what the ailing Ms. Gray needed all along? He wanted to be what she needed too. When she had come down last night and suggested to Chloe that they have a burial at sea for her baby blanket, he guessed how hard it had been for her. Madison had lost her parents to the ocean and still grieved, even though she had fought like the devil not to show it in front of her niece and nephew.

Is that when he fell hook, line, and sinker for her? No pun intended.

She snapped her fingers in front of his line of starry vision. "What are you thinking about?" she asked. "You look all dark and brooding, my hunky pirate."

"Nothing much." How could he tell her?

"You look different somehow."

He tried to smile. "Just thinking."

She bit into her snow cone again, driving him wild by licking her lips.

"I deserve your scrutiny," she said. "I've ruined your show. I haven't heard you talking to the camera lately. I guess America doesn't care about a rowdy dog and a bunch of kids."

"They don't know what they're missing," he said, something in his chest ripping apart. "And that's too bad."

Chapter 24

"How about I tell you a story?" Brandon said to the kids later that afternoon. He scooped up Chloe and tenderly set her on his lap. "Once there was a little girl who got lost in the giant redwoods and didn't know what to do. Then she spotted a small cabin. The girl had hair the color of yours, Chloe, and so she'd gotten the nickname, Scarlet. One day…"

Madison would have thought Brandon had grown up with a pack of brothers and sisters, the way he took to the kids and they to him. The story of Scarlet became a crowd pleaser. Chloe pulled out some picture books she'd brought, and Brandon settled in, reading to the kids and then telling his mother's tales of spiraling temples and bashful dragons. But what were they going to do when he finished? There would be dinner, another meal to cross off the list.

At five o'clock, Brandon leaned forward. "Are you hungry?" Well, how could a kid be anything else? "What would you like to eat?"

"Pizza," they said in unison.

"I can do pizza," he said, which made Madison give a surprised O with her mouth. Where had he been hiding the junk food? Or had the kids broken down his resistance?

She shook her head in disbelief. "Pizza?"

He led them into the kitchen. "Chloe and Tyler, do

you want to help?"

Oh, they really liked Brandon. But she couldn't help being curious about how he was going to pull this off. Would he break another rule, call up, and have a delivery made? Or was he about to commit the cardinal sin and eat cheesy, greasy, artery-clogging food? She'd have to rib him about it, but honestly, she wanted to kiss him and say, "You're a savior, guru dear."

Tyler kept looking through the windows with his hands on his hips. "Can we go swimming in the ocean, Auntie M?"

Madison sighed, thinking of all the arguments she'd had over the years—little things, forbidding her baby brother to go near the water, even when he got older—and how the fights brought her to this moment. A sister playing a mother that had hurt her brother who was more like a son, and how she hadn't known how to change. "I know you don't understand this, Tyler," she whispered. "But I want to let you."

Brandon patted her shoulder. "All will be well."

She heard the peaceful words, and they gave her a ray of hope. She thought of when he had said something similar to that when she went to the hospital. She was better than she had been, wasn't she? Finally, she said the only thing that made sense. "We'll see."

Chloe spread her small fingers on the window. "We could go now. Can we?"

"I need your help making the pizza," Brandon, the prize, said.

Brandon let Tyler and Chloe pick out the veggies for the toppings. A brilliant move on his part. What kid could resist making pizza? They wound up with little dishes of carrots, green peppers, tomatoes, and even broccoli. Brandon added a cup of feta cheese.

He set the mixing bowl down on the butcher block and dropped out the dough. "To knead," he said.

Madison opened the stepstool and stood it close so that each child could take their turn. Everybody dug in and got their hands dirty, and so did she.

After the dough rose, they all got a chance to help with rolling it out.

With flour in her hair and on her face, Chloe said, "I help my mommy cook."

Noticing how her eyes swam with tears when she mentioned her mother, Madison recruited her niece to table-setting duty. Chloe hoisted the heavy plates to their placemats, singing Pharrell's song about being happy as she did. That's when Madison stopped to perk her ears. Could it be? Her niece put her body and soul into singing. She was so young to project that kind of emotion. Not to mention the ability she had to bring forth her own unique style.

Talk about right under Madison's nose. Talent in her own family, and she'd been so busy looking for it in others she hadn't noticed. While taking note, Madison sang along.

Soon the aroma of baking dough, onion, garlic, and cheese filled the kitchen and made Madison's stomach growl. Steam caused condensation on the darkening windows. The soft recessed lighting glimmered over the man preparing dinner and the children sticking daffodils and daisies in a heart-shaped vase.

When they were sitting around the table, Madison felt woozy with the warmth and the laughter. How had she missed all this before? Nothing could make her as happy as now. Was she missing out by not having children of her own? The thought had never occurred to her before she got sick and thought she was going to die. Marriage had never actually occurred either, until lately, and certainly not before Brandon Kennedy.

He would make some kids a wonderful daddy. If her nephew and niece hadn't come to stay, she would have never guessed. Sweet Lord, what had being around the kids done to his face? Tender would be the word that best described it—a genuine superhero. When he had jumped into the dumpster to find Chloe's Mokie, her heart had melted. If there was one act that had sealed him to rock star status, it was his wading through garbage to stop a little girl's tears.

Watching him as he showed the children how to create faces with the veggies on each slice of pizza, she grinned. If she could, she'd freeze the moment so it wouldn't slip away. She watched him as he cleared the table, careful to include Chloe on what she could manage to carry and Tyler on the heavier things.

Madison took a dish from the drainer and dried it. "My compliments to the chef. Where did you study, Florence or Rome?"

"I made it up as I went," he said, and she heard the proud note. "Do you think I should turn pro?"

"I think there's a market," she said, wiping down the counter, and for the first time, she wasn't talking about scoring a deal in good ol' Tinsel Town.

Chapter 25

The next afternoon, Brandon strolled with towels and a picnic basket to a dock not far down the beach. The sky touched the water with sapphire while clouds hung like huge bales of cotton. The scent of salt and seaweed clung to the afternoon breeze, and he closed his eyes a moment, inhaling deep. It had been a while since he'd been able to practice his breathing. The air itself was like a tonic, refreshing him and clearing his head.

Harley lay on the pier, his forepaws hanging over the edge, his head pushed down as he stared at something in the water. Tyler and Chloe, wearing lifejackets, fell into sync with Madison, who held the handle of the overstuffed beach bag over her arm. She walked with her head down and managed to carry the shoebox like it was the urn of some fallen and cherished dignitary. Her blouse had fallen open to reveal the soft ivory curve of her breasts in her bikini top. Those white-framed sunglasses hid her eyes, so he had no clue how she was holding up.

Her emotions lay deeply buried, feelings he couldn't quite pinpoint. Dread? Fear? Because of what they were about to do?

Harley gave a winsome squeal, tremors passing through his body, and Brandon got hold of his collar an instant before he dove into the water.

"Not yet, Harley, boy," he said. "What say we have some lunch?"

He thought he heard "phew" escape Madison's pursed lips.

"Perfecto," she said. "I'm hungry."

Tyler set down his suitcase, spread the blanket he'd carried out, and they sat on the wharf. Brandon had bought fruit, a container of blueberries, four oranges, strawberries, bananas, and four apples. He dabbed some plain yogurt for dipping on each paper plate and divvied out the crusty bread. Although they'd had leftover pizza for breakfast, the children began to eat eagerly, as if starving. Kids, he'd learned, never got enough to eat. Remarkably, they snacked and still could chow down at each meal.

He raised his cup of carrot juice sweetened with pineapple. "Here's to our day."

Madison's hand noticeably shook. "Cheers. May this day bring closure."

Their time spent with Chole and Tyler was drawing to an end. Madison phoned her sister to ask that they meet them at the beach because they were going to take a dip in the ocean. The speaker was on so that he heard Harper's astonished, "You are?"

"Mokie's remains are scheduled to shove off from shore today."

He noted the forced determination in Madison's statement and the hesitation in Harper's. "Wow," Harper had finally said. "This is a milestone for you, Maddie."

Watching Madison now, as she grabbed more blueberries and frantically stirred them into her yogurt, he wanted to say, "I'll take over. You don't have to do this." But the trouble was, he knew she did.

So instead, he nodded. "A real breakthrough."

The audience would get to judge soon enough. The camera guys were on the pier. Waving a hand, Spence was making sure they caught all this tension on film. They couldn't have gotten better footage if they were taping a Hollywood movie. If he had his way, he'd yank Madison out of this scene and walk away with her in his arms. He'd like to knock those cameras on the ground and kick them to their destruction.

Rather than act on his crazy impulses, he snapped to his feet and surveyed the beach. People had taken up residence there. Giant umbrellas twisted and flapped in the wind. Seagulls dove for food while barbecues sent smoke billowing upward. And jet skis and power boats thundered through the water. Watching all this, he broke out in a cold sweat. The smile he had plastered on his face faded as it dawned on him.

Madison could fail.

****

The night before, Madison had slept restlessly. She'd had nightmares of the children falling into the water only to be swallowed whole. Now the swish of the surf beneath her on the pier caused her to shiver. With a finger over one nostril and then the other, she alternated her breathing. No getting out of this one. She'd given her word.

She swallowed the last of her blueberries. "You want to go with us, Harley Barley?"

The super-sized dog lifted his head from his position at the mouth of the water.

Chloe rubbed his ears. "Yes, Harley can say goodbye too."

"Come on, boy," Tyler urged, racing down the dock.

Harley sniffed the air and strung along with Tyler. There was no turning back now. Madison gathered up all the courage she could muster to follow. On the beach, she stripped off her shorts and her blouse and went toward the ocean with the shoebox clasped in both hands. Would the camera catch her knees shaking?

"Madison," Brandon murmured from right behind her. "We can do this."

Could they? These children were her responsibility. What if a storm should kick up unexpectedly and whisk them out to sea? Andrew's image haunted her, all the times she had forbidden his wading in the surf. Denying him had been unfair. Her parents would have scolded her for her fear. *Face your fears and do it anyway.* Who had uttered such total baloney?

Trembling, she stopped at the edge of the shoreline. She dreaded taking the kids one step closer. "Chloe, would you like to say a few words?"

Chloe nodded soberly. "My Mokie was always there for me. My Mokie protected me when I was scared, and when I had to say goodbye to my crib, my Mokie was there. When I slept for the first time in my big-girl bed. When Tommy took my quarter. When Mommy got mad at me for tracking in mud. When Tyler told me that I was stupid—"

"That's enough, Chloe," Tyler said.

Madison wasn't ready. "Do you want to say something Tyler?"

"Okay, okay." He straightened, and he looked so darn cute, so much like Andrew, Madison wanted to hug him. "I was glad Mokie helped out Sissy. He was loyal and brave and true. But now Sis doesn't need him anymore because she's getting older."

Madison snagged Brandon with a stare and held it, pleading with him. "What about you?"

He cleared his throat. Lordy, he was trying to stall, she thought, loving him for it.

"Mokie was a trouper. He spent the better part of his existence in service to his princess. When it comes down to it, that's what any knight does who's worth his salt."

All the speeches were so cheesy and yet so dear.

"My turn," Madison said, wrought with emotion. "Yes, Mokie was a knight, but knowing Chloe, she is more than ready to grow up and be an extra big girl. Chloe is willing to let Mokie go to another baby."

Chloe began to belt the song "Let it Go." She turned the heads of the people on the beach as she sang, her little feet twisting and turning in the sand. Who would have believed the little munchkin would have such a big voice? She sang one relevant verse after another with such passion Madison forgot where she was.

Let it go, Madison! Let go of the pain, let go of the yesterday you could never face. Let it go and carry on!

By the time Madison came out of her daze, she was standing calf-deep in the waves. Smiling, she set the shoebox in the water. "Let it go," she softly sang with the rest. Even some of the folks who had been watching joined in, singing the triumphant chorus. The kids and Brandon and Madison held hands as everyone watched the shoebox sailing out in the current. It rocked back and forth and streamed out to remote and distant waters. In a final determined swoop, it disappeared.

Tyler yanked free and splashed his sister and Madison. Laughing, Madison splashed back. Brandon and Chloe joined in. Harley swam around them in circles, barking for joy.

"This means war," Tyler said, "the boys against the girls."

Madison shouted, "Come on, Chloe. Let's show them what we've got."

Soon, Madison was soaked, but so were her attackers. She felt so gleeful that she jumped up and down in the waves. She even bent her head back as if letting the ocean baptize her. Indeed, she was renewed and reborn.

Her sister called, "Maddie!"

"Over here, Harper." Madison wanted to shout, "Look at me! I'm out here with people I love."

"Oh, good Heavens, you allowed the kids to go in the water." Harper slapped her chest, at once sobbing, then laughing. "It's a miracle."

Pride twinkled in Harper's eyes as she lifted her cell phone and snapped a picture of all of them.

"I'm going to post this on Facebook."

Madison didn't care and would have uploaded it herself if she still had her phone. Hurrah for the cameramen and their Precious Moments shot. The world should know she had felt her fear and had done it anyway with a little help from her family and friends— and that had made all the difference.

She dried her niece off with a beach towel. "I could never have done it without you, Chloe," she whispered, and to her sister, she added, "Chloe should be on *The Voice* or *America's Got Talent*. I bet people all over the country would vote for her."

Harper laughed, clearly enjoying her sister's praise. "I think she'll have to wait a few years before she makes her debut."

"Mommy, Auntie M gave Mokie a funeral, and Tyler talked and so did Uncle Brandon. You should have been here. It was wonderful."

Both Harper and her sister shared a look. *Uncle Brandon?*

Brandon stopped gathering up the wet towels. Was that a flush on his cheeks? She didn't think, with his deep tan, he could get sunburned. Plus, they hadn't been out here long enough for him to redden.

"How was Maui?" Madison asked to divert the attention away from Brandon.

Harper looked a little dreamy. "Divine, utterly and completely..." She paused. "I'll call you later and give you all the steamy details."

They collected their things and headed back up to the house. For a few more minutes, noise filled the rooms, the sounds of scurrying around to get suitcases, the nip and smack of kisses, the "thank yous" and the "goodbyes." Then it was over. Before Madison knew what had hit, a stunned silence had descended on the house.

She sat in her cozy chair and stretched from head to toe. Even the flock of camera workers had taken a break. "It's nice to bask in the quiet, isn't it?"

Brandon shook his head. "It's almost too quiet, don't you think?"

She listened for a moment. "Whoever would have guessed the silence could be so loud?" She glanced at the dog's face pressed against the glass. "I think Harley misses all that noise."

"I do too," he said wistfully.

"I can't believe Chloe and Tyler were screaming for their mom only a few days ago." She smiled, feeling a soothing wave of contentment. "Look at the way things turned out."

"Kids do the darndest things."

He sat with his hands on his thighs, not with thumbs touching index fingers like he usually did. He lounged comfortably like a permanent resident. But for goodness' sake, *Uncle Brandon*? It would mean Brandon and she had tied the knot, gotten hitched. Good grief, they hadn't even kissed.

Chapter 26

If it had been ten years back, Brandon would have offered Madison wine to celebrate her victory. His motive consisted of wanting to relax her enough to pursue a subject he believed she would resist, her parents' death and its effect on her. The best he could do was to suggest a cup of Chai tea and massage her neck and shoulders, an act he'd performed on countless other students. Why not her? But the answer smacked him between the eyes. Madison wasn't just any pupil.

Still, she agreed to the tea. Brandon stuck a pot of water on the stove and studied her through an open bar that separated the great room from the kitchen. Could he approach her after her success over her phobia with questions? Did he dare?

She sure looked awesome these days. Fit and happy. Her makeup worn off but rosy-cheeked and slightly freckled. She was wearing the same clothes she had earlier, but her blouse had slipped off her shoulder. Chloe had lovingly placed her prized scarf around Madison's neck. Her hair had dried in curlicues, rumpled and sexy. She was all barefoot and barelegged, and he wished he didn't feel compelled to do anything that would spoil her pleasure. When she saw him with the tea, she thanked him, took the mug in both hands, and blew at the steam.

She gave a bittersweet smile. "Remember the time

you brought me the cup full of boiled water?"

"How could I forget? I saw murder in your eyes and wanted to run for the hills." For some reason, the memory of it made him melancholy. She had a temper; he'd grant her that. "We've come a long way in nearly eight weeks." He slid in behind her chair. "Would you like a massage? I've heard it said I have magic fingers."

"How can a girl resist?" When he kneaded her neck, she purred. "This is Heaven."

His heart slowed at the touch of her skin. If only they could be lovers. They were together now, and it felt like thunder inside him. No need for candlelight or a word of love, not with Madison, the heroine of the day—of the past two months.

"You sure were a Triton out there in the sea," he said quietly when he longed to shout it from the rooftops.

Her head lolled on her shoulders in a relaxed circle. "I even surprised myself."

He hated to ruin her mood, not to mention his own. "You let go of your fear, kind of like Chloe with her Mokie. So the ocean turned out to be benign. It didn't bite you or steal your lunch money."

While he'd been speaking, her toes had curled against the carpet. God, it was hard to talk about her past. He didn't think she'd ever fessed up before. Too bad there wasn't a little dark confessional designated for baring the soul.

She fidgeted. "Um, well, what I wouldn't give to be far away from the maddening cameras."

"Is that what you want? I think I could arrange it."

"No, the viewers have been with me so far. They might as well hear everything." She stretched her long slender fingers. "I guess I owe it to them, and who knows? My story might help someone else."

They slipped from the house out the back way. Brandon told the cameraman to stay behind. Then he led Madison down to where the ocean roared in his ears. The beach people were gone, had packed up and hightailed off. His feet crunched the tiny, thin shells washed ashore. A lone sailboat darted and rocked about the surf like a toy in a tot's bathwater. He put his arm around Madison, but she shook it off.

"You better stop it, buster, or somebody might get the idea that you really care," she said.

"But I do care, and that's the reason. I don't want our time here to end and—"

"You mean you don't want to walk off into the sunset?" She looked at him, as if searching for any clue the word *care* pushed beyond friendship. Was it pain reflected there in her eyes, or was he wishing it so? Wanting the ache that he imagined there to equal the desire drowning him.

Madison was ripping him up inside. Didn't she know? It was all he could do to keep from taking her in his arms and ravaging her with pent-up kisses. He'd kept his part of the bargain, remained absorbed in his work because doing so was what his show called for, what was necessary. But remaining aloof wasn't what he needed. He needed her.

"I want to know if you're all right," he stated like a clodhopper.

She seemed to have stopped listening to him. Her gaze followed a sailboat, watching it as if fascinated and unable to look away. She hugged herself against the wind, her hair blowing back, the sun highlighting the blonde strands, making them appear metallic and brilliant against the red. Spun gold. The late afternoon shadows danced over her features, rendering it difficult to read her expression, but he thought she'd stopped being angry.

Maybe she'd forgotten him altogether.

A couple of camera guys hailed her, and she began.

"I was seventeen. The allure of theater, dance, and vocal music allowed me to be like my grandmother, Betty Blue—some of you might have heard of her. She sang in a band in the 1950s. Anyway, I craved everything Hollywood. I even posted pages from the *TV Guide* inside my closet.

"My parents, on the other hand, delighted in oceanography. Honestly, I might have followed in their footsteps if I hadn't gone through the rebellious stage. I was tired of being called a nerd because of all my science and biology classes, and so I swung in the opposite direction.

"I haven't wanted to talk about that night. The reason is different than what any of you are likely to suspect. You see, my parents went to Baja to investigate an expected storm. They wanted to find out what would happen when the infestation of mating whales encountered the inclement weather. They put their lives in jeopardy without considering the consequences. A part of me has blamed them for that.

"Harper has never gotten over our parents' disappearance. She's called in psychics and presented our story to reality programs. I tell her it's no use, nothing will bring them back, but she won't give up on the idea they will somehow let us know they are well.

"A few days into the coast guard's search, I had a

dream. In it, I went outside our house and saw Mom and Dad coming toward me, wearing the clothes they'd had on the last time I saw them, but the ocean had left them soaking wet. I asked them if they were coming back, and they told me no.

"I knew in my heart that nobody would ever find them.

"Anyway, to get on with it, an aunt from Cleveland wanted to take us. I guess I could have said yes. Instead, I got a job and attended college at night. We struggled with money. But I managed to finish raising my sister and my brother. Oh, my sister moved out at nineteen when she and Darrin got married. I can't say I was happy when she got pregnant right after the wedding, but she was ecstatic. My brother was more like a son to me, because he'd been only a toddler. As you know, I saw him a week or so ago.

"In the last few years, I've gotten afraid of getting too close to anyone, and so I've been drawing away from my family and my friends and pouring myself into running InSight. I never saw any of this until I started working with Brandon. I'd been avoiding forming relationships because I was afraid of losing the people I love again. It's no way to live."

She nodded, and the cameras drew away from her. "Everything about life before I got a concussion is beginning to feel like memories that belonged to someone else."

Her pain knifed through Brandon, hurting like hell. "Just hang in there, Madison."

"I am. When I woke up in my office, our moments together changed me, charted a different map. Now everything feels right—you being here, you next to

235

me."

Her eyes met his in such a private act of total commitment he teetered, nearly losing his balance. Of course, she didn't actually mean the things she was saying. He'd seen it before, this adoration for a teacher. As soon as she entered the doors of her agency, touched base with all her clients, she'd forget about him.

At this moment, though, with the sky performing its nightly dance of garnet and topaz, she stood out like the star of her own movie, which in truth she was, and he'd never been as caught up in her every move. Of course, her feelings for him were only temporary. She'd put him on a pedestal, but in these awesome seconds, he could believe they wouldn't ever say goodbye.

"You did great." He forced himself to sound light and noncommittal, but he was dying inside, wanting to gather her up and take her anywhere else but here.

She laughed as if to break the ice. "Well, I hope I did all right." Her eyes, caught in the drama of the sunset, were dark and sad. "We only have a day left."

"To be exact, we have thirty-nine hours, five minutes, and forty-two seconds." Had that unabashed declaration really escaped him?

"Are you kidding me?" She grinned and punched him in the sternum. "Now who's doing the counting?"

He touched her mouth with his index finger, his body tingling with need. One kiss, that's all he wanted. Was it so much? A kiss to make it well, a kiss for luck, a kiss to last him for the rest of his life when he wanted—needed—so much more.

Chapter 27

Madison got up before sunrise and sat before her meditation candle. But that chimp mind of hers would not be stilled. Where was Brandon? Already out jogging? Hadn't she shared more with him in the last couple of months than she had any other person? Didn't it warrant some show of emotion on his part? Sometimes she saw sparks in his eyes and believed he felt something for her. But he hadn't budged from his role as a teacher. Maybe she was deluding herself, seeing something that wasn't there. Seeing what she wanted to see.

Essentially, they only had two more days together. Was it wrong of her to hope for a romantic conclusion? The producers got their drama yesterday. The field notes would record the footage with her family and Brandon at Mokie's Memorial Service, labeled as *funny* and *cry*. She couldn't write a better finale even if she'd had a year in which to complete it.

Story, story, story—that's what the writers were after. She didn't need an outline beforehand to know the last day was the time of recapping all that had come before. For confessing what she had learned, and for giving her hopes and dreams for the future.

Sadly, tomorrow afternoon marked the beginning of postproduction. No more cameras, no more Brandon Kennedy.

She chose her attire with care, happy with her reinvented style, more secure with her body than ever before. She gave her legs a showing in a second-act Oscar de la Renta ensemble, believing her gams were now her best asset. She tweaked her hairstyle by wearing it glisteningly straight and adding gold bangles to both earlobes.

Brandon contributed to the morning by serving breakfast outdoors on the terrace where some invaluable crew member had placed white tulips in big bunches. Brandon went all out with herb toast, velouté white asparagus, and Asian pears. The wind had died down, and the air was still and fragrant with the smells of the sea.

He buzzed around as if he had to keep himself busy. "This day will go fast."

His remark caught her like a blow to the stomach. "Yes, it will."

He poured her a cup of his special blend of tea. "Today is about reminiscing."

"Like about when we first did yoga together?" The image of it waylaid her into silence.

"That's right." His grin was bittersweet. "On the beach."

She gave a dismissive tsk. "I was very bad."

He nodded with evident pride. "Not anymore."

Something about all this nostalgia made her joyful, made her sad. "I got a little better."

"More than a little," he said, brushing the back of her hand with his own.

She rose from her chair, dropped her napkin, and slipped past him into the house. She was gone in one quick sweep, ignoring that he'd reached out toward her.

"I told my sister I'd phone her," she said over her shoulder, needing to get away from him. Even though more than anything, she wanted to stay.

Lilly cocked her head at an angle as she plugged in the landline and handed Madison the phone. "There you go, dear." While she dialed, Lilly began the last-minute details in Madison's farewell appearance.

"I've been dying to hear the nitty-gritty about your trip with Darrin," Madison said, wishing to hear anything that would take her away from the present. "What was it like?"

"You mean what was it like to be with the man you love in paradise?" Harper asked. "Well, let me tell you…" And she did.

Madison only listened with a fraction of her attention. She was busy thinking how she'd like to go to Maui with Brandon and dine at a luau and ride horses on the beach and engage in hot sex, preferably the latter. It was such a blissful idea to remain in bed all day with a lover. She'd never stayed in the sack, except when she'd had the flu two years ago. Did that count?

She said to Harper, "Brandon hasn't even kissed me, and our time together is almost up." There it was out in the open and waiting for a response.

"He has it bad for you, Maddie. You can only see it whenever he looks at you. You know that moony look a man gets when he's head over heels done for. Feel sorry for him, why don't you? It's not like Guru Brandon can act on his feelings. How would it look to his fans?"

"Like he's human." She wrapped the phone cord around her hand until her knuckles grew white.

"I don't think his adoring public would welcome

his succumbing to love."

"What if you're wrong? Even Superman had Lois Lane."

"But nobody knew. You've got to keep some things under wraps, at least for now. That doesn't mean you can't play the game. But if you're serious about kissing him before the reality show is over, then get creative. Surely there are some spaces in the house where no cameras dare to reach."

"The bathroom, and how's that for romantic?"

"Well, there you go, then. Men are utterly clueless. You should make the first move. Just catch him in some free-of-the-evil-lens area, like a closet or even the study when there's nobody around. You'd better get to it. You don't have much time."

"I know, right?" She laughed nervously. "I'll see if I can pull it off."

Harper paused a beat. "I couldn't believe it when I saw you yesterday. In the water splashing around as if you did it all the time."

"Yes, who would have guessed all it took to get rid of my anxiety was to hang out with two very precocious children?"

"They had a ball. That's all we heard about last night. Thank you for watching them."

"I should be the one thanking you." Experiencing a bolt of emotion, she leaned against the wall for support. "I never knew what I was missing."

"Maddie, you've come so far. You look better than you have in years, healthy and happy. It seems like you're winning in every way that counts. I'm proud of you."

Pleased, Madison felt an ear-to-ear grin coming on.

"Thanks. Now if I can just get Brandon to ask me out on a date, I mean after this is all over."

"He will, I guarantee it."

When Madison got off the phone, she went to the mirror. She'd lost twenty pounds and looked decent in her clothes. She moved now with agility and ease—no cracking bones or strained muscles—but had her blood pressure lowered along with her cholesterol? She'd meet with Dr. Buckley a week from today. No use denying her nervousness over her lab results.

Would she be able to stick to eating right after Brandon moved out? She'd be free of his watchful eye, and there would be no more cameras. There was nothing to keep her from enjoying a chocolate bar or a cup of café mocha. She could still abstain, she told herself. She had to, just as she had to learn to pace herself at work. All of it seemed overwhelming to her, like embarking on a journey into the center of a volcano.

She had stepped out of her own life for the past two months and would soon be returning. She nibbled her bottom lip. *Hey, wait a second.* She didn't bite her lips anymore. It had been more than three weeks, and she'd formed a new habit. Did it not take one rather absent moment to break it?

She went to her window. In the distance, a young woman was walking down the path toward the ocean, just moseying as if she didn't have a care in the world. Every day was a holiday. That's how Madison longed to look, how she longed to be—not just with Brandon but on her own, by herself.

****

Brandon got a text message from his business

manager. *Call me when you can.* It was close to the end of the programming. Did Jason want to give him a peptalk? Though the story writers handed out a script each day, the impromptu footage was the stuff TV audiences went fruit loops over. Real life always trumped fiction, hands down.

So when Jason asked, "Are you sitting?" he thought his next words would be, "Well, done, buddy." He stood next to the bench near the water lapping not far off.

"The network producers plan to make some changes to *Guru Brandon.* They believe the show would skyrocket up the charts if Madison became a regular. Now don't go protesting until you hear me out. We thought we'd negotiate this deal directly with Madison after production tomorrow. I think she'll approve of a script that shows her going about her normal day at work. Meanwhile, the two of you play up the sparks that are already flying. This season's trends were about getting to the nitty-gritty. If we could milk more of that—"

"No." He balked at the crazy scheme, digging his feet in the sand. "The producers want to change the entire concept of the show."

"Sometimes you should go along with them, buddy. Go along or get the show canceled."

"What are you saying, Jason?" Weak-kneed, he collapsed on the stone bench with his head in his hands. "Are we in danger of going under?"

"The ratings have taken a dip in the past year. But you knew that, didn't you? Isn't it why you pushed to recruit Madison?"

"No," Brandon said, thrown off balance. "I was for

Madison because I thought I could help her, period."

"Well, if you want to keep your show, you've got to choke back your ethics and come on to Madison. Guide her so when the bigwigs approach her, she'll say yes."

"No dice," Brandon said, Jason's demand sparking his rage. He got up and trod the beach where pigeons scrambled, their wings fluttering. "I won't string her along to get her to agree to a deal."

"You can just this once. Think how much Madison would love a red-carpet premiere, how much she'll welcome making more money. By putting on a little, you could ensure her the exposure she's always wanted for her agency. Not to mention, buddy, you'd see your name in lights. No more worries. You two could start a new breed of reality TV."

Defeated, Brandon said, "I've got to go."

The realization came to him like a mortar tank mowing him down. He had to tell her about the network's plans. But when and how? He wanted to take her out and buy her a singing bowl. Actually, he longed to give her more. But it would look like he was making her a teacher's pet. If he had his druthers, he'd have gotten her a mandala, so she could use its patterns to center her thoughts. He'd purchase mala beads or a ring of hessonite garnet. All of those things would benefit what still seemed challenging and elusive for her, sitting to meditate.

Her yoga routine had improved so much he didn't have to worry. She could even manage a headstand. Well, she did have to brace herself against the wall, and she couldn't balance for very long, but still, there was much more he wanted to teach her. It would take a good year to pass on all the knowledge she needed. They didn't have twelve months to spend together. Frustration stole his breath. The agreement had been under-planned.

How much knowledge could he squeeze into so little time? It was too bad her niece and nephew had shown up. Harper should have had her head examined for asking her sister to take them. But honestly? He wouldn't have traded the time they had spent with the kids for anything. Their input had led to Madison's getting into the ocean, and that had led to her breakthrough. Nothing he could have done would top that. He couldn't be happier. At this point, the last thing he wanted to do was upset her by telling her the studio execs' absurd intentions.

****

Restless, Madison found Brandon busy writing at the kitchen table with Harley spread out over his feet. The man and his dog painted such a familiar and welcome picture her throat felt raw with the knowledge of his being missing in less than forty-eight hours.

She swallowed down her emotion. "Am I interrupting?"

"No." He gestured woodenly toward his list. "I've been scheduling out a postproduction plan for you to follow."

"You mean after you take off for the greener pastures of someone else's habitat?" She had tried to sound devil may care. Instead, she'd just come off as jealous.

I don't want to share Guru Brandon, get it?

He stuck his pencil behind his ear and patted the chair to his left. "I realize you must be feeling a little uneasy about my leaving."

"No, really? Is it that time already? I suppose I'll have to find myself another kill-me-with-gorgeous mentor. How about your competition. Do you have any? Do you think some other yogi might take me on?"

His shoulders stiffened. "I think it's time you got back to your clients."

She slid in next to him, trying not to inhale that earthy scent he wore—or was the aromatic concoction his natural chemistry? An eclectic blend of male hormones, the Lord be praised for creating it.

"So," she said, drumming the fingers of both hands on the table, "what kind of madness have you cooked up for me?"

"I'm giving you a timer to keep track of the length of your practices, but you can use your smartphone when you get it back."

His reference to a digital device was still another reminder that she'd soon be returning to the land of the free and—*choke*—techno gadgets. Her stomach flipped as she felt herself losing control. Would she fall under their manic spell the second she touched them?

He wasn't looking at her. "Eventually you should be able to improve your health even more, but it takes dedication and commitment."

The saliva in her mouth dissolved. Would she make it on her own?

"The trick," he was saying, "is to guard against distraction."

Her mind, before the guru, had been all over the place. She would never have had time or the inclination to change.

"Madison, as you pursue the principles of Eastern

thought, you will be inclined to draw more positive people and experiences into your life."

She recalled her clients and how much she cared for them. She hadn't thought as much about them. Not lately.

"I've made a list for you to use when you shop at the market."

Did he mean for her to go by herself? That would be like going to battle and forgetting to bring a weapon. Without someone over her shoulder saying, "Stay clear of the potato chips and the pretzels," she would fail for sure, wouldn't she?

"Remember, Madison, food has the power to make you content, whole, and nourished."

She knew what she was hungry for, and it wasn't food. Contemplating the taste of Brandon Kennedy's mouth had become addictive. She could bite him. He looked that delicious, especially now with his hair in loose waves over his pensive face. If only she could read his thoughts. Did he share her regrets?

"I've got a real treat planned for you this morning." He rested his elbow on the table, his head in his hand as he studied her, his eyes narrowed conspiratorially. "It requires a trip into town. Are you up for it?"

Is this where he kidnapped her, and they disappeared into some waiting jet bound for Acapulco? "I can't wait," she said, knocking her shoulder against his solid brick of an arm.

He drove her to one of those new age shops she would have avoided before she'd met him. It was off the beaten path, quite some distance from all the local souvenir traps. She'd have scoffed at the wafting incense if she hadn't been wishing for something like it to burn while she struggled to uncomplicate her thoughts while meditating. Some sandalwood wouldn't hurt, or what about patchouli, frankincense, or jasmine? What was it Brandon had said?

Oh, yeah. "Stimulate the senses, quiet the mind."

A sophisticate of a woman in a batik tunic that accented the white in her A-line haircut and the silvery-blue in her eyes approached them. "Is there something I can help—oh, aren't you Guru Brandon?"

"I am." His face reddened, and he turned his head quickly. "The last time I was here, you carried a small selection of tambouras."

Madison said, "What is a tamboura?"

"A singing bowl," the woman said as if glad she could supply the answer. "Or you can call it 'the chanting of om.' " She led them behind a curtain where there was a collection of Asian statues surrounded by planters of long grass. She picked up a small brass and wood bowl and ran a wooden mallet along the rim.

The bowl strummed, echoing like a flock of angel harps.

"I love it," Madison spoke up. "But what do you do with it? Let it sing for its supper?"

Brandon picked up another, scrutinizing it. "These are used in meditation along with other stimuli. Which one do you prefer, Madison?"

She listened carefully to all five. "I like the smallest one the best. It's soothing and ethereal." She leaned toward the purse she had dropped near her feet and rummaged through it. She pulled out her wallet and snapped it open.

"I've got this," Brandon said, flipping out some cash. "I want you to have it."

He was buying her a gift. She bet he didn't do this with all his students. She felt honored like she earned the Yoga Master Prize. She felt touched like he was her lover and not a TV personality. Her heart hammered, and waves of appreciation pulsed throughout her.

"Thank you," she said, moved to tears. "I love it."

Chapter 28

Supper—or their last hoorah—consisted of peas that Madison shelled herself. She had to admit it relaxed her to prepare fresh food, a domesticity her great-grandmother might have known. Maybe Madison and her contemporaries did pluck open the microwave a bit too much, and maybe those frozen blocks some people called food should be avoided at all costs. She did as he instructed. She divided the peas in half, threw them in with the simmering wild rice spiced up with cumin, pepper, and turmeric.

Would she have these meals after Brandon had gone? "Do you eat by candlelight when you are by yourself?" She threw an array of veggies in a steamer. "Or do you never eat alone?"

"Candlelight induces tranquility. Then of course, as you know, there's eating in silence."

Was he attempting to shut her up? The closer their last hours drew, the more professional-sounding Brandon's speech and mannerisms became. He appeared to be holding himself at bay.

She longed to shake him and say, "Oh, where, oh, where was the Brandon who let down his hair and played with Chloe and Tyler? If you see him wandering around in a confused state, please bring him back to me. Another man has taken his place, a stick man, polite, passable, but heartbreakingly not my man."

She wanted to rid herself of this Brandon who was a replica of the model guru he'd been when they had started out.

"I hope you know how much I appreciate all you've done for me," she said. It was a more personal thing to say, something that might gain a more personal reply.

He turned toward the stove and hauled the rice from the burner. "Do you feel you met all your goals?"

No, not all, I wanted to get together with you.

"Well, we'll soon find out when I pay a visit to Dr. Buckley on Thursday. Would you like me to call you?" On second thought, was there any life after tomorrow?

"If you'd like, although I might be aboard a plane to my next assignment." He paused, angling his head casually. "If you want, you could leave a text or an email."

She frowned in confusion. "A text or an email, somehow that seems like taking a step backward."

"I think you've developed strong enough habits that you'll be able to handle some digital conveniences. Just don't let them become an addiction."

No, you're my addiction!

He gave a nonchalant dip of his hand. "You can even visit me on my website."

"Just like that, you shut me out?" She slammed down the spoon, shaking the table. "What's wrong with you?"

He blinked as if she'd smacked him across the face. "I don't know what you're talking about." His smile never made it to his eyes. "Tomorrow you'll begin your life travels alone, a shining new experience, one you're more than ready for."

"That's. Just. Fine." Unable to take any more, she ran from the kitchen. "I'll look forward to it."

"Madison!" He dashed up the stairs behind her, but she shut the bedroom door in his face. And purposely made sure her stereo speakers were blaring "School's Out for Summer."

Chapter 29

An hour later, Brandon ran beneath the moon casting light on the crest of the sea. Usually, the scene had a cleansing effect on him. He drew energy, gazed in wonder. Not tonight. Racing with intensity, he burned up all his oomph. He hadn't kept track of how far he'd gone, maybe a mile at full speed, before, spent, he dropped to his knees on the sand.

Harley, who had kept up, bouncing joyfully along, now plopped down and cuddled his huge head on Brandon's lap.

He scratched the dog's velvety ears. "Hey, boy, I'm going to miss you." He glanced over his shoulder in the direction of Madison's house and felt a pang. He'd miss that woman!

He hadn't ever gotten as close to a student. Oh, he always became consumed with each new case. He tended to be obsessive about fixing his patients, but before Madison, he'd been able to remain neutral and proficient.

The truth was he took pride in his work. He loved helping people, especially Madison. It was safe to say she was his prize pupil, and he wished the best for her, but after tomorrow he would most likely never see her again. She would return to work, and like most students with a crush on a teacher, she'd soon forget all about him. And that was okay, he told himself resolutely. It was the way it should be.

Madison hadn't understood that he was backing off for her sake. But he had unintentionally hurt her, damn him. Right now, Guru Brandon was out of control and pathetic. And all he could think about was that he was letting her down by not telling her about the TV network's proposal. He couldn't rightfully go along with it, though. It was wrong. But if he didn't give her the chance to say yay or nay, wasn't that even worse?

The dog stared sympathetically at Brandon and whined as if he understood his dilemma.

"Too bad dogs can't give advice," he said with an almost instantaneous realization that there was a man who specialized in guidance. His uncle. Timothy Kennedy known to his parishioners as Father Tim.

It had been the priest who had gotten Dad help for his drinking problem. If not for his uncle, there would have been no AA meetings, no sober dad. And if not for his uncle, Brandon wouldn't have made it to the audition where he landed the part in *Lies and Destiny*. Uncle Tim had been there when Brandon's cancer-ridden father was taken off the respirator. His uncle's steady flow of encouragement had been what led Brandon to quit the soap opera and journey to India to search out a new beginning.

"Follow your heart," his uncle had told him more than once.

Brandon needed help determining the right path.

He found St. James Rectory in his contacts and made the call. His agitation lifted the moment his uncle's familiar Irish brogue came on the line. His pleasure at hearing from his nephew was evident. After catching up a little, Brandon relayed his discontent.

"I'm confused," he confided, and the second the words left his mouth, his shoulders lightened of their weight. "Madison is more than just a student. She's a friend—maybe more than that. I'm not sure. But I know she's reaching out, but I can't respond. Everything inside me is all jumbled, and I'm afraid to open up, worried I'll say something I'll be sorry for later."

"You fear getting hurt?"

"I don't know. It could be. I'm circling around her because I don't want my feelings caught on tape. It's an impossible situation. She no doubt thinks I'm a total jerk."

"I see."

"So what do I do?"

"When the cameras aren't around, you should tell her the truth, let her know you care about her. Just keep an eye out for any busybodies."

"I know. The network is more interested in Madison's sex life than her health. My relationship to her isn't the only problem. The execs, misled by the camera footage, are hot to trot over a spinoff promoting the two of us as lovers."

"What about the original theme of your show?"

The question hit him in the gut like a hot poker. "It's not pulling in the ratings."

"I'm sorry, Bran. Is there anything I can do?"

"I have to warn her about the studio's plans, but even if she agrees to their ideas, I don't want any part of it." His gaze dropped to the surf. "I can't fake emotion, no matter how I feel about Madison."

"It sounds like you need time to think things through. But you have to be straight with her. She'll lose all respect for you if she finds out you knew and didn't say anything."

"Yes." He got to his feet. "I will. Thanks a lot, Uncle Tim."

After he hung up, Brandon slapped his thigh, and Harley fell into stride with him. Tomorrow he'd have that talk with Madison.

****

Madison hadn't slept well. Her dreams were like trying to see through a dark sheet of glass. She awoke to thirst and wandered downstairs for a drink of filtered water. She'd fallen asleep in her clothes. She ran her fingers through her disheveled hair.

She discovered Brandon slouching in the easy chair and did a double take. He didn't have a candle before him, nor was his body in the lotus position. He simply appeared to be thinking, his eyes distant as he stared past her.

She snapped her fingers in front of his face. "Brandon, are you okay?" He didn't look well. In the lamplight, she could see the shadows under his eyes as if he hadn't had any sleep.

"Hi there," he said, "I could ask the same of you. You left in quite a huff last night. Were you able to work through your anger?"

"It's our last day together, our last morning." *You donkey, don't you get it?* Talk about clueless; he took the cake.

"I know," he said and hung his head. "People get used to routine."

"That's right. It takes three weeks to form a habit."

There was so much they were not saying, so much left undone.

His eyes were bloodshot, and he closed them as if

not wanting her to see he looked like he'd been up the entire night drinking whiskey and shooting pool. "You probably are feeling a little afraid, Madison."

"Big-time." Her own voice sounded small, but then there was that knot in her throat...*I want you to stay!*

He slapped the arm of the chair. "I've got an idea." He motioned to her, his face filled with that boyish wonder she'd come to cherish. "Let's go watch the sunrise."

"I'm game." She followed him into the gunmetal darkness where the air didn't stir, and the only sounds were of the ocean roaring in the distance. Harley had lumbered out behind her, licking her heels.

He said, "There's a certain kind of freshness in the air. Do you feel it, do you smell it—tell me."

She walked with him. "Always the instructor, even to the end."

She was so close to him her thigh scraped against his, close enough to inhale that male testosterone that was exclusively Brandon Kennedy. Their fingers touched, sending a surge of electricity throughout her, making her miss a step. As if it were instinctual, he took her hand in his. She noted the texture of his rough palm against hers. No eyeballing cameras had snuck behind them to their destination. She had him all to herself. Imagine that? What she could do, if he let her.

They had front row seats, their backs to the misty waves. Harley, never a morning dog, rolled over in the sand and went back to sleep.

They took stock of the light show just getting ready to start. She shivered in the chilly morning air. Seeing her, he wrapped his arms around her, and she thought she'd do something dumb like tell him how much she cared. She couldn't help laying her head on his mighty shoulder. It felt good to cuddle with him, natural and intimate.

He said, "The first thirty minutes of sunrise and the last thirty minutes of sunset, it is safe to look straight at the sun."

"They're always telling people not to take in the sun with the naked eye."

"And it's true, but the first and last half hour won't hurt you. In fact, it's the great healer of the mind and the body. Watch the sun. Don't you feel its energy balancing and getting rid of toxins?"

The hell with the sun! What she felt was Brandon's body heat radiating through her, tightening her muscles, skimming up her spine. That kind of warmth should come with a warning—*exposure might cause side effects*. Maybe she could have blamed it on chemistry or like attracting like—called it a lethal injection. She was dying for want of him.

She managed to say, "I see a halo around the sun."

"Feel it vibrate?" he asked, turning to look at her, and his eyes turned molten-blue. Somehow, she didn't think watching the sky had anything to do with it.

The heat had gathered at the sweet place between her legs—another side effect of her being close to him. If this didn't end up in a kiss, she didn't think she'd be able to bear it.

Drawing in a long shaky breath, she said, "I do feel the vibration." Oh, did she!

"Being out in the middle of nature, with the birds and the sea creatures, it does something to a person, don't you think?"

"Amen to Mother Earth," she said dreamily.

"There's harmony in the sounds." His breath seemed to have caught in his throat.

"Yes, a more beautiful melody could not exist."

"Do you feel your eyes blur? It's the sun cleansing you."

Cleansing? Try heating up as if some crazy so-and-so had switched on the gas. She moaned, "My eyes have become pools of marvel." No, that wasn't right. They were pools of longing, no mistaking it.

His voice came out as if he'd been running at top speed. "Are you feeling better, Maddie?" Panting, he pulled himself away and looked down at her, lust in his gaze.

"Hey," she said and reached up to play with his hair on the back of his neck with her fingers. "Is there something you'd like to—?"

His lips lowered and met hers with a kiss so sweet and urgent she felt she would dissolve into the sand. The strength of his hands around her shoulders made her body quiver. She ached for him with a desire stronger than any craving she'd ever known. Coffee be hanged, she'd replace it in a heartbeat for a daily taste of him.

He moved his tongue along her throat and down her neck, exploring, learning. "I want you," he said, and she reached up for his face and held it in her hands with temptation so strong it made her body cave against him and her head tip back toward the burning sky.

A man's voice came out of nowhere. "Hey, you two, ever hear of getting a room?"

Brandon shot to his feet. Just as quickly, Madison saw the runner jog past, his shoes kicking up sand. Harley raised his rump in a perfect downward-facing dog and woofed.

A new day in Santa Monica had most certainly dawned.

Brandon groaned as if waking up. "I am sorry, Madison. I shouldn't have...I am sorry." He headed back toward the house.

When she'd caught up with him, she found him stuffing his things into his duffle bag.

He didn't turn to look at her. "I'll be out of here in a couple of minutes."

"You can't just leave after we just shared that hot kiss."

Some of the TV staff had come in through the front door. Willie asked, "Don't you two want to say something before we remove the cameras?"

"Hold on," Brandon said, zipping his bag. "I—"

"Wait a second, can I say something?" She raked her hands through her hair and bit her lips to bring color since she didn't have a spare second to race off for lipstick. She didn't wait for anybody to shush her. As the cameras lit, she got right to it.

"When I awoke after I hit my head and saw Brandon for the first time, he seemed almost too good to be true. He wasn't only good looking. He had a way of calming and easing all my fear. But it all changed when he moved in. You see, he tried to remake me, starting with what I ate. For the first couple days, I believed he was starving me to death. I guess I wasn't very nice, but he stuck it out. I don't know if anyone before me ever tried to bargain to get her way, which didn't work of course.

"I don't know when exactly I got aboard with his plan to get me well. I'm just glad I did. If I hadn't, I never would have gotten to know my niece and nephew, wouldn't have known how wonderful they are. I might not have been softened up enough to take Harley, and that hound dog has been one of the best things that ever came into my life. I wouldn't have been able to talk about my mother and father's death. There I said it. A month ago, you never would have caught me uttering a peep. If I learned anything from Guru Brandon, it was how to trust and how to love, and I just want to say thank you from the bottom of my heart."

She turned to Brandon in the doorway. His face held a mixture of joy, pride, and what was the other? Could it be pity? He shook his head and punched his fists against his rock-hard thighs. He backed onto the front porch.

"I'm sorry, I can't do this," he said.

Then he was gone, leaving behind a confused Madison and the purr of the ever-ready cameras.

Chapter 30

Madison must find Brandon. Why had he left in such a huff? Where would he go? She paced back and forth while the staff removed the camera equipment. What if he got in a wreck? No, he wouldn't allow his emotions to get the better of him. She unplugged her charged cell, intending to call him, but cursed remembering she didn't have his number. She searched everywhere for the business card he'd given her the day they met, but it must have gotten accidently tossed out during the decluttering process. She telephoned Harper to inquire.

Harper listened, then said, "No, I never got it. I called the station, and they must have gotten in touch with him because he called me, but my cell didn't display his number. I guess they like to keep everything private. Why, Madison?"

"He just left without saying goodbye or anything."

"Do you know why?"

"I was thanking him. Well, actually I was confessing all he'd done for me to the cameras, and he flipped out. It was as if I'd called him a rotten example of a human being. It doesn't make sense. We kissed this morning on the beach. Brandon had been a willing participant."

"That's a shame, baby. I'm sorry. I wish I could help. Brandon will probably be back after things blow over."

"You didn't see his face when he left."

More confused than hurt, Madison got off the phone with her sister and approached the cameramen. "Do you have any idea where Brandon went when he stormed off?"

The men shook their heads, and Spencer said, "Not a clue, but he should have stuck around. The interviews weren't over. We're going to need to catch up with him."

"Do any of you know where he lives?"

"We don't have that information, Ms. Gray."

"Maybe they have a record of it at the station." Without waiting for an answer, she took off, her Mustang beating a track down the Sunset Strip toward Hollywood.

Forty-five minutes later, an office assistant with a low ponytail and a fringe of wheat-blonde bangs over golden brown eyes greeted her. "Brandon's inside with Dan Harris. I can't disturb them. It's against policy."

Madison breathed a relieved sigh. Soon she'd talk to him, find out why he fled. "I'll wait here until they finish."

The assistant straightened a file of papers. "It might be a while."

Hardly able to contain her impatience, Madison said, "That's all right."

She took a seat in a chair too firm to be comfortable, thus adding to her irritation. Heated voices drifted from the other side of the closed door. She longed to figure out what they were saying. She got up and walked around the office, paused behind the office assistant, and scrawled down the number on the telephone. Finagling, she asked to use the restroom in the corridar, and once inside, used her cell.

Madison pinched her nose between her fingers and faked a Brooklyn accent. "We've got a package on the main floor that's too big to bring up. Could you sign for it?"

"Oh, all right, but I hope it's not another piece of furniture for Mr. Harris's office. If it is, you're going to have to get someone to deliver it."

"No, no, it's nothing that ginormous."

She slipped back into the office as the assistant left. "I should just be a second," the woman said, smoothing the pouf of hair at her crown.

Madison opened her purse. "Don't hurry on my account. I've got a book to read."

With the woman gone, she crept to the door and opened it a crack. She could make out Dan Harris, a man she'd met at social functions and charity events. He was tall, big all over, wearing a blue dress shirt and slacks that accentuated his short waist. His face was broad and ruddy, his lips dark, eyes a gray that sucked up the blue of his shirt. He'd been pouring himself a coffee, and he set it down on his desk.

He lowered himself onto a plush leather chair that squeaked with his weight. "I still don't know how you managed to lasso Madison Gray, but it was the best move you ever made. Securing her saved your ass, let me tell you. The editors say the footage from the last couple of months is the best thing you've ever done. The producers all agree on the show's reinvention. With the spinoff we've got in the works, you two will make reality-TV history."

Brandon paced, yesterday's shirt unbuttoned and

wrinkled. "I'm telling you I don't go for the idea." He rubbed his forehead. "Madison won't like it either."

"Not even if we allow her to oversee every creative detail of the promo?"

"You'd be changing the show's entire dynamics. Plus, I've heard her say she'll be glad when the filming stops. She's tired of being on stage every waking moment."

"What do you mean?" Dan stabbed a pad on his desk with a pen. "I know Madison Gray. She lives to promote her clients. And with the fireworks between the two of you, *Hollywood loves the Guru* will be a huge success." His heavy lids lowered. "I can see it now. The cameras follow Madison through her day at InSight, noting her change, while you go on to treat another case, but you both meet each day for lunch or dinner." He opened his eyes and tilted his head to the side. "Who knows, maybe the two of you will get married with the wedding broadcast so that the ratings tip the scales and earn you another Emmy."

Brandon sped up his pace. "This idea of a spinoff is absurd."

"People love a good romance."

Brandon eased up. "Even when there isn't any?"

"Come on, Brandon. You can't tell me you aren't enamored with Madison."

"I care for her the way I would any pupil. No one is more pleased that she's doing so well, but that's as far as it goes. I never cross the line."

"Are you saying you're not in love with her?"

"Of course not. Ms. Gray is my student, end of story."

With her heart racing, Madison sucked in her

breath and glided into the office like she didn't have a care in the world. "There you are, guru."

Dan's elbows jerked back in his chair, his body flailing against the leather cushion, then his hand ran back and forth beneath his desk. Good Lord, was he searching for a panic button?

She jammed her arm across his. "What's the skinny here? Am I the last to know you two are in cahoots? I believe you need my signature. A contract is not a plaything, Dan. I'll sic my lawyer on you if you try anything underhanded."

The office assistant stuck her head in the doorway. "I'm sorry about this, Mr. Harris. I got called away..."

Acting as if this were an ordinary day, Brandon crossed the room and handed Madison a bottled water. Did he actually believe it would lower her boiling point?

He was shaking his head, the scam artist. "I meant to tell you about the producer's harebrained scheme, but I just didn't want to upset you."

"How considerate of you." Dredging up dignity from every part of her reserves, Madison straightened her shoulders. "I suppose the kiss you stole at daybreak was intended for some hidden camera."

"No, I—"

"You kissed her?" Dan Harris laced his hands together and dropped them behind his head. "I certainly hope you got it on tape."

"The kiss was a ruse," she snapped. "A maneuver Brandon planned to sway me into saying yes to your"— she made the quote sign with her raised fingers— "'harebrained scheme.' Well, I'm done. My time is up and right on schedule. There will be no more shows—

no *Hollywood loves the Guru* or anything else. All this time, Brandon, you've lectured me about being sincere. You're the biggest phony of them all." She passed him a scowl intended to cut him down to size. "Shame on you."

"Madison, does this mean…are you…?" There was a pause. He seemed to have lost the ability to stay calm, his hands visibly shaking. "We need to talk, you and me."

Purposely, she glanced at her mother's watch. "Sorry, I've run out of time. By the way, I won that bet with Audrey Powell. Doesn't matter, you can go back to her now. I'm sure she'll be waiting for you with open arms. In fact, maybe you could use her to spice up your show. You know, fake an attraction as I did with you."

"You don't need—"

"I don't need to what? Admit that I played you the same as you did me? We'll do anything for good *press coverage*. Isn't that how it goes?" Her temper spiked, but she suppressed it, not wanting him to see her blow a fuse. She paused in the doorway, casting him an icy glance. "I want the crew gone before I get back to the homestead."

"Please wait. Let me explain."

"Oh, and just so you know, my next stop is for coffee." Even suggesting this, she felt sick inside. "Then I'm going to buy myself the biggest Angus steak on the planet, polish it off with a bottle of champagne and a chocolate mousse. And after all those calories digest, it's hot fudge sundae time."

She doubted Brandon had ever been at such a loss for words. With his face as white as the walking dead, unruly curls hanging in his eyes, he said, "I want to—"

"It doesn't matter now what you want." She fired him a hard-edged glower. "You forfeited that privilege." She inhaled down to her toes, steepled her hands—imitating him—and nodded. "Namaste, asshole."

Tears rose to their breaking point. Brandon was trying to head her off at the elevator, so she took to the stairs. *Don't cry over this*, she told herself. *Don't let him see what he's done to you by not loving you. Don't give him the satisfaction.*

When she got to her car, he was on her heels. "Maddie, please listen to me. I've had to hide any feelings I had for you."

She shook a finger at him. "You don't get to call me Maddie. Don't you dare. That name's reserved for people who love me."

"I'm trying to explain."

"I don't care, Brandon. You planned to use me." She shook her head in disbelief. How could he? And yet he'd been shunning all her advances. She'd just been too stupid—or blind—to notice, but now it all made sense. "That's why you were backing away from me this morning. You don't want me. You never did."

Her heart in pieces, she didn't look at him as she sank inside her car and skidded off, gravel flying out from the tires.

Chapter 31

Anger with himself rose up inside, cold and dark. He'd never known this degree of self-loathing. He'd do anything to erase her tears of utter disappointment in him. She was right. He'd been a complete ass not to have told her everything this morning like he had intended.

He hadn't meant to kiss her, hadn't planned to, yet he wanted to do it since the first time he laid eyes on her. He'd been pushed to the brink by her exquisite face at sunrise. It'd made him break his vows. Then he'd let her down by storming off the way he had, but what else could he do? He couldn't take it when she'd said he taught her how to trust.

There was one thing he could take care of, and now was just as good as any to begin. With the blood pounding in his veins, he returned to Dan Harris's office, determined to do right.

Looking hopeful, Dan got up from his desk. "Did you work things out?"

"I don't like the way this went down. The show's turned into a farce. I'd like to see all the episodes with Madison scrapped."

Dan's eyes opened wide. "Are we just supposed to throw out two months' worth of work because you pissed off your costar?" He opened the bottled water Brandon had tried to push on Madison, took a pull, and slammed it on the desk. "Those are the breaks, Kennedy. You knew that going in."

"I never was in favor of deceit."

"Then you shouldn't have signed the contract." Dan sat down and wiped his brow with a handkerchief. "Listen, we can work this out."

"You don't know Madison. She's had a lot of troubles, and she's had a difficult time getting past them. She's a decent person, a wonderful human being, and a…the last thing I wanted was to hurt her."

"Have you fallen in love with her?"

"Who said anything about love?" Brandon tried to smile, but his facial muscles rebelled, and he ended up with what must have passed for a sneer.

"You don't have to say a word. When is the last time you slept? When did you change your clothes or shave? Man, get some pride in yourself, will you?"

"Just give me all the film, or better yet we'll destroy it together." Brandon wanted some leverage, but he didn't have any. He should have stolen the reels, then built a bonfire in the sand and destroyed them. He rubbed his temples. He'd never even gotten to say goodbye to Madison, as if there were ever a way to part on amicable terms.

"I can't allow you to destroy the tapes," Dan said, sounding sincerely regretful. "You'll forget about all this mess once you begin your next assignment."

While pacing, something dawned on Brandon, and he froze in the middle of the room. "There's not going to be another assignment."

"What kind of crazy talk is that?" Dan said with a flick of his hand. "You're not thinking straight. I have a feeling it's due to a certain woman you've been shacked up with for the past sixty days. We're all susceptible, you know? Give us a classy babe like Madison, and we forget to sleep. Even you, the king of cool, are prone to turning into a lovesick schmuck."

"I've been a hypocrite. The show is as hokey as all the other reality crap on TV."

"Telling the truth is overrated. It's not like you aren't a good life coach. You are. But you have to follow the rules of the trade and then forget about it. Look, you've earned a vacation for all your hard work. Go off to your Himalayas, hang out with the other swamis, and I guarantee you'll come back with a whole new attitude. You don't have to worry about taking time off, not with all these episodes you have built up. I'd say you're good for a few months of total vegging."

"Thanks for the offer, but I don't think I could return to the program no matter how long I'm gone." He lowered his chin. "My contract is up this month."

Dan guided Brandon and sat him down, then turned his chair around to sit eye to eye with him. "Listen, it's glamorous in an exotic way for a yogi to sit on a mat in the middle of suburbia and talk about detaching from material things. But it's freaking lunacy to be homeless and talking about the joys of being hungry." He nodded. "You get the picture?"

"Right." Brandon stilled. "Lately the show, it's not enough."

"You go talk to Madison." Dan twiddled his thumbs as if deep in thought. "After she simmers down, you might be able to convince her how you feel about her."

"I don't know. I'm worried because she was so out of her head when she left here. I'll blame myself if she actually goes on a food binge. We had her schedule worked out for after today. I hope she sees it. I hope she's all right. She's got to be."

"You'd better figure out how to break through to her." Dan rubbed his chin. "What if she hits rock bottom and you're not around?"

****

The first place Madison headed was Oceanview Market. Brandon had used her. Imagine that, and all along she'd believed—or hoped—he was crazy about her. It had been an act, a trick of the trade. He probably did the same with all the women on his stupid show.

As she marched down the aisles of Oceanview, she felt unleashed. Left unguarded, she could eat anything that struck her fancy. Here was the golden day she'd been waiting for, the day when she didn't have to pay an ounce of heed to Guru Brandon.

She tore a box of coffee pods from the shelf. Next, she hoarded candy bars, sodas, and cookies, the brownies freshly made in the bakery, a peach pie, and cupcakes. She went for the beer, and to celebrate her freedom, she grabbed a bottle of rosé. She hunted down the old-school greasy potato chips. No pansy baked chips for her. No siree!

She asked the butcher to pick out the biggest porterhouse and followed this up with Italian sausage, linguica, wieners, and pork and beans. She wasted no time filling her cart with sodas, mostly rootbeer. In a stupor, she wandered into the dairy section. Nothing would satisfy her like a potato heaped with sour cream and butter. She hoisted up a tub of chocolate chip ice cream and a jar of hot fudge topping.

She stood in line, and because Brandon had taught

her to meditate while doing so, she didn't. Instead, she talked to the heavy-set lady in front of her about the joys of sleeping in and eating late. Without thought, she scooped up packages of every kind of gum and hard candy.

The sales clerk had a head full of braids and a squeaky voice. "You've got a big family to feed, I'll bet," she commented.

"No, it's just me." Why did that make her feel more than a little pathetic?

The woman in back of Madison tapped her on the shoulder. "Girl, you're too healthy to be eating all this food."

"I can eat anything I want," she said, and who knew? Maybe she could after shocking her system for a couple months with veggies and yoga.

"Lucky you." The woman lifted her hands in the air. "I just see food like this, and I gain ten pounds."

"Yes, lucky me," she parroted, "always the winner."

She stopped to buy a real-deal pizza. No more healthy wannabes, not for this woman of the new page. From now on, her philosophy would be if it's not rolling in grease, it's not edible. Yeah, she might clog her arteries. She might even die of gluttony, but she'd go out happy and loving every last morsel she ate.

When she shoved into her house with one of the ten bags of groceries, she noticed, too soon, that all the cameras had vanished. It hit her. No more interviews. What a shame. She had so much to say now that she was unplugged.

"Look at me; this is the way I unpack all the good stuff." And to demonstrate, she laid all her junk food across the bar as if creating a subject for a still-life painting. "This is called, 'On the Way to Hell, I Stopped for a Quick Bite.' "

Harley nuzzled her side, and she dropped down to his eye level. "My goody doggy, my bestest dog," she said, rubbing his chin. "It's just you and me now."

Why was she missing those damn cameras?

Sweet Mary and Joseph, was it her imagination, or did her dog look devastated? His eyes were all watery, and he hung his big cumbersome head. Crazy mutt, didn't he know a good thing when he had it? Her throat closed. Didn't she?

A knock sounded at the door. She jumped, her heartbeat surging into the danger zone. She hadn't shut the door tight, and so it swung open, revealing her latest shame.

"Madison, what are you doing?" Brandon asked mournfully.

She held her hand up to stop him in his tracks. "Stay right there, hotshot. You're barred from my house! Don't you dare come any closer, or I'll sic my dog on you."

Harley loped over and leaped, his paws on Brandon's shoulders, licking his face.

"Hey, guy," Brandon said and then stretched his arms around the dog. "Madison, let me come in. You can't break all your good habits because you're mad at me."

"Get over yourself, guru, or I'll call the cops and have you arrested." She parked her hands on her hips. "All that talk about Karma, do you recall? 'Madison, don't take more than one toothpick. It's bad Karma to steal. Madison, don't cut Joe Blow off on the freeway.

273

It's bad Karma. Don't say you're fine if you're not; it is bad Karma to lie.' You know, Brandon, I'm not fine right now, because all of your aphorisms were a line of bull. And you know what?" She scowled. "It's a wonder you're not falling-down dead with bad Karma."

"Madison…" He started across the threshold, but she shoved her hand toward him.

"It was all for the sake of fattening your wallet, wasn't it? Everything you said, it was just for those ever-loving cameras. Well, the show's over, sweetheart."

"Let me in and we can talk."

"No, now get out! I never want to see you again."

"But, Madison…"

Those telltale tears threated to expose her. "Get out, I tell you."

He closed the door, and she let out a breath. She'd forgotten to breathe today. No wonder her heart wouldn't stop hammering; her breathing had been too shallow.

She turned to the invisible camera lens. "This is the way to cook up some beef," she said and plopped the red meat into a frying pan.

While it fried and spit hot oil, she stuffed a couple of enormous potatoes in the microwave and went around putting away her groceries. She did pour some Frosted Flakes in the dog bowl for Harley.

"Why shouldn't you have a treat as well, Big Stuff? Maybe I'll give you some of this mouth-watering steak." She stuck a fork in the meat, and the sight of the blood running into the pan gagged her. Why was the beef so tough? Had the butcher given her a bum steer—literally?

The potatoes needed to be microwaved longer, though the steak appeared done. Madison uncorked the champagne, poured it into a fluted glass.

"Cheers, to a new way of life."

What she meant by it, she wasn't sure. Was it cheers to a new way of saying *adios* to the confounded *Madison Project*? Or cheers to a new way of life without Brandon, the lying SOB? She cranked up Pearl Jam on the Bluetooth speaker and got ready to scarf everything down.

The steak spread across her plate like the bottom of a shoe. The potatoes blew up in the microwave, and what remained was flat and hard. Hunger caused her stomach to growl like a mad dog. Speaking of which, why was Harley staring down at his bowl like she'd dumped a good piece of the kitchen sink inside and asked him to eat it?

"Brandon has ruined you too, hasn't he, Harley-Quin?"

She was admittedly famished, having not had a bite to eat all day. But did she go for the steak or the pizza at her fingertips or even a chocolate bar? No, she was craving—with every cell in her body—those damned vegetables.

All this honest-to-goodness food, and in her mind, she saw an emerald-green, plump zucchini, a bright carrot, and a sprinkle of feta cheese.

"What is wrong with me?" She gulped and picked up her glass of champagne. She heard Brandon as if he spoke over her shoulder. "To drink this would be like ingesting turpentine." Holy St. Christopher, what had happened to her? It did reek like chemicals. It was all in her head, no doubt, but it didn't stop her from dumping the bubbly down the drain. Next, she trashed Harley's cereal and replaced it with feta cheese over veggie kibble.

She chomped a big bite of raw carrot. "Here's looking at you, kid." She collapsed in her chair. "I'm damaged. Brandon's made it so I can't stomach junk food."

Harley looked up at her. Who said dogs didn't understand people language? Big Stuff's sympathy unraveled her tears. On top of everything else, her dog got her misery. It was touching and sad, and she found herself hanging on to him as she dissolved into racking sobs.

She wept over the man who had done her wrong. She wept for her illusions of him and for her wish that this morning had never happened. Remembering the kiss, how passionate it had been and how triumphant, she skidded into a greater funk. Brandon had been acting. "You can't trust actors," a former boss used to tell her periodically. "You never know when they're on stage."

If only she hadn't taken Brandon Kennedy in and fallen for him as hard. If she hadn't, she wouldn't be crying the blues to a dog who listened with more than his heart.

****

What Brandon needed was a drink. Yep, the guru needed something more than sitting on a yoga mat and trying to find enlightenment. His drink of choice used to be beer, a tall frosty one on a summer's day—just like his dad. God forbid! How long had it been? Not that he resembled his father. Oh, he'd gotten pie-eyed after Dad's death. It was all part of the grieving process, he'd told himself. Even now he reasoned taking a nip was part of his missing Madison.

There were things he hadn't told her. She knew nothing about his family, the family that was now gone. Brandon first associated the word Dad with the pop of a beer can. If his father had received medical attention for his PTSD...if there was no such thing as war...if, if if....

Okay, Dad did drink too much when he and the guys in his band got together to jam, but it was just beer. Some nights, though, he'd hit a point of no return, and a dark look would cloud his eyes. It would take days for him to come back to knowing where he was. No one messed with him until he surfaced again, the same dad as before. After his mother died, though, Dad hadn't returned to the land of the living for months. But Brandon wasn't his father.

No, Guru Brandon was a fraud. He should have spoken up this morning and leveled with Madison. Instead, he'd played the part of the stoic guru right up to the disastrous end.

Feeling sorry for himself, he pulled his car into the parking lot of A Table for Two.

The restaurant was on the second story, dimly lit inside, with large windows so that the town was visible outside. It was a part of Santa Monica where the hour of the day tossed shadow and light along the row of shops where Madison and he had passed just yesterday.

Brandon became aware of a bombshell of a waitress laughing as she scribbled an order from four admiring men. She took one look at Brandon, slid her coffeepot from the table, and drifted over. In a cloud of perfume, a little cleavage showing, she leaned toward him.

"I know you, hon," she said. "You're that yoga guy."

He felt as if a look at his face would reveal his guilt. "You've got the wrong man."

"Too bad." She set her coffee pot on the table. "I'm plumb in love with Guru Brandon."

"He's not worth it."

"What can I get you, hon?"

"How about a shot of your best whiskey?"

"You want that? But you're a health freak." Her hands went to voluptuous hips. "You can't fool me, mister. You must got you some serious woman problems."

That he was contemptible must be written all over his face. He couldn't date Madison—she'd never have him anyway. Just as well, he told himself. Why violate his moral code? Why get involved with someone who would never work out? And what was all this talk about love?

She was a habit, the first thing he saw each morning. What man didn't want a beautiful woman at the break of day? Happy? He could be happy without her. Joy was a state of mind, or so said the fortune cookie. A guy had to find his own pathway to truth. Life wasn't meant to be all valentines and roses. His spirits dropped to his shoelaces. Who was he kidding? Without her, the future unwound before him like a prison sentence.

After the waitress brought the glass, Brandon sat staring into the long black hole of Jack Daniels. He remembered then when he'd been seventeen and had found his dad coughing up blood, a two-quart bottle of whiskey on the washing machine beside the sink on the back porch.

A biopsy showed what Brandon had feared. The oncologist claimed the many years of alcohol consumption combined with the tobacco use created a kind of poison. Dad mumbled an apology to Brandon when the doc diagnosed cancer.

What had Brandon been thinking? A man couldn't drown his troubles in booze. Of all people, he knew this to be true. When he sobered up, this mess would still be there goading him worse than before.

He left A Table for Two without ever taking a single swallow.

Chapter 32

*The real meaning of enlightenment is to gaze with
undimmed eyes on all darkness.*

~Nikos Kazantzakis

Madison awoke to Harley whining. She'd fallen
asleep with her arm around him like he was her big,
warm security blanket, her—*choke*—Mokie. When she
sat up in her bed, she found his majestic form standing
in the open doorway.

"You have to go outside, bubba?" That job had
become Brandon's designated honor, but her memory
flashed the awful events of the day before. "Come on,"
she said, determinedly tugging on her running shoes
and her shorts. "Time to boogie."

They tore out the back entrance and headed to the
ocean. The world was just starting to wake, the sun a
fireball to the east. She looked straight into it because,
God Almighty, she couldn't look anywhere else.
Remembering how it had been—was it just
yesterday?—her chest constricted with pain. *No use
sulking.* She set out with Harley into the crisp golden
glow of the beach.

Who would have thought a couple of months back
she would be running at breakneck speed? Today she
loved the way the air felt against her face, the
fragrances, and the taste of sea salt on her lips. The

seagulls flew over, casting shadows and calling out to each other as they searched for breakfast. Other joggers passed by, their dogs clipping their heels. Harley knew his place with the rest and kept a steady *clomp, clomp, clomp*. It was amazing that all of nature seemed to work together to form a whole.

A mile down the beach, she stopped. She was panting, her lungs burning in a healthy way. She'd read about dopamine and adrenaline, the runner's high. She'd never felt it until now, the bliss state. It was like toys at Christmas. She could get used to this, praise be. She couldn't help but flaunt a goofy grin all the way back to the house.

What was she going to do with all the junk food she'd bought? She heard it then as it drummed into her head. "Donate it," Brandon had said whenever she cleaned out a drawer or a closet. She boxed up all yesterday's lack of better judgment and set it in the back of her car. She'd take it to the food bank in East LA.

Afterward, she still had most of the weekend in front of her. Respectively, she could get some gardening in, do yoga to her heart's content, and meditate for as long as it took for her to enter Nirvana. Yeah, fat chance on the latter.

Her cell phone rang. She ignored it when she saw an unknown number but ended up, after a heated debate with herself, listening to the message left on her voicemail.

Brandon sounded desperate. "I have to talk to you. Please call me."

Her throat tightened. "Not on your life, guru."

Once she entered the house, her landline trilled in

its high-spirited ring. It would be Brandon again, but she dashed toward the Chinese table. Good thing because she saw Harper's number across the small screen.

"How's my favorite sister?" Harper asked when Madison snapped up the receiver.

"Good, considering." She relayed all the events from the previous day.

"Are you kidding me?" Harper said after she told her about the wrongdoings of Guru Brandon. "What a rat. I just don't understand it. When I saw him, he was besotted, make no mistake. He was besotted with you and unhappy because of it."

"Well, maybe we should have shot him and put him out of his misery."

"Madison!"

"Don't you get it? First and foremost, Brandon Kennedy is an actor. Being an agent and working with a herd of great pretenders, I should have had his number."

"I'm sorry, baby," Harper said, as usual ignoring that Madison was the eldest. It was that nurturing maternal thing her sister had about her. It kicked in at times when needed the most, like now. "You know I'd take away your pain if I could."

"I'm okay. I am still eating like I was in training to run a marathon."

"You go, girl." Harper sighed so loud Madison heard it through the wire. "Darrin's boss wants to take us out to dinner. I don't suppose you're up to having the kids for an overnighter."

"I would actually." It would fill up the hours so she wouldn't have to think about anything else. "I'll let them help me make dinner. It will be fun."

Right on schedule, the children raced up the sidewalk to greet her, their arms spread to hug her. A far cry from the first time they'd been dropped off, they allowed Harper to leave without making a fuss.

Darrin stuck his head back inside the house. "Maddie, you look terrific."

"Thanks," she said with a smile and turned to find the kids on the couch, petting Harley, the kiddy channel already in full swing.

Chloe showed off her fingernails, each painted a different color, a rainbow of pastels. "I don't suck my thumb anymore, so Mommy said I could get a manicure."

"Welcome to the girls-just-got-to-have-fun set," Madison said. "I like your sparkly sequined Hello Kitty top. Is that new too?"

"No, but these are," she said and took out a package of felt-tip pens.

Madison got off the couch. "Do you two want to draw some pictures?"

Tyler said, "I can draw the Yankee's logo."

Madison opened the door to the kitchen. "Okay, I'd like to see it."

They settled at the table and just started in on their masterpieces when Chloe asked, "Where's Brandon's yoga mat?"

Tyler shot his sister a frown. "You weren't supposed to talk about him because it will make Auntie M feel bad."

"I'm sorry," Chloe said, her lower lip jutting out. "I forgot."

Madison dragged a hand through Chloe's

corkscrew curls. "It's all right, sweetie."

She couldn't let the kids see how tormented she felt. Would there always be something around to remind her of Brandon? He was everywhere in the house, but she had to get past it. *Move on, sister.* Nothing's worse than a cheater and a liar, she reminded herself, and the pain of it left her broken and exposed.

With a sudden idea, she picked up the pad of paper, some pencils along with the felt-tip pens, and said, "Let's go to the ocean and sketch."

"I'm going to draw a rescue boat," Tyler said.

Chloe tippy-toed around the kitchen in glee. "I'm going to find a seashell."

Madison, the kids, and Harley spent the next couple of hours on the beach. The late afternoon was so lovely Madison could have sat for hours. Chloe had done half a dozen pictures, and Tyler had found a few boats to sketch.

"Look at all the colors in the rocks," Madison said as she drew. She hadn't drawn anything since she took an art class in high school. She'd forgotten that sketching an object made her really see it. It also made her lose track of time. She'd never be a professional artist, but she didn't care, not today. It wasn't always important to be the best. Sometimes the advantage came in being outdoors, in using all five senses, and in being with those she loved, her niece and nephew. Who could ask for more?

Chapter 33

Brandon opened the door of the motel near the sea. The wind blew and fluttered into the room like a ghost. A couple days ago, he'd have calmed down by signaling Harley for a jog beneath the stars. But tonight, his memories were all he had to keep him company.

The story he had told Madison about his past was a load of bunk. To be honest, his father was one of those unsung war heroes. Soon after his discharge, he'd followed Ravi Shankar to India where he learned to play the sitar. He ended up marrying a beauty from Bangalore, with a string of names but whom he called Shar, in a ceremony too close to his release from the army.

Sure, Paul Kennedy was a little bit laid back, but hey, it didn't keep him from seeing Shar got her trips to the ocean. A pair of fishing poles and Dad and Brandon left Maa alone to do what she loved best. Spin her tales onto a yellow legal pad in a flow of blue ink.

Despite that Grammy and Aunt Sally didn't believe in his mother getting published, Dad told anyone who'd listen, "My wife's the next Pearl S. Buck," and "Isn't Shar's writing as good as Pearl's? And doesn't she have the culture down?"

Did he even read a page? Maa wrote about India, for crying out loud. Well, of course she did. Her biggest fan was Brandon, who could recite every word. No getting around it, his mother would have won awards if she had lived.

Home, in those days, consisted of a little 1920s bungalow in Pasadena with a Douglas-fir floor, a stone fireplace, and a nook Dad had built for Maa's desk. When Dad got back from India, he put together a band, cut a few records, and never had to try hard to come up with a hit that made the charts. Maa loved him. She called him *Laadla*, even when they fought. She hated to lose him to the drink. Her way of coping with the tough times was to make up stories.

"A ghost of our ancestors lives in the cellar," she'd say, though they had no cellar. "A ghost named Alexis-Nathan." And when Dad fell in with his demons, the admiral came to visit. The Christmas of '89, Alexis-Nathan anchored below for two weeks. Maa pushed his fables. Was it any wonder with Dad's song lyrics, Maa and the admiral's stories, Brandon often quoted other people's words?

His parents had been a nice-looking couple—Maa, petite and dark, her smile adoring, her face lit with health and vitality as she looked up at Dad. The perfect match. That was until Maa couldn't get out of bed one morning. Yeah, sometimes Dad stayed in the sack till the afternoon with a hangover. But Maa was the strongest of the two; then she wasn't.

To see Shar Kennedy, his beautiful, generous mother, ill and weak was terrible. Her future as the next Pearl S. Buck fled along with her unfinished books. All that promise, all her love, gone, and her fourteen-year-old son left alone with a damaged father.

A chill now sliced through Brandon, as if the wind had been a prayer. It didn't matter how grounded he believed himself or whether he practiced yoga or *Ujjayi* breath. He couldn't get warm. His guilt over what had happened on *Guru Brandon* hit him like the wrath of a dark ninja.

And now an even stranger sensation gripped him so that the hair on his arms rose. Out under the starry sky, his precious mother stood on the water staring at Brandon, unaffected by the wind. Brandon's gut twisted as he pushed, head bent, toward the image who remained as quiet as a statue. Brandon closed his eyes and rubbed them with his fists, then looked again.

There was no one now. Had it been an illusion? Was it a figment from his past? He glanced from the cliff to the sand, shadow to shadow. Maa had vanished from the face of the earth, but had she been there at all? Most likely not. But somehow, for the first time since her death, he allowed himself to experience all the emotions over losing her. And that led to his sorrow over having driven Madison away.

Chapter 34

On Monday, it rained. Madison listened to it as she sat in the darkness meditating. She let her gaze fall on the candle and uttered her mantra. At first, she was aware of the pain in her lower back. *Did I pick up Chloe the wrong way and strain a muscle? Did I sleep wrong? Is this arthritis setting into my bones? After all, I'm not as young as I used to be.* Her thoughts shot this way and that like pinballs in an arcade game.

She kept with it, though, and after some time, her mind began to still. She experienced a peaceful feeling that stayed with her even into her morning shower. This was the big day. Today she returned to her old life. That sounded overwhelming. Could she still run an agency? Would it be like riding a bicycle? Would her leadership qualities kick in right away?

She walked into her closet, but instead of reaching for her yoga pants or shorts, she went for one of the three powerhouse suits she had left. They were from when she'd been on a fad diet that she'd stuck with long enough to warrant this trio.

Note to self, stop at a thrift store after work and get a couple suits, preferably in colors other than black. She no longer needed to appear slimmer.

Satisfied, she started to sweep her hair up in her trademark bun, and that pesky Brandon settled near her ear, saying, "I like your hair down."

Wearing it on her shoulders was less trouble. Madison wouldn't need hairspray. All those chemicals in the hairspray, she might as well be smoking. *Smoking? Didn't she still have that pack stashed in the desk drawer?* She could light up now. Somehow, though, just the thought of that first drag made her sick to her stomach.

She ate her blueberries and later her yogurt, and gathering her purse, knelt to say goodbye to Harley.

"Hey there, my action-hero dog, you watch the house, you hear? You scare the heck out of any bad guys if they try to break in."

Right. The gentle giant would probably lick them to death.

The rain was nice, the traffic not so much. Madison had forgotten how stressful her commute to Hollywood was each day. No wonder she used to pull over to the side of the road because she was hyperventilating. *Breathe*, she told herself firmly, and she plugged in her cell phone and selected a cut that mimicked the sound of a waterfall. *Breathe!*

She was about to pull into her spot reserved in the parking lot, but someone other than herself had moved in on it. Her shoulders immediately tensed. To make matters worse, the only space left was under a messy tree almost a mile away. Her stride shouted at her murderous intent. She'd get that minion, all right. Halfway to the office, with her yoga mat and healthy lunch, she stumbled in her high heels. Panic shot through her, making her lose her breath.

What was she doing? Traveling in reverse?

She should be enjoying the walk in the drizzle, not stewing like the old wobbly Madison. She lifted her face to the sky. It felt good. She felt good.

Note to self, stop to smell the roses. A proverb, she thought. Was she using too many of them lately? Picking up bad habits from a recently discarded guru?

She entered the office to find her assistant holding a steamy cup. "Here's your coffee, Ms. Gray."

"Thank you." Madison held the mug and inhaled. She smiled. It smelled wickedly delicious. "You got this from that trendy café, Let There be Coffee?"

"I did. It's the way you like it, straight black, no froth, no muss."

"I said that?" Geez Louise, it made her sound like she was ordering a blackboard.

"You did. Have I done something wrong?"

"No," Madison quipped, inhaling the magnificent brew. "It's just that—just that I—I gave up coffee after I got sick." Regretfully, she pushed the cup toward her assistant.

"Oh, I'm sorry, I didn't know." The young woman seemed eager to please, big brown eyes blinking attentively. "Can I get you something else, tea or hot chocolate?"

Madison sighed and ran a hand through her hair. "I'm fine...what's your name?"

"It's Allie—well, Allison Montoya, but you never called me by my name."

Surprise caused Madison to flinch. "I didn't?"

"You usually call me Hey. Hey, this coffee is cold. Hey, get into my office, stat. Hey, order a chili dog for me."

"I did that, Ms. Montoya?" This knowledge hurt. "Well, who did I think I was?"

"I don't know," Allison said with a self-conscious

laugh. "Maybe the boss."

"The boss from hell. Hmmm, I'll tell you what. You drink that coffee if you'd like, Allison, and come into my office so we can have a chat."

Allison's dark eyes widened. "You want to talk, Ms. Gray, about your clients?"

"Not now. I want your input." Madison cocked her head to the side. "How long have you worked for me?"

Allison shuffled from one foot to the other. "I'd been your assistant a little over three months before you left."

"Five months now. Unbelievable. I think it's time I got to know you."

The more the morning progressed, the more Madison felt like a stranger in her own existence. First off, she had to clear out her drawer full of snacks she no longer ate. Peel off previous calendar pages. Lob the whiskey from the cabinet down the drain. Needing fresh air, she pried open her window and saw a jogger below on the boulevard. Immediately, she suffered a pang of longing for the beach. Sounds battered her nerves, the roar and hissing of traffic, a siren bringing to mind her emergency exit from life as she'd known it sixty-three days ago.

This was the day to reconnect with her clients. She should be jumping up and down, but the files felt heavy in her hands, sticky. Her throat ached at the prospect of making all the necessary calls that would establish her once again as the head honcho. Reading page after page, she discovered, much to her surprise, people had moved on without her.

By ten o'clock, when she was so weary she could barely see straight, an associate stuck his head in her office to inquire about her health. His name was David Abrams. He was single, handsome with an Ivy League style, gray eyes, and a well-groomed head of sienna-colored hair.

"Do any of my employees take breaks?" she asked.

"Well, of course they do, Madison. It's the law, and you know what a stickler you are for playing by the rules."

"Of course I am." Never let it be said that Ms. Gray didn't abide by *the rules*. Too bad David hadn't seen her hiding in her closet with a forbidden cell phone on the first night of shooting *Guru Brandon*. He'd change his tune. She was halfway out the door when she caught herself. "Exactly where is the breakroom?"

"I don't think you've ever been there before." He waved a hand to indicate the elevator. "It's downstairs, second door to your right. Do you want to call a meeting in there?"

"I just need a breather, understand?" What she wanted for starters was to get to know the staff that worked for her. She picked up her shoes by their ankle straps.

"Yes," he said, though it was evident by the confused look on his face that he didn't at all. "Would you like me to escort you? It would be my pleasure."

"No, that's all right. I should be able to find my way in a building I've worked in for a few years, shouldn't I?"

He rubbed his hands together. "Do you want me to bring in some glazed doughnuts?"

"God, no," she said, squishing her feet back into her unforgiving shoes.

"You seem different, Madison. Your hair, I like it.

And your complexion..." David was eyeballing her body. "I see you've gotten some sun."

Oh, sweet Lord. Heat sprang into her cheeks. "The beach is close to my house."

"You never...well, that's awesome." He presented her with a straight white grin. "I hope whatever you're doing, you keep it up."

Always before, she'd been too busy to give a man a second look, and now she wasn't, was she? Why did she feel like she'd be two-timing if she flirted a little?

Brandon Kennedy, be hanged! She was going to start fresh, dating, getting to know nice men like David Abrams. That way, she could put a certain teacher behind her. Maybe she'd have a baseball team full of boyfriends. How about that? Be the belle of Hollywood, whatever that meant given she'd been away, and trends changed faster than the weather.

Still, she batted her eyes. "Thank you." Wasn't that how a woman toyed with a man? Funny, she felt out of sync in an ever-modernizing world. Had it always been that way, she asked herself, as she limped down the hall in her tight shoes.

She'd developed a toughness that enabled her to do her job. Men usually saw her as a threat, which was an element not conducive to romance by any means. She'd let her guard down when she met Brandon. She'd given up her deepest, darkest secrets, thinking of him as the real deal.

But she'd been mistaken.

The elevator ponged, and she slipped inside its dark, mirrored walls, needing to get away, and it was only a little after ten.

When she entered the breakroom, she found two

twenty-something-year-old women talking in a huddle at the table. They seemed to be having men troubles. Oh, how she could relate, but when she spoke up, the women jumped, crumbs flying from the package of soda crackers they'd been sharing. They took one look at her and skedaddled out of the breakroom.

Making friends, didn't they have self-help books on the subject? Honestly, the way her staff reacted to her, she must have been truly the boss from hell. So much for her belief that she could begin her new life by being liked.

Look what happened when I wasn't looking...

Brandon had stressed people needed other people to be well adjusted. Since she'd been in the breakroom, she counted three employees who had been about to enter. They spotted her and took off like she'd been about to write them up for loitering. Discouraged, she sauntered back to her office. She spent the morning pouring over the applications of potential clients. She made a few calls, arranged some appointments, and then, bored, stared out the window at the rain.

Blame it on being away for too long. People used to ask her opinion or her help throughout the day, but now it seemed everyone had forgotten her. She'd have to work to win them back to trusting her judgment. She had suffered a collapse, after all. Maybe it explained why even her office assistant was treating Madison as if she were breakable.

Don't excite Ms. Gray. She might just up and fall on her noggin.

At noon, at her desk, she ate the soggy salad she'd brought from home. Then she rolled out her mat, kicked off her impossible shoes, and struggled to sit in lotus position in her straightjacket of a blouse and skirt.

Note to self, keep some yoga clothes at the office.

Allison Montoya came in and immediately averted her eyes at the sight of Madison. "I'm sorry." She patted her blonde bob. "There's a man here to see you. He doesn't have an appointment, but I thought maybe you'd want to see Mr. Kennedy."

Madison's pulse shot up. Brandon must be just outside her office. She could imagine him with his too-good-to-be-true body and his devilishly fine looks. He had that star quality. Allison probably didn't watch much TV, or she would have recognized him from his weekly show. But Allison had to recall his appointment with Madison two months ago, no doubt believed Mr. Kennedy a savior of the first order.

"Tell him I'm meditating." Madison struggled not to topple while folded into her pose.

"You don't want to see him?" Allison sounded surprised.

"Not today." *Not ever!*

When the door closed softly, Madison fell into a long, "Ommmmmm." She drowned out his voice. She lifted her eyes to the sky outside the window. "Ommmmmmmm."

When would he get the hint? She wasn't about to stop. "Ommmmmmm." She was doing perfectly well, had all his teachings down—couldn't he hear? She'd become an old hand at living clean and green. She just hadn't gotten the hang of mixing her old life with her new.

As the weeks went by, after many attempts and failures, she managed to get Allison to go to dinner and see a chick flick with her and had a nice time. They talked, laughed even. It was fun breaking bread with somebody other than Harley-Quin, bless his big heart.

Madison kept her appointment at three that first Thursday with Dr. Buckley. To be prepared, she'd arranged to have her lab test done a few days before.

Dr. Buckley smiled and seemed a lot more lighthearted than the first time Madison had met her. There was none of that staring down her nose with solemnity. Instead, she shook hands as if Madison had graduated at the top of her class.

"You did it, Madison. Your blood pressure is perfectly normal, and your cholesterol is down to a decent level. Your kidneys are functioning well, and so is your liver. If you keep up the good work, you're going to live to a ripe old age. I can almost guarantee it."

Madison felt like flying a kite. "Hooray for that."

"You did the right thing by working with Guru Brandon. It's made all the difference."

Okay, there was one thing in his favor.

In the following weeks, she joined a book club. It didn't matter that the last time she'd read a novel, it had been *Middle March* back in college, a book as big a doorstop. Reading, she discovered, was better when it wasn't mandatory for a grade. She joined the gym and got herself a hot pretty-boy trainer. It did wonders for her ego when he flirted with her. At least, she thought it was flirting. He stared at her a lot, and not in a let's-improve-the-body sort of way, but rather like he thought her already fit. And wasn't she?

In time, she stopped, or so she hoped, being regarded as The Wicked Witch of bosses. She arranged for her staff to take power naps and to incorporate meditation breaks into their schedules. She even hired a motivational speaker to address the benefits of maintaining a healthy work environment. Her own body strength kept improving, especially when she added a treadmill desk to her office décor and used it throughout the day. Soon, she opened an account so she could charge the life-changing desk and offer it to employees who wanted to switch. Over the course of a month, morale soared as her staff adapted to Madison's health boom.

During the evenings, she still found herself thinking about Brandon. And not just at night. There were times during the day when she thought, *I've got to remember this so I can tell Brandon.* Then she'd recall, with a thud back to earth, that they were no longer together. But bedtime held an even greater trigger for heartbreak. She'd wander downstairs for a glass of water and believe she saw him in his favorite chair, looking like he had when he slept. Hair tousled. His dreamy mouth turned up at the corners as if he were about to tell a joke. Where had he gone when he fell asleep? She had always wondered.

And where was he now?

Chapter 35

At eleven o'clock on the nose, while Madison settled the last dispute from disgruntled clients, Allison's voice chugged wearily from the intercom. "Sorry to interrupt. An Audrey Powell out here. Needs to see you. Won't go away. Sorry."

Madison's first impulse was to yell, "Tell her I won the bet," but she caught herself in time. Before Brandon's teachings, she'd have said that or something just as dismissive. Since then, she sent loving kindness during her meditations not only to her loved ones but to the worms.

May you live with ease. May you be happy. May you be free from pain.

Just as I wish to, may you be safe. May you be happy. May you live with ease.

May your life be filled with happiness, health, and well-being.

Madison purposely relaxed her shoulders. So what if the two of them had had that scene on the terrace? So what if the leaked footage had gone viral? She'd gotten the last word, hadn't she? Although her practiced loving kindness wasn't quite authentic, she was getting there—even if it were more a case of faking until making it.

She extracted a sigh. "Tell Ms. Powell to come in."

Audrey entered with an unexpected smile and set a

check for a thousand dollars down on the desk. "There you go."

Madison snapped it up. "What's this?"

"I owe you," Audrey said, "for making me see myself for what I was." She rolled her eyes. "A b-e-e-t-c-h."

"You're welcome, I think. To be honest, I don't understand. Money wasn't part of our deal." She handed it back to Audrey. "To be blunt, I don't want it."

"I promised you a feature story in *Powell's Review*. I don't know if you still want that, but you did stick it out. You deserve a reward, whatever you wish."

"Nice of you to accommodate me, but as I said, I don't need a handout." Madison clasped her hands together tightly. Her tongue felt suddenly thick. "As far as our bet, you not seeing Brandon, it's not my concern. Do what you want. I don't care anymore."

"Don't you?" Audrey collapsed on the loveseat and heaved a sigh. Even at that, she was still the ingénue with her wholesome Grace Kelly looks.

"What do you mean?"

"I got to see some footage that makes your claim seem bogus."

"Listen, if you came here to gloat—"

"I came here to...apologize for my abominable behavior. I shouldn't have shown up at your house, shouldn't have barged in. I shouldn't have said the things I did."

"Is this a ploy, Audrey? Because if it is—if you've got a camera camouflaged along that ruffle on your blouse—I don't want any part of it. I just don't, you understand?"

"No, it's nothing like that." Audrey's shoulders drooped. "The fact is, I wanted the press coverage for my small publishing house. I have employees counting on my drumming up business, and I just wasn't coming through. I don't expect you to understand."

"But I do," Madison admitted. "We have more in common than you might think." She cleared her throat. "When you called me a big bag of wind, the truth hurt, because I, too, would do anything to score PR for InSight. My antics to get attention were deplorable."

"Seriously?" Audrey looked like she was about to fall over.

Madison shrugged. "You know, when we initially met, I wanted to be friends. I mistakenly believed we could get together after the filming of *Guru Brandon* and have coffee. I thought now here is a woman dear to my own heart."

"When I saw myself on YouTube, I wanted to take a gun to my head. You have no idea what it's like to see yourself as the nightmare you really are."

Madison wanted to laugh. "Oh, don't I?"

"You had every right to kick me out. What a terrible scene I made. I'd like to say I was genuinely worried about Brandon, but I'd be lying. I was thinking about myself." She brought a hand to her throat. "The things I said, and Brandon was right about me. If I don't learn to get real, I'll never be happy. You can't practice yoga and berate others, you know?"

"I do." Madison passed Audrey a plate of sliced apples. "The toughest lesson I've had to grasp was to wish everyone well. It goes against my nature—or it did."

Audrey tilted her head. "Whatever it is you're

doing, you look fantastic. I wish I could get the sort of help you have, not from Brandon—too much water under the bridge for that. Are you and Brandon still together?"

"No, we haven't spoken since that last day."

"Wait, what?" Audrey's brows shot up. "But how could that be?"

Madison set her cup on the saucer. "By any chance, have you seen him around?"

"I haven't." Audrey shook her head. "Where is he, then?"

Madison had been equally split on wishing Audrey could divulge his whereabouts and praying she wouldn't know. "I expected you to tell me."

"Well," she said, "one thing is for sure. He couldn't have gone very far."

"Why do you say that?"

"Watching the footage of *Guru Brandon*, a person would have to be blind not to see how much he cares about you."

Funny—not in a ha-ha but in a tragic sort of way—Madison hadn't noticed it. Another thing of which to be thankful? Too bad, some chances only came once.

****

One Saturday in late June, she'd been at Tyler's championship little league game, and they were walking to the parking lot when Harper asked if she'd seen any of Brandon's earlier shows.

"I'm sorry. I just don't go for self-torture." Madison was a terrible liar. She'd been watching him all right.

She had downloaded the first season from Netflix. It was incredible how good Guru Brandon had been in the initial episodes. She had sat on the couch with her feet tucked underneath her, eating rice cakes, watching the man she had given her heart to instructing a lady named Emma who had agoraphobia after being a victim of a mass shooting. Madison realized, halfway through, it was the same episode she'd seen while channel surfing. Brandon got Emma out of her apartment for the first time in ten years.

Madison wanted to stand up and cheer after it was over. Sometimes, his patients had children. Madison found herself with a dopey smile because it was like watching Brandon play with Tyler and Chloe. Again, the word "natural" came to mind. He'd gotten down and played, laughed. Was it all part of his charisma, his being perfect dad material? Madison laid her head back against the couch and closed her eyes. She imagined what it would have been like if Harper had dropped the kids off and there had been no Guru Brandon in the house. Things probably might not have turned out as well as they had.

He could have left her on her own with her niece and nephew. He could have said their presence on the show went beyond the call of duty, but he hadn't.

"Thank you," she whispered to his television image.

Shortly after the first season, Madison had noticed a difference, although minor, to each of Guru Brandon's performances. The show would be about three-fourths of the way to its conclusion when Brandon would invariably turn to the audience and say something like, "I don't think so and so"—whoever the show was about—"is going to get well." Or "I was afraid of this happening" and blah, blah, blah. Or he'd throw his hands up in the air. "This isn't going to work," he'd utter rather melodramatically. How unlike him.

It seemed expected that Brandon act negatively. She'd caught him a few times spewing gloom and doom to the camera while working with her. He had stopped all that nonsense somewhere along the last month. But with her, toward the end, he hadn't needed to say a word. She'd added all the drama needed just by the turn of events. The arrival of Harley. Chloe and Tyler's appearance. Her confessions.

It was merely speculation on her part, but had the format of Brandon's show changed through no fault of his own? He wasn't a fake, or she hadn't thought he was until that day in Dan Harris's office. She tried to get a grip on her conflicting thoughts, but it was like trying to prevent a flood with a teacup.

The production company notified her that her stint would launch in sixty days. Although she knew this was her cue to promote herself on social media, she found herself shying away, which was so unlike her. It was just that hanging out with Harley, jogging, and practicing yoga were now her priorities. When she wasn't working at keeping herself fit, she was attending Chloe and Tyler's swim meets.

After a particularly exciting event on a day so warm no amount of water could quench Madison's thirst, she got inside her car to transport Harper and her brood home. "All set?"

Harper buckled the kids into car seats in the backseat. "So, Madison, have you been watching episodes of Guru Brandon?"

Madison's stomach clenched. "I've seen it a few

times."

Chloe said, "I want to see Uncle Brandon. Can I, Mommy?"

Harper turned in her seat. "He's not your uncle, Chloe."

"I want him to be," Chloe demanded.

Glancing into her rearview mirror, Madison saw the sincerity in her niece's eyes. "It's okay, sweetie," Madison said.

We all could learn something from kids. They followed their heart and didn't pretend to dislike somebody. *Maybe it's how we all are supposed to be.* Out of the mouths of babes? Maybe Madison should take notes.

Chapter 36

One full month after production, with no trace of Brandon, Madison began to worry in earnest. As far as she knew, the postproduction follow-up hadn't happened, which was strange. She'd expected a call by now—or a dozen—telling her to show up for film edits and to record voiceovers. A requirement stipulated in her contract but not acted upon.

Why?

Not that she wasn't doing fine on her own. Even now, after her power nap, she could take down any studio director who stood in her way. And do it peacefully. Maybe she merely wanted to show off. Say, *hey there, guru, watch me wheel and deal with a slice of calm and a chip of vitality thrown in.* After all, she had changed. Didn't that warrant his approval?

At the very least, he'd been a friend, hadn't he? Just because he hadn't returned her affection didn't mean she should excommunicate him from her social realm.

She tore down a post-it note that said to call the network and another with the same words written in red felt-tip pen and still another with three explanation points tagged to the end of the sentence. Well past time, she decided, and placed the call to Dan Harris. If his assistant remembered Madison's little prank to get inside Mr. Harris's office, she didn't let on.

Sure enough, soon Dan's "Hell-o" came on the line. "Madison, what can I do for you?"

"I wasn't sure when that ghastly production I was in was due to air. Forgive me for being blunt, but I'd hoped never." Would he be able to tell she didn't actually mean it?

"It seems you got your wish."

"What do you mean? Did a little bird carry the footage away?"

"You and your lawyer will be getting paperwork to sign. Until further notice, we've shelved it."

"Is there some reason the network decided not to run a show that was supposed to bring in a deluge of new viewers?"

A pause crept into the phone, one that lasted such a long time sweat beaded along her upper lip.

"You don't know, do you?" Dan asked, and she could swear she heard him grinding his teeth. "Brandon quit the show."

"I think we may have a bad connection. For a second I thought you said Brandon *quit*. I know that can't be since his shows are still airing each week."

"They were taped at an earlier date. No, Madison, he didn't renew his contract with us, and frankly, I don't like it one bit. I haven't heard a word. When I tried to call him, his phone number had been deactivated. I know we had our differences, but it didn't mean I didn't care about him. If I could have given him what he wanted, he most likely wouldn't have walked out."

"What was it he asked for?" She had the feeling she already knew.

"He believed the show strayed too far away from

its original premise."

She agreed with Brandon. Nervously, she fiddled with a paperclip. "Do you have an address?"

"I went to his apartment to talk some sense into him, but the manager told me Brandon had paid off his lease and split. She didn't know where."

Her heart thudded as her sense of urgency increased. Should they file a missing person's report, contact the police? "He couldn't have fallen off the face of the earth."

"I know it, but wherever he's gone, it doesn't look like he wants to be found."

Oh, God, was she actually wringing her hands? "Well, thank you for speaking to me. The last time we met, it wasn't under the best of circumstances."

Another one of those frustrating pauses. "Madison, you're what led to his leaving. Find him and bring him home. He's one of the good ones. He helped a lot of sick people get better, you know?"

The implication of what Dan said had her head spinning. Had he cared about her? "I'll call you if I get in touch with him."

Afterward, she hurriedly scrolled through the Wikipedia information on Brandon Kennedy (Guru Brandon). Even though the content read like an advertisement, she discovered he'd been born and grown up not that far away in Pasadena. That was a start. Hopefully, she'd be able to track down some family, but his mother and father were both listed as deceased.

She spent a better part of the day on the phone trying to locate anyone who could tell her something about Brandon. Had he returned to his hometown very recently? But although she finally did hook up with a former classmate, the only thing he was able to tell her was that Brandon had an uncle. A priest at St. James in Pasadena. Madison promptly called the church and was connected to the warm voice of Father Tim Kennedy—praise the Lord for small favors. He had seen him—would miracles ever cease?—and agreed to meet with her.

She took the next day off work and headed to Pasadena, the home of the Rose Bowl. She turned off Interstate 210 by the mountains that surrounded the Los Angeles Basin.

The church was in the heart of Old Pasadena. It was an architectural treasure of old-world splendor with its many columns and aged brick. A walkway led her to an adjoining rectory. The pleasant aroma of roasted chicken welcomed her as she followed a white-haired lady in a gingham apron to a room where a priest sat watching last Sunday's 49ers game on TV. He hit the remote as she entered.

"Madison, welcome." His smile was big enough to light the room without flipping a switch. "I'm glad you could make it."

Timothy Kennedy looked to be in his mid-sixties. He had sandy brown hair, a high forehead, kind eyes the same blue-willow color as Brandon's, a nose that could have been broken maybe more than once, and a handshake that was so vigorous it rattled Madison's insides.

"Thank you for seeing me, Father. So you're Brandon's uncle?"

"You bet, on his father's side." He gestured to a worn but cozy rocker by the fire. "Have a seat, why don't you, dear."

The springs pinged a little when she sat. "You said you saw Brandon. When was it exactly?"

"Toward the early part of summer. June, I think." Father Tim looked worried as he leaned back in a high-back chair and rubbed his thighs with his big strong hands. "He gave his notice at the network and followed it up by coming here."

"Why?" she blurted.

Father Tim sighed. "He felt lost and didn't know how to go on."

"What did you tell him, Father?"

"I told him to pray about it, and he would find his answer."

She wanted to get Father Tim's take on Brandon's resignation. "Did he tell you why he quit?"

"He wasn't satisfied any longer with the show's direction." Father Tim eyed her intently. "He talked about you. He had good things to say, to be sure, but he felt he had hurt you. It was eating him up inside, if you don't mind me saying. I hadn't seen him like that since his father died. Did he ever mention anything about his parents?"

She shook her head. "No. Wait. He told me a little about his mother."

"That she was ill? Safe to say, he didn't have an easy childhood. He grew up faster than any kid has a right to."

"I did read that his parents had passed." They had much more in common than she'd thought, a lot of which they could have shared—given the chance.

"Brandon took care of his mother, and later he had to watch over his father. My brother had a drinking

309

problem. My nephew's childhood wasn't always like a scene from Currier and Ives, that's for certain, but I think it's what shaped him into the caring man he is today."

"Speaking of today..." She couldn't stand hedging around a second longer. "Do you have any idea where he is?" She hung onto the arms of her chair. *Please say you do!*

"I wish I did." He leaned back. "I don't mind telling you, Madison, I've done more than my share of praying for him. The last time I saw him, he was so down at the mouth."

A sliver of ice worked its way up her spine. "Do you think he might be across the world somewhere?"

"You mean off in some hermitage trying the make the world a better place?" He smiled at her, a slightly crooked smile. "Wherever he is, I hope, for his sake, God's granted him some peace of mind."

She pressed her knees together to keep them from noticeably trembling. "I do too, Father." She needed to be alone before she did something embarrassing like burst into tears. "I have to go." She got up and took the priest's hands in her own. "Thank you for seeing me. If I hear anything, I'll give you a call."

She passed the camellias and inhaled their bittersweet fragrance in the humid air. On impulse, she took a sharp right into the cathedral. Looking around, she filled with awe. There were deep niches and statues and beautiful hand painted murals. She felt cocooned in reverence, steeped in silence. She dropped into a pew near the back where she hid in the shadows. In her heart stirred a raw, throbbing pain.

She buried her face in her hands. "Oh, please. I

didn't want to love Brandon. I didn't want it to matter that someone dear could be stolen from me again. I can't have another person I love go missing. I can't go through it a second time."

Chapter 37

Because of Madison's reminder of how fragile life was and how quickly it could vanish, she found herself getting in touch with old classmates, rekindling relationships, and plunging into the unfamiliar territory of forming new friendships. One such alliance was with her former foe, Audrey Powell.

At first, it was the phone calls back and forth that bonded them together. They both grew up in Southern California, both adored shopping, and were struggling businesswomen. But the two had more at stake than commonalities. The news exclusive to Madison's recovery was often a topic. Both women were excellent at brainstorming. They developed a couple of paragraphs devoted to Madison's past, the shakeup—or as Audrey so aptly put it, "the call to adventure." That meant an account of Brandon's rescue and Dr. Buckley's death sentence.

Because of their growing connection, when Audrey telephoned one afternoon to say brokenheartedly, "My mother was killed in a hit and run accident on Abbott Kinney Boulevard. I have to identify her body, and I have no one to turn to," Madison didn't hesitate, heading straight to Audrey's South Olive Street apartment.

Madison drove while Audrey prattled on about the hospital making a mistake. When they reached their destination, Audrey asked Madison to accompany her. Madison knew too well what it felt like to be alone and afraid. Once inside the morgue, a policeman lifted a sheet, and Madison held her friend tightly so that she wouldn't fall over. Finally, after much deliberation, Audrey nodded. But when the policeman went on to ask if her mother had been suicidal and Audrey grew so flustered, Madison asked the officer to postpone his line of questioning.

Who would have believed in a matter of ninety-something days Madison would be taking Audrey Powell home with her? And yet it felt like the right thing to do, the only thing to do. They ended up walking the beach and talking way into the night. Audrey told her about the unresolved issues between her mother and her. For the first time in a long while, Madison thought of her own mom and the conversations that still dangled without resolve.

Madison spent the next few days cooking for her friend, nutritious meals that Brandon had passed down to her. On the day of the burial, the sky opened and deluged the mourners in the cemetery with autumn rain. Beneath her designer blacks, Madison's skin shivered. The disaster brought back more memories of her parents. They hadn't had a funeral. She'd been too young, too shocked, and in too much denial.

After dropping Audrey off in Venice Beach, Madison's thoughts tugged at the notion of being granted a "second chance" for a decent send-off for her mother and father wherever they were. Yes, Harper might benefit from a ceremony like the one they'd given Chloe's Mokie. Closure was what her sister needed. Couldn't the same be said for herself? It wouldn't hurt.

She turned on her phone and made a call. "Hey, Harper Lee, how about you and me giving Mom and Dad a farewell service? I mean…I know you—"

"I'm in," Harper fired back.

Life, Madison thought, was strange. After all these years, who would have thought she and her sister would be joined together to lay their parents to rest?

The following Sunday, after a night at a hotel in Baja, with Madison's backpack loaded down, she said, "Beautiful day." Her voice sounded oddly cheery.

Harper lead-footed it down the beach, her hat flapping in the wind, a big straw bag over her shoulder. "It's serene—perfect for a *bon voyage*."

As if there were such a thing. *Oh, yes, let's just wave goodbye after eighteen years of our mom and dad being stuck in the sea.* They were orphans, after all. Harper had made a picnic lunch. Madison had asked her to prepare black rice with a fresh coconut to lend a tropical nuance. She had collected sand in a bottle.

"Each pebble, connected to all the rest, makes a beach," she said, which was so Brandon her laughter almost spilled out for anyone to hear.

They walked with the sky on all sides of them, clouds darkening everything. Madison had the sense that she had lost days, maybe even months or years, out of her life. As if it were yesterday, she remembered her parents studying the migration patterns of the whales who returned to the exact spot in Baja every spring. The whales came to gestate, to mate—not that their sex life mattered to Madison one whit. Oh, she had once loved the mammals. It hadn't been unusual for a mother whale to lift her calves up for her to pet. Yes, there'd been a time when whales were her friends and extended family. But it was hard not to picture an abnormality, some fictitious Moby Dick swallowing her parents, boat and all.

Madison now glanced at the wristwatch Mom had given her hours before their disappearance. Back when Harper had first spotted it, Madison had told a vague version of the transferring of ownership without mentioning the ugly words that transpired. "I'd come of age, so she gave it to me," Madison had said with plenty of bluster. Harper mentioned how weird it was their mother had passed it on that day of all days.

If Madison didn't open up now about what had really happened, she never would.

"I've kept things from you, Harper, the things I said to Mom." The guilt that lay buried rose fresh and raw, overwhelming her.

"You made me pinky swear not to talk about it, and so I didn't. You were the last to see them after all. Wasn't it just a couple days before your senior ball?"

"Yes." Madison bit her lip until it throbbed. "Mom was her sparkly, spunky self, dancing around my bedroom and clapping at the sight of me in my formal. Anyone else would have thought she was the adolescent in the family with her enthusiasm. I didn't even want to go to the dance. I had to study for a chemistry test and let her know about it. She reacted by unbuckling her watch and strapping it to my wrist." Madison tapped the clockface where a funny-looking whale blew bubbles. "She gave it to me to remind me not to take myself so seriously."

Harper laughed softly. "You could be a royal pain."

"I know. She wanted me to babysit that afternoon while she and Dad made a quick trip to study the whales. Because it was storming, I was frightened and hollered, 'You shouldn't have had Andrew. You should have gotten rid of him before—' I never finished. The hurt in her face. I had devastated her with my stupid outburst." Tears choked Madison. "I didn't mean it. More than anything, I wish I'd gotten the chance to tell her."

"Listen, Mads, if you think about Mom, you'll realize she forgave you immediately. And if you really think about her, you'll know she saw through your words to your fear. But thank you for telling me. It explains a lot."

Harper let Madison lead the way into the lagoon. It took only seconds to feel the sand squishing through her toes, but then her hands clenched around the handles of her backpack were sweaty and shaky.

Madison started singing the hymn "Amazing Grace," and it felt good to sing again after all the silence, broken only once by Chloe. Afterward, Madison, with her hand chained to Harper's, waded farther out into the lagoon.

Kelp twisted around their ankles, and brown pelicans swooped past in a wild swoosh while the water churned both warm and cold. The air was moist and sweet where the currents swarmed together. Thousands of varied species meshed far below where the sea existed in constant darkness, lifting at times, her parents used to say, to the sunlit sea.

Hadn't Madison witnessed something like it when she'd awakened in her office? Brandon had prompted her to talk as he lit the incense, but there was a gap in her consciousness—a place she had been trying to fill ever since.

She now lifted her chin. "Marian Boyle married Joseph Gray in 1975. They were the last of the flower children and the war protesters of UC Berkley. Upon graduation, the couple moved into a boarding house in Daley City. They worked hard to complete their PhDs, and in 1982, their dreams became a reality. They opened a whale watching company on a little strip along the Oregon Coast called Depoe Bay. I was born in the small coastal town, and three years later, you came along, Harper."

Her sister picked up the cue. "Joseph and Marian loved teaching. They taught us to observe the sea life up and down the Pacific Coast. But their passion was humanizing the gray whales. They moved to Santa Monica where they became professors at Pepperdine. And though they occasionally achieved recognition in some local or esoteric seafaring publication, what gave them joy, beyond all else, was raising us."

Madison picked it up. "Mom and Dad worked a sixty-hour week, never tiring, and they probably would have gone on with their happy, productive lives for many more years—if that lousy storm hadn't demolished their boat."

She hadn't meant to fall into such wallowing resentment, but as bitterness left its bad taste, she took her parents' binoculars from her backpack. They were so old, so rusted that they worked like fogged kaleidoscopes. It didn't matter because she wasn't looking for anything specific. She peered into them, facing out to the horizon. "Can I see clear to China?" she called, remembering when she'd faced the ocean with Brandon—when he'd hugged her on the beach. Something strange was happening. Madison saw the cabin of a boat. Static came from the radio into her ears. The engine sputtered, and three inches of water sloshed on the deck.

She dropped the binoculars to the front of her thigh. Her jaw firmed tightly.

Harper stepped forward. "Madison, what is it?"

Startled, she looked again. "Nothing." Only bluish white. She remembered the dream that never went away about her parents returning to her, and suspected it wasn't a dream. Replacing the binoculars in her backpack, she then took out the bottle and spilled half of the sand into the sea. Harper dumped the rest.

Both sisters smiled through their tears, puckered their lips, and blew kisses.

"Mom and Dad are here!" shouted Harper.

Madison threw her arms out to the sides, feeling free in a way that she hadn't in years. "They're alive and they're everywhere!" The clouds opened, and sun poured down like a shaft from Heaven. And all at once, two glistening whales breached, their magnificent bodies haloed in soft golden hues.

Chapter 38

Three days after giving her parents a memorial service, on impulse, Madison stopped at the new age store where Brandon had bought her the singing bowl. Lately, maybe because of her newfound spirituality, she couldn't get over the feeling Brandon was somehow near. It was probably wishful thinking, stemming from her desire to see him again. It wasn't as if she'd find him here among the Sanskrit cards and the chakra posters, for goodness' sake. She hadn't gone that far over the edge. But still, she could swear there was a connection, no matter how slight.

That same high priestess that had waited on them before glided over as if she had wings on her sandaled feet. Today the woman wore a serape, and her platinum hair was brushed back in a bun at her nape. Her gray eyes widened with recognition the closer she came to Madison.

"I remember you," she said enthusiastically. "You were with Guru Brandon, and he bought you a lovely singing bowl. Are you using it?"

"I am. Thank you for asking."

"Do you like it?"

"I sure do. In fact, that's why I came in today. I thought I might purchase a mandala to help me focus during meditation."

"Surely," she said and opened a glass counter. She

removed some stiff muslin with healing images on them. "We have silver, white, burgundy, and amber. Now you want to hang the swatch so that it is facing you. You can use it as a visual stimulation for minutes each day."

"That sounds like it might help." Madison chose the burgundy because it looked especially rich. "I like this one."

The woman wrapped it in tissue. "Is there anything else I can help you find?"

"Yes, are there any spiritual readings that I can study?"

"We have many choices over there in the bookcase. May I recommend a title that comes from the Yoga Sutras? It has only a part of the Sutras' 196 aphorisms. It's divided into four sections called *padas*."

The more Madison learned, the more she wanted to know. "I'd like to see it, please."

The woman took it from the bookshelf. "The first *pada* gives you the definition of Yoga. 'Yoga is the practice of removing afflictions of the mind.' "

"I'll get this book as well."

"As a matter of fact, I have something." She smiled like a gypsy, wistful and all-knowing. "I saw Brandon three days ago. He stopped in to buy some oil burners."

Madison stared at the woman for a long, shocking moment, then looked down so that the blush she felt rising to her cheeks wasn't apparent. "Are you sure?" She hoped the lady didn't hear her heart clamoring. "Are you sure it was him?"

"Well, there's not another Guru Brandon, is there?"

"I guess not. Did Brandon say why he bought the—what did you say? Oh, yes, the oil burners and the books."

"No, he didn't, but I thought it might be for some of his students. You were his student, weren't you?"

The priestess should know without Madison having to say a word. She was psychic, wasn't she? All women who worked in a shop with crystals and tarot cards must have a third eye. It came with the territory, didn't it? This woman was no exception.

"Yes," Madison said, "but I haven't seen him for a while."

She left the incense-clouded shop, her feet dancing for joy. Once inside her car, she phoned Father Tim and then Dan Harris. "Brandon didn't go far. He's right here in Santa Monica."

But if he hadn't gone off to the Bay of Bengal or some temple in Tibet, what was he doing? And why hadn't he contacted anyone?

****

A man could go mad missing a woman this intensely. In time, the knife-sharp need would lessen—it better. He'd quit seeing Madison everywhere he looked. No longer would her smile haunt him. Her profile wouldn't cut through his thoughts at the darndest times. Her body in motion, those nice curves, that flame of hair—he'd eventually forget, wouldn't he?

He worked hard on his new project every day, ate a little dinner, and went to bed with the chickens. Occasionally, he leafed through the pages of *Autobiography of a Yogi*, reading about the life of Paramahansa Yogananda and consuming himself with learning. And that led him to meditate with a pencil in hand. Inspiration followed, refueling his imagination. He transformed the images given to him by his mother through her stories. His new venture excited and involved him. His plans set him dreaming, scheming, and he thought of some of the patients he had attended to during the taping of his show. He'd let some of them down.

The woman who wouldn't leave her apartment—what was her name? It came to him then, Emma. Had he honestly helped her? The story writers had made such a fuss, but he privately suspected she'd end up going back to her screenwriting and not venturing out. He wondered if he helped anyone. Look how things with Madison had turned out. He'd failed her.

On Sunday, toward the end of September, he went to High Mass at St. James, then left the cathedral to corner his uncle before he got caught up in the afternoon football games.

No one, though, could deny the depth of his uncle's feeling when he saw Brandon and gave him a tight embrace. "Good to see you, Bran."

A half hour later, the two sat drinking hot apple cider in the rectory. With direct sincerity and unrestrained emotion, Brandon told Father Tim what he'd been up to. His uncle listened, asking questions and giving advice and encouragement.

Diplomatically, his uncle scooted his chair closer to him. "Have you talked to Madison? She's worried sick about you."

The mere mention of her name sent a wave of adrenaline kicking through his veins. "Have you seen her? Is she okay?"

"She's blossoming. You should see."

"I am happy to hear that." Brandon set down his mug. "I can't tell you how much."

"Then get in touch with her. Do it now. Do it before it's too late."

His shoulders grew rigid. "I can't. I don't deserve her."

"Listen, son," his uncle said, grabbing his wrist. "You can practice virtue, and you can read dogmas, everything that's known this side of paradise, but when you're as in love with a woman as you are, how can you be happy?"

As usual his uncle saw past all the roadblocks that he'd installed to keep his feelings from derailing him. If he were ever to find total peace, wouldn't he have to find his way back to Madison? The problem? He didn't know where or how to start.

Chapter 39

One night in late November, Madison sat curled up with Harley. No, she shouldn't have allowed the dog on the couch. No, it wouldn't happen again. But it was nice having the snuggly Harley next to her, especially when she was about to watch the tapes of the episodes they had filmed those two months last spring.

She had talked Dan Harris into letting her borrow them. He owed her after all. No one else would be watching them, so what would it matter? Nobody would miss film that would most likely be shredded, and because of her business, she did have an advantage. Plus, she'd become Dan's friend. But what was the real reason she wanted to watch her lessons? Simple. She was curious, not to mention she'd see Brandon again. She hadn't been able to find him, so this was the next best thing.

With the tissue box on her lap, she hit the remote. "Okay, let her roll."

A few minutes passed by and she thought, *was that tightly wound lady me?* How had she not known how bad she'd looked? She didn't even recognize the shrillness of her voice. It had a frantic quality and a jolt that hurt the ears. *The Taming of the Shrew* flashed to mind. Was this the person she had presented to the world? *For crud's sake, kill me now!*

She had been out for a good fight in those first

days, while Brandon, saint that he was, stood by, patient but firm. Sweet Almighty, the way she'd carried on about the food. Brandon should have thrown the skillet at her. Madison watched with fascinated horror. Her face had been so pale it appeared mask-like. Had she been aware that she'd been as overweight? A wave of shame struck her with such force her stomach pitched. She flattened her back against the couch and instructed herself to breathe.

At nine o'clock, as was her habit, she went to bed. Her nightmares were full of images of the woman she'd been, and she viewed herself in snips and pieces, conscious that the old Madison no longer existed. Glad of it—thankful for that April that had changed her life.

Just before her morning meditation, she read the spiritual teachings from the Yoga Sutras. During her breathing practice that day, she felt gratitude for whom she had become. Weeping followed, a pouring out of the rest of her pain, distilling her, and bringing forth the deepest serenity she had ever known.

She spent her day acutely aware of being in the moment. She didn't judge; she merely saw what was happening—the light was red, and the cars were jam-packed all the way to her turn off—and then she let it go.

When she arrived at work, Allison awaited her with a list of problems. First off, there were ten messages just this morning from irate clients. Tony D'Angelo had torn his contract in half and threatened to quit if he didn't get the part of Christopher Reeve in an upcoming movie. Heidi Throne had torn off the set in her wheelchair because she got into a fight with her leading man. And the eighteen-year-old singing sensation,

Saratoga (one name), had stormed into the agency with her white cane tapping the floor before Allison could stop her, saying her new album deal had fallen through.

Madison patted Allison's arm with reassurance. "I'll take care of it."

When Madison entered, she found a hysterical girl wailing into her cell phone. "They said I was a flash in the pan, a one-hit wonder."

"Are you ready to talk to me?" Madison asked. "Or would you rather spend your day wallowing to whoever will listen?"

"I'm a failure," the girl said with a grim look on her angelic face.

"A failure at eighteen, is there really such a thing? The only way you can fail is to give up on yourself. And remember, there's always room for growth no matter what your age."

"That's easy for you to say, Ms. Gray. You never failed at anything in your life."

Madison laughed until tears gathered in her eyes. *Would you care for me to tell you about some footage from a recent reality TV show...?*

Chapter 40

That evening, Madison decided to take a different route home. She got off the freeway early and headed north up the highway that flanked that fabulous aquamarine sea. The winds had quieted on this Thanksgiving eve, making her in awe of her surroundings. Debussy played softly from the car speakers. She had a lot to be thankful for, she thought. It was then she saw a new sign just off the road. *Shalimar Yoga Studio*.

Was it a sign or was it a *sign*?

She'd heard the art gallery had sold. She wondered who bought it, and what a perfect place to practice. It was up there on the ridge that looked out at the ocean from every window. It would be great to pick up some different postures and to have instruction and be with other people who were yoga enthusiasts.

She had time to inquire. It wasn't like she was cooking tomorrow. Harper prided herself in her homemade pies and mouthwatering turkey. As she got out of her Mustang in the parking lot, a group of women flowed from the building. Maybe Madison could catch someone before the studio closed for the holiday. She held the door open for stragglers carting their yoga mats and their bottled water. She entered the lobby, noticing the tasteful oil painting of an orchid, the rich teakwood floors, and the sculpture of the ancient god Shiva displayed in the corner.

No one stood at the counter. Probably most everyone had gone to get a head start on their holiday baking. To the left, a light shone through the doorway and pooled like moonlight on the floor. Hoping to find someone still lingering about, she entered, and a sense of tranquility instantly struck her. She felt she'd moved into a place of deep relaxation. The walls matched the sea which was visible from every angle. On the left wall was a scroll painting, on another a single branch of a birch tree. The entire room was a study in Oriental aesthetics. In the far window, she saw then a man standing with his hands on his hips.

He wasn't just any guy, though. He was the very same one whose mere presence had soothed her that long-ago day in her office. Of course, she wanted to run past the bronze lanterns and leap into his arms, but he hadn't seen her come in. She had time to study him there at the window. His back was slightly bent, which was so unusual for him, and he appeared lost in thought. She tiptoed closer and heard his long sigh.

He straightened suddenly. "Madison?"

Her heart leaped. "How did you know it was me?" she asked, stunned.

"That scent of citrus leaves, deep, dark woods, so shocking, so sublime, could only be you." He turned around and tilted his head. "You must be following the things I taught you, because, sweet damn, you're beautiful."

He hadn't taken his eyes off her, which made her all warm and tingly inside.

"I could say the same of you." *You knock me off my feet!* "I came in to see about taking some yoga classes,

328

and here you are."

"I bought the place. Do you like it? I did some redecorating. What do you think?"

She pivoted around in a circle. "It will do," she said with a grin.

"I guess I'll take that as a compliment." He looked at her like she was the only other person on Earth. "And you, Madison, have made some self-improvements. Your dress, it's soft, blue, and accents the healthy, honey-rich tone of your skin. Your hair's grown out even more, and it shines. Your eyes glisten…"

They took a step toward one another, both uttering the other's name. They started to laugh.

She waved a hand. "You go first."

"I hung around, trying to see you. I wanted to ask for another chance. You'd made it clear you wanted nothing more to do with me, but I kept calling and showing up at your office. You never responded to my messages or let me through the door. I didn't blame you. I am so sorry I didn't tell you everything from the beginning."

"Dan Harris told me how opposed you were to the producer's big plans for us."

"I should have called Dan. I guess I was pretty down. I got the idea of buying the gallery because I've come to love Santa Monica, with its people and its charms, but mostly I stayed because I couldn't forget you, no matter how I tried."

"I know what you mean. I guess you could say I'm doing fine by myself. I've kept to the schedule you wrote for me, and I've even incorporated more, but I still miss you." She paused. "It's the little things, isn't it? There's nobody but me to play ball with Harley.

Chloe doesn't have anyone to give her a piggyback ride when she comes over. Tyler doesn't care for my rendition of your pizza. And I...I don't like looking at those coastal sunsets all by my lonesome."

He took her hand, smoothing her knuckles with his thumb. "I miss seeing you in the morning. I miss sharing meals with you and playing with the dog and the kids. And I know what you mean about the sunsets. Without you, they seem washed out, even drab. I'm sorry too, that I never told you...you were so open with me. But I didn't say it. I never even mentioned that I love you."

"Love me," she said, shocked. Had Brandon actually just said the L word?

"Most men have a tough time talking about love because the word that follows on its heels is commitment. I felt I had no right. After all, I'd be leaving you for another assignment after our time was up. Then I quit the show, and things were different."

"Different how?" she murmured.

"Now I would give anything to commit to spending the rest of my life with you."

"Oh, Brandon..." Her heart swelled, and she choked up and couldn't speak.

****

His body was pressing against hers, his hand running firmly up her lithe back to bring her close. Their mouths met, and he fell into a sacred place, the one reserved for her and him—the place that had been waiting all this time. He'd believed there was no way back, but he'd been wrong, thank the Heavens and the deep blue sea.

The moon outside had started its slow climb to

travel in its nocturnal cycle, and below them on the highway, people were whooshing by in their cars. It didn't matter. Nothing did. His world was only her, and he meant to keep it that way from this day forth.

He whispered her name in her ear and inhaled deeply of her fragrance, the power of it doing crazy things to his head. He touched her cheek and felt the heat of her skin, like being near fire. Regret flooded through him for all that lost time since they'd been apart. He'd have to make it up to her. What could he do but kiss her harder, and the kiss seemed to transcend all time in waves of undulating passion and pent-up need.

Her kiss was a dizzying drug. Her body went lax in his arms, and he held her like there was no tomorrow. Her mouth opened to his and then drew back to entice and to tease. He kissed her slowly, deeply, as she wrapped her hands around his neck. She tilted her head, and he brushed his lips over hers—the touch of her tongue driving him wild. He shuddered with need. He kissed her harder, a kiss that punctuated his hunger. *I'll take you now*, it demanded like a steamy romance novel. *I need you now.* Such a Tarzan thing to say, so opposite of the controlled man he had been. All the time he had been separated from her, all the misunderstandings, all the pain, dissipated like smoke. As if it had never existed.

"I've missed you," she said. "Did you know that?"

He nuzzled her ear and kissed her jawline. "I'm so glad you came in tonight."

The door opened with a snap and a swish.

"Brandon, are you still here?"

"Yes, José, I am." He whispered, "It's the janitor." He hugged her tight before letting her go. "I wonder—

it's been so long, and I have so much to tell you—so much that I should have let you know before. Would you have dinner with me?"

She angled her head. "What did you have in mind? The hamburger place—what was it called? Oh, yeah, Goodtime Charlie's. That was where I changed my mind about you."

"You mean, when I went scrounging through that dumpster?"

"I mean, when you made a little girl smile and a big girl swoon."

"You were impressed?"

"I was starstruck." She closed her eyes and opened them again with a dreamy look. "You knocked me off my feet when you made pizza for the kids and me. That was a red-letter, write-home kind of night."

Half his mouth lifted in what must appear a sappy smile. "I could cook for you again for old times' sake."

"I bet you didn't guess I've memorized all your recipes and have been eating green for quite some time."

He ran a finger over a cheek glowing with evident health. "I could tell." Her nearness drove him to experience involuntary tremors of arousal. "I'd say you deserve the gold for your dedication and your achievements."

"And you want to reward me by preparing something out of the loop and very special?"

The double-meaning in her words sent his spirts soaring. "You betcha."

"Would you like to follow me to my house, or do you remember how to get there?"

He laughed. "I think I could figure it out."

Chapter 41

Soon afterward, Brandon was using the groceries Madison had on hand. He chopped and steamed and fried like a top ramen chef, while Harley danced around Brandon as if afraid of him leaving again. And how could she have let him go? What a catch he was with his competency and his tricks of the trade. Here was the man who had brought about the change in her. Not to mention that he was smoking hot.

She fell into sync with him, paring an avocado, creating curls from a carrot.

"We're a great team," he said.

"Who would have guessed when we initially met?"

"I remember," he said, flashing a conspiratorial wink her way. "You were so ready to give up your trashy diet in favor of living clean."

When they finished the preparation, Madison put a little B.B. King on the stereo system and lit some candles.

She gave him a questioning look. "Maybe you'd rather eat in silence."

He shook his head. "I have discovered that silence can sometimes be overrated."

They had eaten a soup filled with chickpeas, mushrooms, and zucchini when Madison put down her spoon. "Brandon, Father Tim told me a little about your dad."

His face grew serious. "Did he say he was a drunk?"

"He told me your dad was an alcoholic and sick and you took care of him."

"I did more than taking care of him. I tried to fix him. I have a problem with wanting to fix other people. It's gotten me in a lot of trouble."

"But you're good at it."

"Not if I get so emotionally involved that I wind up hurting someone. There's a fine line between caring for another person and enabling. I am prone to the second. I've been working on it. I hope to mend my ways."

"You mean you're not perfect, Guru Brandon?"

He snorted a laugh. "Not by a longshot."

He told her then about his mother and father, a subject he said was difficult. He wasn't a far cry from her in his experiences with loss. It bonded her to him stronger than before. She reached across and took his hand, giving him her support, an act she had been waiting to do since she drove to Pasadena and entered St. James Rectory.

Together they cleaned the kitchen until all the chrome and glass sparkled.

"I missed walking with you," he said.

"I think one of the most difficult things about us not being together was being at the beach without you." She raised an eyebrow. "Do you think you could teach me to meditate in the moonlight?"

He gave her a wicked once over. "I could think of better things to teach you in the moonlight."

So hot! "I'd like to know all the teacher has to teach me."

She had waited so long to be with him; she wanted

everything to be special, even their prelude on the beach. She couldn't have asked for a more beautiful night. They skirted the shore and then doubled back toward her house. The moonlight streamed down, making the sand appear like glistening snow. He had taken her hand, and the warmth there made her swoon with happiness. He was really here with her, and she'd never let him go again.

His lips brushed her knuckles. "You're too good to be true."

He pressed up against her, the feel of his exquisite body driving her a little mad.

Her face drew close to his. "Show me," she dared.

He dropped a kiss on her lips, like a hint of what was to come, and lifted her into his arms. The ocean behind them throbbed as if in time with her rapid pulse. Moonlight illuminated his face like when she'd seen him that first day—that same slash of cheekbone, eyes focused, full lips parted with his breathing. Right now, he was everything he had promised from the start. And after all this time, she would know what it was to be loved by that guy who made the girls in the shopping mall and on the beach go crazy with lust.

She couldn't help but utter a laugh, glad for the pounds she'd shed, pleased that he carried her with such ease. "What are you thinking of showing me, muscle man?"

"A little Zen and other pleasures."

"Hmmm, sounds like a plan."

"Uh-huh," he said and pushed open the back door of the house. "One I never stopped thinking about."

He approached the winding staircase, and she said, "This reminds me of the night I fell asleep at the kitchen table and you carried me up the steps. It was all just so Rhett Butler of you."

To her delight, he toted her up the steps. "All the better to love you, my dear."

"You realize you're hauling me off to my meditation room."

"I take it you still practice?"

"You won't recognize the place with my altar, posters, and prayer beads."

"I'll be damned," he murmured. "You continue to impress me. I think I'm head over heels for you, lady."

His words went straight to her heart. He put her down in the dark of her bedroom, and she lit her candle and opened the windows. The sound of the ocean played its passionate introduction. She reached up and cupped his rough face in her hands.

"Maddie," he said with a shuddering breath. "The first time that I saw you, I thought you were beautiful. I wanted to make love to you from the beginning, but that camera…"

"That flipping people-are-watching," she said, and for some reason, that whole idea heightened her already out-of-her-head desire. Having waited months for this, she found they were both ripping off each other's clothes. He pushed her against the wall, dragging down her skirt, lifting off a shirt, both of them clearly frantic with long-awaited need.

"I've craved you for so damned long," he said.

He was a golden Adonis cast just for her. And she fell back on the bed with him, and she let him take her, her legs clasped around him. Stars crashed against stars as she moved under him, her heart pounding. For too many hours in too many days, she had needed this so that now her greedy mouth claimed his and her fingers clung to his back.

They rolled on the bed until she was on top of him, her hands ripping through his hair, savagely now stealing more kisses. It only aroused more hunger. She tasted the salt of the sea on him, laced with night and the heightened sense of more to come.

Given time, it seemed everything became intense— the satiny smoothness of the sheets, the hard texture of his palms on her flesh, the spirals of hair on his chest. She felt it all like her skin had awakened to his touch, and she felt it with more awareness than she ever thought possible. She could exist solely on sensations. It made her happy and reverent at the same time, like capturing sacred scripture in the fingertips of her mind.

That floating feeling of which she'd become accustomed while practicing meditation flowed over her, but this time Brandon wasn't downstairs or far away, and she wasn't by herself. Aware now of what they could give each other, she moaned with pleasure. A journey proved more poignant when it became two together as one.

He embraced her and rolled until they had exchanged places. Underneath him, the tide of her passion, the rise and fall, grew until she couldn't stand it. Her climax when it came was like the Santa Ana wind as it rose and then exploded out to sea, creating endless waves and ripples. She groaned with ecstasy as he plunged deep into her, causing her to draw up and give all of what she had. His breath was hot and sharp as he kissed her possessively. He took her with the need rendered from months of unsated lust. Falling back, she gazed at the light show behind her closed eyelids, bright flames like the sun rising against dark sky.

He buried his head in her hair. "I love you, Madison Gray."

With her heart still jackhammering, she said, "Well, it's about time."

"No better time than the present."

She smiled, experiencing those contented aftershocks that came after the finish of great sex. "Who would have thought of us as such compatible lovers?"

They slept spooned together, a perfect fit like they were created to do so, and in the wee hours of morning, he grabbed her again with the frantic heat that had initiated their first round of lovemaking. Would she ever get enough of him?

When the morning light slanted through the blinds, she didn't pop out of bed in favor of doing meditation. Brandon looked at her, whiskers shadowing his jaw. What he must be thinking, she thought.

She rolled over the opposite way. "Don't look at me. I have morning hair."

"I find your morning hair a big huge turn on. I always have."

She turned back. "Seriously? But it's messy."

"The way I like it, that fresh-out-of-the-sack look."

****

He had to remind himself he was the man who had always kept himself in control, depriving himself of his need. Desire for her had been something to reckon with, to tame. He'd been able to restrain himself, to act with discipline, but now with her, there was no holding back his primal urges. His mind was so clouded with her, with only her, he forgot all else except the increasing roar of her breath in his ear. He watched her face in the glimmering light and delighted in the pleasure he saw there. How he had waited and dreamed of watching her shiver and moan. She was his. Finally. And at long last.

He ran a finger down her cheek. She was beautiful, he thought. "The lady doesn't know of her many attributes." He leaned toward her, moving his mouth over hers, testing the softness and lingering over that faint peppermint sweetness. Like a sculptor, he had to touch her, to explore the mythical body she'd formed by sticking to her health plan. He had been her tutor, after all. As a student, she'd excelled beyond his wildest dreams.

His hard thigh brushed against the firmness of hers. He remembered his stipulations for his ideal woman. Little had he known then that her fire was what he needed in his life all along. Her passion roused him and made him stronger than when alone. She stretched, arching her back in such a sensuous way he sighed in appreciation.

Ordinarily, he'd have risen from bed to meditate before dawn. Not this morning. At this moment, his mind only sought the sight of her. Hadn't he dreamt of this for ages, or so it seemed, in his motel by the sea? All his reading, all his seeking, hadn't given him the incredible high she instilled in him with her mere presence.

The blinds kept the world at bay, hiding them. The ocean sounded from outside—not chaotic or even turbulent but a roar as steady and as whispery as a secret. The urgency he'd known before was just as quiet now. Though his need was mounting once again, it came in continual, slow waves like the surf rolling toward the shore. He ran his hands along the spine Madison had straightened so perfectly with all her months of yoga. If he were to name this lazy lovemaking session, he'd call it "Exploration and Discovery."

Her soft groans and murmurs followed his probe of those sensitive places on her body, of that blue, shadowy spot just below her clavicle, of her smooth neck and velvety earlobes. Before this, he'd spent months guessing what would turn her on. How had he stood it? And how had he borne his own ignorance about the things she could do to him? The deep pleasures she so readily gave now. His breath escaped in a hiss. He had never known a woman who could set him off with just one touch.

Touch me once, touch me twice, the verse of some old love song had come to him when the fire of desire took hold, and he moaned. He pressed into her, and she moved with him at his leisurely pace, which agonizingly had him craving more. He wanted all of her, yet he wanted to stay in this place, so hazy and blissful, while all else faded away as if it had never been.

It seemed like a veil had lifted, and he drifted in a cloud. All reason had left, and only his senses remained. He hoisted himself up straight-armed and stared down at her, enjoying her hunger. He lowered himself, and his breath rasped against her ear. He'd started to increase his pace but stopped and began again slowly. He was blocking his own needs to pleasure her.

"Brandon," she whispered, "I want you now."

"Your wish is my command, m'lady."

He lost himself in his deep plunging thrusts, and all

his built-up tension exploded at the same time she reached her peak. He fell back in contentment, his mind emptying of all but the knowledge of her lying at his side.

Chapter 42

Madison usually spent every holiday at Harper and Darrin's ranch-style house, when she'd taken an actual day off, but she had never brought a man with her before. Now she was bringing the love of her life. The kids came running when they spotted the Mustang from the window, and laughing with apparent joy, Brandon scooped them up in his arms.

"You two have grown leaps and bounds since I saw you last."

Chloe nuzzled her red-blonde head against his shoulder. "I knew you'd come back, Uncle Brandon. I told Mommy and Daddy."

Darrin, always the cordial host, stepped onto the porch and held out his hand. "Good to meet you, Brandon. I hope you stick around this time."

"I plan to," he said, setting down the children so they could hug Madison. He wore a royal-blue cable-knit sweater that stretched deliciously across his broad chest and brought out the striking hues of his eyes.

They were just about to go inside when an Uber pulled up to the curb. Harley, who'd been prancing around the group, took off in a run with his tail straight out behind him like when spooked by the garbage can, and Madison cried out. Then she spotted her brother in his military uniform. He was getting out of the Uber. She worried Harley, The Hulk, would knock her six-foot-two brother off his feet. But Andrew stayed put, hugging the monster dog and patting his fluffy back.

Madison wasted no time running to her brother. "What a surprise!" She smacked a kiss on his freshly shaved cheek. "Can this holiday get any better?"

Harper appeared, wiping her hands on a dishtowel she had slung over her shoulder. "We've got quite a lot to be thankful for this year."

The table was set with an extra chair. "Just in case," Harper had said this morning on the phone to Madison. They hadn't gotten any calls from Andrew but never gave up hope.

"Look at you." Andrew held Madison at arm's length. "Anyone would think you were in love." He gave Brandon a grin. "Your teacher, huh?"

When they were sitting around the table, with its gleaming silverware and delicate crystal, faces shining, everyone talking a mile a minute, Madison thought of what Father Tim had said about Brandon's childhood not always being a scene from Currier and Ives. She felt so glad she could share this landmark Thanksgiving with him. He kept smiling at her, and she didn't think she'd ever seen him as happy.

Harper put down her fork. "It's tradition around here for us to take turns saying what we are thankful for." Of course, being the ringleader that she was, she started, "I'm thankful we are all here, and that Andrew is with us."

Darrin carved the turkey. "I'm thankful for the second honeymoon I got to spend with my lovely wife, thanks to Madison and Brandon."

Andrew fiddled with his fork. "I'm thankful that Madison decided to take Harley. I wanted him in good hands."

Harley looked up with his soulful eyes; his ears perked, tail swatting the floor.

Brandon lowered his head. "I'm thankful for Madison who taught me much more than I could ever teach her."

Tyler spoke up. "I'm thankful my soccer team came in first place this season."

Chloe said, "I'm thankful for turkey."

Yes, Madison would be eating turkey today. Mostly she stuck to her diet, but there were exceptions. "I'm thankful for second chances," she said, her throat knotting up in a tight ball. "I never knew what I had until I nearly lost it." Her eyes misted. "I love you all."

To think she'd almost missed out. Maybe everyone should have a major shakeup at least once. It did wonders for how a person looked at things, not to mention it was the day she'd met the man who brought her back to life, Brandon Kennedy.

Epilogue

April 1st, late afternoon. Weather breezy at seventy-five degrees. The wedding of Guru Brandon to Madison Gray began production at the beach in Santa Monica. Cameras. Let 'em roll. Showtime.

Shakier than she cared to admit, Madison tucked her arm through her brother's and steadied herself to take that final plunge—that do or die. She'd never thought the day would come, yet here it was. She'd broken her own rules when she said yes to Brandon's on-bended-knee proposal. But then who could say no to a man who pops the question in LAX? What a zoo of onlookers. Everyone wanted to see her reaction to the sign Brandon held up. "Madison, will you marry me?"

Holy smokes, all she'd done was go to Philadelphia on business. "Yes," she said, "Oh, yes!" After all, she hadn't been about to argue with a man wearing a Burberry raincoat—so very Professor Higgins of him, her classy one and only.

The best things could not be rushed, and planning this wedding was one of them. Madison's brother had had to get a leave to walk her down the aisle. She liked to think her dad was close, maybe on the other side of her. She smiled at the thought.

Of course, doing it up right meant a seaside bash. The tent, just in case of rain, the musicians in Panama suits playing a calypso version of "Here Comes the

Bride" while the seafoam sizzled in accompaniment. Nothing like a beach wedding surrounded by friends and family. Oh, and oops, a TV production crew swarming around.

Just what had happened was a long story with lots of legal mumble jumble. The condensed version was she had opted to finish her segment of *Guru Brandon*. Her goal, just as before, was to influence others to improve their lifestyle choices. The money Brandon and she had made by the airing of "The Madison Project" would go to their favorite dog rescue, Mosley's Mutts. Thus, this was the last episode, a finale and a wrap, and in two months' time, the viewing public would be able to click on the entire season.

"Watch out," Andrew said. "Don't run into the camera."

"And upset all of America? Not a chance." Still, she veered a little to the right. Her flat shoes kept her feet grounded—well, almost.

He clamped her arm to steady her. "You all right, Mads?"

"Don't worry, I may have a case of the wedding day jitters, but I'm not about to keel over. Not this time around."

Just six more feet to the small platform and the wedding party. Could Madison make it? Thank the stars above she was in her walking shoes with her brother to lean on. Because if...there he was, Brandon Aran Kennedy, achieving the effect of absolute calm, absolute elegance, and the fever of nerves raging inside her lessened.

The officiating monk gave a quick bow of the head. "Ready to begin?"

A new attack of anxiety caught her, and she couldn't, for the life of her, find her voice.

"Let's do this thing," said her knight with his killer smile.

Because they wanted to cover all the bases, they planned to say their wedding vows tomorrow in the Catholic Church. With Father Tim presiding, of course, and just the two of them in attendance.

"Love is the force that moves the universe," the monk said. "Love is the power that maintains all that we know. Love unites us all. Love is what brings us into ecstasy. Love completes our being…"

Harper was the maid of honor. Since their farewell send off for Mom and Dad, the human steamroller had stopped trying as hard, though her next move, she claimed, was college and a nursing program. Any hospital would be lucky to get her. Nobody could nurture people like Harper Lee McGregor. She straightened the train of Madison's wedding gown, helpful sister that she was, and Madison slid a hand behind her back with a thumbs-up.

Out of the bridesmaids—each adorned in vintage Coco Chanel—Audrey Powell was Madison's first pick. Something different about her BFF on this day. She seemed more attentive, less distracted. It might have a lot to do with her hunky date with his British accent—what was his name? The intro had been a blink. Liam, she remembered. Liam James.

Note to self, throw bouquet in Audrey's direction.

Maybe the two women should start some sort of support group, maybe call it Dying to Live or something like that. There were so many women out there who were stressed out and whose lives were unbalanced. She'd bring it up to Audrey soon after the wedding.

Chloe, in a burst of exuberance, tossed orchid blossoms over her head. Well, kids would be kids. Speaking of which, Madison had been late this month. She had a feeling if the pregnancy test proved positive, Brandon would decide to break out plenty of flaxseed ices and mommy-to-be yoga. The prospective daddy-to-be was grinning now at Tyler who was adorably tuxedoed and carrying the rings as if guarding the royal's jewels.

Madison barely knew Brandon's groomsmen. They were made up of a couple of guys from his old Pasadena neighborhood, a colleague from New York, and a guru, flown in from India. The only exception was Willie. With his hair combed and no camera lens jetting from his shoulder, he looked like a regular Joe as he winked at her.

She scanned their guests beneath the tent. Father Tim was smiling largely from the front row and Jason Bennett—the romantic—had tears in his eyes. Andrew sat on the outside aisle, and beside him, Harley took in the service with his sweet, noble face. There was Dan Harris with his trophy wife, and Lilly, her hair piled atop her head like scoops of strawberry parfait, and some of the former reality TV staff members. Allison sat next to Spencer, his wife, and their twin boys who were shooting spit wads into the crowd. Some guests were Madison's clients, each probably wishing to score a moment in the cameras.

The paparazzi had made quite a to-do over the guru and his student getting hitched. Brandon couldn't have kept a lower profile with his new yoga studio, but someone had spotted them together. Maybe José, the janitor. Or maybe when Madison showed up to take a class, and Brandon had kissed her. Not that any reporters jumped from the Oriental screens, but one of the students had lifted her cell phone to catch a video, which made the six o'clock news.

The presiding monk now nodded at Madison. "It is time."

Madison looked into Brandon's eyes. "When I was a child," she said, "love was centered on myself and fulfilling my own need. When I got older and met you, I did things to make you happy, but I needed something in return. When I didn't get what I expected, it hurt. I continued, though, to love despite the pain, moving past the desire to get something back. That's when I learned what it truly is to love."

Brandon took her hand in his. "Even in the beginning, you were special to me. It didn't matter what you did or did not do; my love flowed out to you effortlessly. My love for you is not a rational thing. It has no boundaries or conditions."

Some sacraments signified a major transition, and the wedding ring was no exception. Brandon slid the platinum ring on her finger. "With this ring, as in ancient times, I promise to love you."

"And carry me across the threshold?" Madison couldn't help asking. She wanted it all, and why not? She'd waited long enough for all the ritual life had to offer.

He looked at her for a moment without speaking. "That and more, you'll see."

With a quaking hand, she slid the band on Brandon's finger. "With this ring, my love is set now and eternally."

Finally, the "you may kiss the bride" came, and Brandon moved his face toward hers, stroking her temples. "Take it slow, ace," he said, and it gave her a thrill the way their eyes and mouths lined up. He taste-tested her lips and then deepened the kiss, crushing her against him so tightly her breath caught and her eyes watered. Her man was always doing something unexpectedly spectacular.

Then the monk introduced them as "Mr. and Mrs. Kennedy," and it was music to her ears. For a second, though, she flashed back to that day when she'd forgotten who she was. Who'd know by the following year she'd be Mrs. Brandon Kennedy?

The cameras zoomed in for a close-up. By now, Madison had learned that pure glamour didn't come from a more flattering angle but in being uniquely herself.

After the guests had gone and night had set in, Madison and Brandon strolled down the beach, just the two of them. The ocean sprang forth dark and luminous, the surf crashing as the wind fingered through her hair and her lightweight clothes, chilling her to the bone.

"You're cold." He removed his jacket and wrapped it around her.

She spied the tattoo on his arm shimmering in the moonlight. *Samsara*. She had possessed things but longed for something else or wanted more of what she had. But now she felt content with the present moment. Relaxed and unworried. It was what Brandon had and she had sought. She hadn't completely known that until now.

With a deep breath, she pulled the jacket around her, feeling a sudden giddy wave of happiness. "I'll tell you this, guru. I'm a child again on the threshold of wonder."

Just as he had promised, he scooped her up into his arms. "Well then, let's begin, Mrs. Kennedy."

A word about the author...

Born in California, award-winning author Melody DeBlois follows the sun. When she isn't swimming laps, she's writing sweet and sassy romances. Her heroines are self-reliant and smart, and her heroes are kind by nature and love dogs.

She lives in California during the summer and spends winters in Arizona with her husband. She has plotted her novels while hiking the beach or trekking across the desert. Her most treasured possession is family.

Thank you for purchasing
this publication of The Wild Rose Press, Inc.

For questions or more information
contact us at
info@thewildrosepress.com.

The Wild Rose Press, Inc.
www.thewildrosepress.com

To visit with authors of
The Wild Rose Press, Inc.
join our yahoo loop at
http://groups.yahoo.com/group/thewildrosepress/